CW00740950

# SECRETS OF SWANFIELD HOUSE

ELAYNE GRIMES

Storm

PUBLISHING

This is a work of fiction. Names, characters, business, events and incidents are the products of the author's imagination. Any resemblance to actual persons, living or dead, or actual events is purely coincidental.

Copyright © Elayne Grimes, 2024

The moral right of the author has been asserted.

All rights reserved. No part of this book may be reproduced or used in any manner without the prior written permission of the copyright owner.

To request permissions, contact the publisher at rights@stormpublishing.co

Ebook ISBN: 978-1-80508-792-2
Paperback ISBN: 978-1-80508-793-9

Cover design: Rose Cooper
Cover images: Shutterstock

Published by Storm Publishing.
For further information, visit:
www.stormpublishing.co

*This book is dedicated to Edana Minghella. Forever loved.*

# ONE

Marcella 'Marcie' Mosse hadn't been home for almost a year, and she'd forgotten how long it took to drive from Inverness to the remote Highland village of Strathkin.

That spring morning she was blessed with clear weather as her hire car swept through a landscape of craggy, snow-capped mountains. Descending an alpine-like valley, the road wound around and weaved in and out of dappled tree shadows, until she reached the brow of the hill before the village. Marcie pulled into a parking area alongside two motorcyclists who were taking photographs from the elevated viewing platform. Further down the hillside beneath their feet, the rocks lessened, and a lush green depression reached down to the glen of Strathpine. Strathkin Loch was glistening, and in the far distance, the small weekly ferry pulled away from the pier, heading out to the Summer Isles before it would lurch across The Minch to the islands beyond.

The motorcyclists drew away with a roar. A buzzard captured Marcie's eye as it circled above. 'A *tourist eagle*' she heard her uncle Callum say in her mind. She watched the bird swoop in the cool spring air and glide into the glen on a scavenging hunt.

Climbing back into the car, Marcie steeled herself for the emotional moment when she finally laid eyes on the sign for Swanfield, her family home. From this distance, she could see her uncle Callum's small croft house, Sweet Briar, set behind a low drystone wall he'd painstakingly put together over several warm summers and harsh winters. The small white cottages scattered around Strathkin Loch could only be reached by a narrow single-track road that weaved through the estate. In days gone by, Strathkin had been an important port and a tourist destination. Now, many crofts and farmhouses stood empty, long abandoned enclaves of a forgotten past. Many of the remaining inhabitants of the cottages and crofts in the village still worked on the Strathkin Estate. Often, even in summer, in this remote and unforgiving landscape, fires would be lit, and stories woven into the fabric of the Highlands were exchanged over thick tea and thicker slices of homemade cake; some still communicated with smoke signals. *If the chimney is smoking, do drop in. If there's no smoke from the stack, I'm out in the field.*

Pulling away from the lookout, Marcie drove slowly down into the village, rewarded with magnificent views of the loch and the lush greenery.

The roadside verges were adorned with stunning red campions, flowers she remembered from her childhood and native to this part of the country, while late blooming daffodils stood tall in groups like a welcoming guard of honour. At the bottom of the hills that rose either side of the road, blankets of bluebells covered the lower slopes, and the occasional glimpse of white flowered wild garlic were visible in the woodlands she passed, and she slowed the car to remember their position in case she decided to venture out to pick them later. Down near the water's edge stood The Strathkin Inn, the scene of many a winter ceilidh and midge-ridden summer barbecue, and now owned by childhood friend, Heather McLeod.

Marcie had thought of her three best friends from the moment she received the news about her grandmother the night before. She knew in her heart that she would need them around her over the coming days, and had been in the process of constructing her message to them in her head when she saw a Highland pony high up on the ridge. Isabella 'Bella' Forrester's unmistakable long, lean shape was clearly visible even from a distance. Marcie smiled as she watched her friend carefully steer her broad-backed pony down from the ridge. She and Bella had fought like sisters from their early days at school and even now did so in ongoing text 'battles'. Her uncle Callum said they bickered because they loved each other like family, and of course he was right.

Beyond The Strathkin Inn was Lochside Croft, home to the Balfour family, Dina and Ruaridh and their four boys. Dina was the only one of the four best friends to make a success of love and marriage so far. With her engagement to Simon, she was determined to be next.

She breathed a heavy sigh, puffing out her cheeks, and recounting what had brought her back to the harsh and humbling Highlands of Scotland. A not too unexpected death. Marcie knew she should have come sooner – what remained of her family meant everything to her – but for a long time she had been distracted by her job, and now it was too late.

It seemed like a lifetime ago, another world, yet it was only last night. In a heaving pub, Marcie had tried to catch her boss's eye in the packed bar of The Queen's Larder, her usual Friday night haunt and the scene of many a raucous leaving party.

When she reached him, Henry Steyn immediately started praising her for her diligence and good work. He was unusually tactile, his arm casually draped over her shoulder, but then he did appear to be several glasses in.

'What's the latest with your grandmother, Marcella? Am I losing you for a couple of days? A week? My favourite lawyer in chambers.' Henry's voice was slightly slurry like he'd come back from an exceedingly long lunch, his daily copy of *The Racing Post* clearly visible and still folded haphazardly in his jacket pocket.

Marcie smiled weakly. His *favourite lawyer*, who'd just been overlooked for promotion – again.

'Things aren't looking great so I'll be away next week, but I can reassure you I'm up to date. Everything is under control.'

'I wouldn't expect anything less,' stated Henry, a hiccup ending what could have been a lengthier discussion.

She remembered, too, Simon, her fiancé's reaction when she had filled him in later, over a glass of wine, about being overlooked once again.

'*Boo!*' Simon had said softly into her ear.

'I'm not sure I can keep up this pace. Not with everything else that's going on...' she had begun to say.

'Heard anything today?' he'd asked, concerned, a comforting hand on her arm.

'I'm sure Uncle Callum will call soon when it's time for me to say my goodbyes, but I've booked a flight for tomorrow, just in case.' She drank down the last of her wine, and her fiancé immediately swapped glasses with her. She let her tongue dance over her lips then leaned up to give him a kiss of thanks. She felt a buzz in her clutch bag and released the vintage velvet clip to retrieve it.

The caller rang off before she could answer. Simon's phone rang and he immediately picked it up. His face told the whole story as he gently shook his head. Marcie leaned back against the panelled wall to steady herself. She knew her grandmother was dying; she had just hoped it wouldn't happen so soon.

Today, she had taken the first flight to Inverness. As the aircraft heaved and strained its way out of a stormy London into the calm, clear air, she caught only glimpses of the cities below through breaks in the soft, white, fluffy cloud.

Passing over the undulating green hills of the Scottish Borders, she felt an almost physical relief. She had asked her uncle not to travel from his Highland home to collect her from the airport. Instead, she booked a hire car for the long drive to Swanfield.

And here she now sat, hands gripping the steering wheel of her 4x4, at the entrance to Swanfield, readying herself. Despite the sad circumstances, a real smile graced her lips for the first time in weeks, maybe even months. The feeling of homecoming was palpable.

The car crawled down the long driveway to the large baronial style farmhouse, if you could call it a farmhouse. It had been added to over the years so often that it was now a spider's web of a residence, most of it empty, some of it crumbling. Still, today in the bright greyish light of spring the red sandstone shone like a beacon, tempting her in, weaving its spell. But this was a sad type of homecoming that Marcie had hoped wouldn't be for some years. She swallowed hard as she brought the car to a stop. Smoke rose from the chimney as if the house had sighed a welcome. She stepped into the cool air.

When she turned, her uncle stepped from the threshold and just like in her childhood, he opened his arms in a warm gesture. She dropped her bag and ran towards him, the last few steps almost a stumble as she fell into his open arms. Taller than her, he enveloped her into the kind of bear hug he'd started giving the night her parents died. For some time, no words were needed.

'Oh, lass,' he said eventually with a long sigh.

He led her into the vestibule. Marcie could almost hear bustling from the kitchen and smell the inviting aromas of home baking from her childhood. She imagined a table groaning with doorstep sandwiches and hot soup and fruit cake, but the kitchen was silent and bare save for the sound of a wall clock and a tartan throw over the large plaid reading chair. The wood-burning stove was lit on this April day and gleaming with a welcoming glow, logs crackling and popping.

'It was very quick at the end, lass,' said Uncle Callum as he flicked on the kettle ready to fill two waiting mugs.

Marcie took out two cups and two saucers from the dresser. 'If you're going to make it...'

'...make it right!' they both said together, recollecting her grandmother Lisanne's hatred of tea in a mug. From the top of the small fridge freezer, she lifted down an ancient teapot, a silver Carlton, with an old-fashioned spout and a firm black handle.

Marcie opened the old Christmas tin sitting near the kettle. It was empty. The tin was normally filled with a festive treat; a thick slab of plump fruit cake that had stretched into spring then summer, to be eaten at any time of day. Cake was always on offer in her grandmother's home, and on leaving after a visit, a paper parcel wrapped with a hessian bow was thrust into your hand for the long journey south. The heady whisky smell still pervaded her senses looking at the empty tin.

'It was in the freezer,' explained Uncle Callum, holding up a large square block of fruit cake. 'Took it out last night.'

He handed her the square. The aroma of a whisky soak pierced the air, making it even more inviting.

They both flitted around the kitchen on autopilot – knowing the other's steps, like a familiar dance. The slow cooker bubbled in the corner with a hearty venison stew for later but for now, it was time to take stock of a different kind.

Marcie cut two thick slices of the cake and sat down while Uncle Callum took the tray to the table, now balancing a teapot and two china cups and saucers.

'I want to know and don't want to know at the same time,' she said, pouring the thick brew.

'There was no suffering. Mum looked at peace. I can call and you can go and see...' Uncle Callum offered.

The thought horrified her. She shook her head.

'The minister will be here tomorrow,' began Callum, 'but everything has been put in place as per her instructions, you know. He just wants to run over some final details. Old McGhee from Strathdon wants to know if we're happy with the obituary but to be honest I've not had a chance to look at it. I'm sure we'll be happy with what he's proposed. He's the professional.' *Old McGhee*, thought Marcie, known locally in the area as *The Despatcher* being the funeral director of choice for the three villages that made up the area that surrounded them: Strathkin, Strath Aullt and Strathdon.

'How long will you stay?' he asked, stirring sugar into his tea.

'I don't know. I mean, once the funeral is over, once I see everyone, see the girls, catch up.'

'Just the girls? You'll see himself, no doubt, for old times' sake?' he quizzed.

'Yes,' she insisted with a knowing smile, feeling colour rise in her cheeks. Her feelings for Ruaridh Balfour had stayed with her longer than she had expected them to, but distance and time and her love for Simon had diminished any possibility of romance that had once been thought of as a foregone conclusion to many in the small village they all called home.

'Do you ever think what would have happened, if you had stayed?' Callum sat down on the wooden chair at the table, and Marcie sat opposite, leaving her grandmother's chair empty as if she was about to return from the room next door.

'You mean, would I have married Ruaridh Balfour?' she asked her uncle. They caught each other's eye. She had left. She had moved on. But being back now, it suddenly felt as if she had been transported back a dozen years.

'He's had his fourth, you'll have heard no doubt,' Callum

said with a smile and a raised eyebrow to his niece. 'They don't hang about, the Balfours. He's one of four, himself. He's a hard worker, Ruaridh. I don't know when they find the time.' He finished with a look in Marcie's direction, and she tried not to return it.

'Callum!' she scolded, red-faced, then they both giggled.

Ruaridh Balfour. Over the years, she had asked herself many a 'what if?' over the bold boy she'd grown up with, and Callum knew that, too.

With the absence of a mother, and with a strict grandmother who wouldn't discuss such things, she and Callum left nothing undiscussed on their frequent walks and climbs, and it wasn't just her uncle's assumption that she and Ruaridh would marry and carry on the Balfour tradition of raising teams of boys and building their family to tend the farm.

Travelling back and forth on the school bus to the nearest school ten kilometres away, Marcie and Ruaridh were once inseparable. The four girls – Marcie, Bella, Heather and Dina – and the three boys – Ruaridh, Jamie MacKay and Ruaridh's brother Ross – were all from Strathkin stock and formed easy friendships. They looked out for each other and became a tight-knit group almost as soon as they were introduced.

It was inevitable that Marcie and Ruaridh would become the golden couple. In their differences, they complemented each other; she was determined and focused on her future, while he was carefree and fun. After cheeky teenage banter and childhood dramas, they started to sit together on the long bench seat at the back of the bus, holding hands with dreamy looks and stolen kisses. They'd talked incessantly of their future children and houses and holidays to far-off places where people from their little village rarely ventured. Ross Balfour, Ruaridh's older brother, was the first and only Balfour to escape, leaving for a holiday in New Zealand never to return, and his name was now talked of in hushed tones.

Marcie's plan was always to leave Strathkin to continue her education, as her mother had done. But her first year away changed her; she found that there was a life, a good life, a great life, beyond the confines of a rural Highland existence. During her first Christmas back, at the yearly ceilidh, she had become bored with the music, the dancing, the faraway look in Ruaridh's eyes, the glazing over when she talked about politics and big city living. In turn, she saw his frequent glances over the room to Dina, who was trying not to catch his eye. Marcie knew at that moment that she had lost him, the boy she had yielded to, and he to her, just three years earlier. She left him to go sit at Bella and Heather's table, where the drinks were flowing and the raucous laughter was attracting disapproving tuts from other tables. It was where she belonged, with her girl posse, and she never looked back.

They'd never talked about it – this separation of sorts. She and Ruaridh had drifted apart like couples often do when distance is placed between them. His engagement to Dina hadn't been a shock, even at such a young age. The proposal happened on a remote Uist beach that Marcie and Ruaridh had talked about during their dreaming days. It was a place just for the two of them, they'd said, away from the prying eyes of village life. Did Marcie have regrets? She didn't think so. Her love for Simon was different. It was comfortable. It was steady. It was fun. And wasn't love about being happy and content? That's exactly what she saw in Dina and Ruaridh the last time she was here to 'chase the sun' with Uncle Callum, her yearly trip north on the longest day when the sun never sets. Marcie's midnight picnic and camp out with her uncle in the most northerly part of the mainland was just for the two of them – a time for reminiscing and planning and drinking a little bit too much Talisker.

.  .  .

In her grandmother's kitchen, Marcie carried a box of wine bottles to the long farmhouse table. She was glad to have had a few moments with her uncle alone. Work had been all consuming and, not for the first time, she had a swell of regret in her heart that she hadn't made it *home* sooner. Striving for promotion, had she prioritised her work over this? Had her diminishing family played second fiddle to the demands of her career? Marcie wiped away a tear in this, her grandmother's kitchen. She recalled her recent phone calls with her uncle, when he had been updating her on her grandmother's condition, they had had sometimes been laced with what she could only describe as creeping moodiness that was so unlike him, even in the circumstances. Marcie felt certain there was something at the heart of it, and she was determined to get to the bottom of it during her short stay. They were close, closer than some fathers and daughters, because of the cards they'd both been dealt. And they were also both talkers, so Marcie knew that whatever it was that was eating away at him, they would resolve it together.

She checked her phone. Her friends had all replied, though with no actual words. Heather and Bella shared thumbs up for a seven o'clock rendezvous. Dina's response was a face adorned with hearts along with several wine glasses. Just when you wanted to dislike the woman who married the former love of your life, well, you had to love her even more. Marcie had been blessed with friends who fell back into familiarity no matter how long she'd stayed away. She smiled and took herself off for a bath. Despite the sad circumstances that had brought her back to Strathkin, Marcie realised it was probably just what she needed – an injection of what she called her *Highland normality*.

As she sank into the hot, soothing water, she realised the days ahead would be melancholy but also filled with endless possibilities.

# TWO

Marcie gazed at herself in the long mirror affixed to her bedroom wall. She wore a black shimmering dress and heels, with perfect make-up and her hair piled high. *What am I doing?* she thought to herself. This was a country night in, not a night of jazz and dancing at The Crazy Coqs. She pulled off her dress and threw on a cream cashmere jumper and a pair of tight jeans, just as she heard a firm knock at the front door. She ran downstairs and opened the door to two people she'd known since childhood: Bella, with her wild auburn hair and huge blue eyes, and Heather, blonde with startling ice-blue eyes that made her look Scandinavian. The women screamed at each other and then dissolved into hugs and kisses. Marcie felt like she was fifteen again.

'Look at you, for goodness' sake!' exclaimed Marcie. Both women were dressed as if for a night out in a swish restaurant – exactly the kind of outfit she had just slipped out of.

'I never get a chance to go for it these days, so I dusted off the good stuff,' said Heather, beaming in front of her friend and giving a little twirl of excitement at the chance of being all dressed up.

'She looks like a member of ABBA.' Bella laughed and they let out a shriek of laughter that could easily scare nearby cattle.

Before they'd regained their composure there was another rat-a-tat at the door, and Bella opened it to the vision that was Dina. Bella and Heather took an extra-long sideways glance at Marcie as she gazed at her one-time rival.

A long embrace by the four friends followed. Afterwards, they were silent for a moment, not wanting to break the spell between them but knowing that at some point they had to acknowledge why they were all here.

Dina held up a tin. 'Cheesy biscuits!' she exclaimed, and they laughed.

Marcie ushered them into the sitting room where the fire was already roaring and light jazz was playing on Spotify.

Always their first drink of choice, Marcie popped open a bottle of champagne and they raised their glasses to reunions and homecomings, Dina, mother of four, supplementing her filled flute with a sturdy glass of sparking water that she nursed. The four friends settled into their favourite seats from long ago, kicked off their shoes and made themselves at home. They all knew this house, Swanfield, well from their childhood years.

Marcie looked around at these three strong women who graced her home, chatting animatedly between each other like of old and all seemingly on different subjects at once, and smiled.

Heather had been her best friend since their first day at school. A few years ago, her disastrous first marriage took her away from Strathkin for a time. Everyone knew it wasn't the great love match Heather claimed it was. She simply wanted to escape the bad weather and her father's black moods. She came home several months later, tail down, and was welcomed back by her father, whose manner, from the shock of losing her, had become milder and gentler and more accepting after he realised what he had been missing – the loving nature of his wayward daughter. After that, she introduced a vibrant music scene to the village through her family's business, The Strathkin Inn. For a time, the pub was a beacon for music and the arts, but its vibrancy quickly disappeared. Ever the entrepreneur, Heather created a small, almost handmade museum at the back of the pub about the history of their village. But tourists were rare and when they came, they moaned about the lack of Instagram-mable features, while staying in one of the most picture-perfect landscapes in the world. Since the death of her parents, Heather had made the best of the business as she could, but Marcie knew it was hard going.

Bella was a horsewoman of some renown. She owned the trekking centre, another struggling business. Bella had inherited the property, the ponies and their tack from her parents after they retired. But the changing weather and the chance to travel further, cheaper, meant that, like Heather, she, too, was finding the older she became, the struggle to keep her business successful and profitable was becoming less tolerable. What had started as infrequent, it was now almost a daily occurrence that she would canter to the high ridge, look down upon Strathkin and wish, *if only I had had the chance to live another life.*

And then there was Dina, the girl voted at school the most likely to be a great success, with the model good looks and the perfect temperament. Ignored at school by Ruaridh, it was only when Marcie left that he was captivated by Dina, the woman who had been in his orbit for so long but somehow only in the shadows. After Dina got together with Ruaridh, she had made amends with Marcie over long nights and roaring fires. Dina and Ruaridh's relationship had been a blessing, in a way, because it had prompted Marcie to look elsewhere for work and love, and she'd even come to thank Dina for the life she had now.

'So, what's the gen?' asked Bella, always the most forward, the most up front. 'How long are you here?'

'Until after the funeral, I expect. There's...' she began.

'Nothing to keep you here anymore?' finished her friend, her head cocked to the side and an expression of expectance.

'It's not that. I don't want to cramp Callum's style.'

Bella made a face to her friend as if to say *what?* She then laughed with a shake of her head.

Dina, unusually, was the first to stifle a giggle, hand firmly placed over her glass of champagne. 'Style? Does Callum have a style?? He's sixty what...?'

'You know what I mean. He lived here with Grandma Lisanne for a long time, and I'm sure he has plans for the place. To expand or sell part of it. I'll be welcome back for holidays and the like, but it'll be Uncle Callum's place now and I have my other life.'

'What's your *other life* like?' asked Dina, now cosying up with a thick tartan throw, eagerly awaiting the intimate details of her friend's London life.

'One glamourous party after another, no doubt,' said Heather, feigning an arrogant air, arm outstretched as if putting on long, elegant gloves but, like Dina, leaning forward and hungrily waiting to devour the details.

'Don't believe what you read in the hairdressers' magazines,' said Marcie. 'We live a quiet life now.'

'Now?' asked her best friends in unison, thirsty for any gossip about their friend.

'When Simon left—'

'Simon has left you?' all three shouted in unison.

'No! Simon left the law. He quit the firm. It was all getting too much, the pressure, the long hours. It's not for everyone and he felt he wasn't getting the cream of the cases. It's still very much like an old boys' club in some of the firms, including mine.'

'But wasn't that why you wanted to join *that* firm? One of the best? You wanted to shake it up?' asked Heather.

'Hmm,' mused Marcie. 'I started with great intentions, but it didn't work out like that.'

'Well, are you supporting him or what? Taking up the reins, so to speak?' quizzed Bella.

'No, he's working in a bar.'

The three friends turned to her, all open-mouthed.

'He's what?' asked Heather incredulously.

'After all those years of study, nose in a boring book,' said Dina with a shake of the head, gazing into the fire.

'Did he really quit, or what?' quizzed Heather, looking for a story behind the story.

'His friend owns a couple of bars so he's managing one of them. He loves it, to be honest. The pressure at the firm was too much. I thought he was going to have a breakdown. He's much happier, so much more relaxed.'

'Did he ditch the expensive Italian suits?' asked Bella with a wink.

'Jeans and T-shirts,' qualified Marcie.

'I'd like to see that,' agreed Heather, gulping back the last of the champagne. She stood up. 'Cocktails!' she announced and disappeared into the kitchen.

'What's going on with your stuffy old law office, then?' Bella went on. 'I thought they were completely taken with your fabulous, good looks, sense of style and that haughty Highland air?'

'Yes, well, it only works so far. I got turned down for promotion.' Marcie said it so quietly that Heather glanced to Bella, who gave her a thumbs down gesture.

Marcie contemplated her glass then looked up to see her three friends waiting in anticipation of where the conversation was going.

'The last time you were here, didn't that happen?' Heather thought aloud.

'Yes, well, it happened *again*,' said Marcie with a sigh and a large gulp of champagne to help the news go down. She wasn't used to being what she considered a failure in her work life. She had strived and worked hard to get to where she was. And now she had to admit to her friends that the bright lights and big city life that she craved may not be all that it was cracked up to be.

'So, are you throwing in the towel and joining Simon?' asked Dina. 'Serving up the pints to the weary traveller like Heather at the Inn?'

'Not yet. I love my job. I love the law. I feel I'm doing what...' She trailed off. She wanted to qualify her statement by saying that she was doing what her mother had given up for her.

Growing up in Strathkin, her mother, Catriona, had always dreamed of being a lawyer. She flew the nest as soon as she could, to go to Edinburgh University, qualifying near to the top of her class in law. It was in her first year at practice that she met the charismatic Malcolm, and that was the end of her law career. Marcie's mother retreated home, baby already on the way, and settled into a life of domesticity in Swanfield. It was her dream to return to the profession she loved, and she was encouraged by her mother, Lisanne, who had unfulfilled dreams of her own. But all of their dreams were destroyed on a last-minute trip south. Rebelling against a long car journey, Marcie stayed in her room in a semi-sulk when her parents set off. And never returned.

The chink of glasses brought Marcie back from her reverie. Returning from the kitchen, Heather set down a tray of cocktails on the long broad table in front of the hearth.

'Now, we need to drink these quick, before the ice melts. It's roasting in here.'

She handed the first to Dina, who held it up against the light of the fire. 'My gosh! I can't believe you've still got these!' Dina exclaimed as light danced across the cocktail glass painted with an image of a stained-glass window.

'How long ago was that?' asked Bella, holding up a glass with painted flowers in dazzling colours.

Marcie remembered the evening before Dina's wedding when Heather had brought a box of cocktail glasses and paints as part of a make-do hen party. Marcie held up her glass and saw the swan that her grandmother had painted onto the glass so beautifully, so lovingly ten years before.

'I can't believe you still have this either, city girl!' Bella laughed as her fingers encircled the red-thread friendship bracelet they'd made for each other in this very room on her sixteenth birthday in a party arranged by Lisanne at Swanfield. They held up their arms and saw that they all still had the same bracelets around their wrists, fifteen years later. The women exchanged knowing smiles, and Dina whispered to Heather, 'How many have you had?'

Heather giggled. 'I snuck an extra one. You know, the mixologist's treat,' she replied, stumbling drunkenly over the word.

'So, Simon is managing a bar, a kind of gastropub?' asked Dina in a rewind moment.

'Let's be straight, you're going to marry a waiter,' stated Heather, no stranger to the vagaries of hard graft, split shifts and long hours. 'You could move back, and he could work here. I've just lost two bar staff.'

'Makes sense, you've no customers,' qualified Bella in a throwaway line that sounded a little fiercer than Marcie imagined she'd intended. As a sudden and unexpected silence descended on the four, Marcie suddenly felt tension in the room. Unseen glances were shared until Marcie decided to break the mood that was taking over.

'Business not good?' she asked gently, not wishing to add to the strain that had suddenly befallen them.

'With everything going on in the world in the last few years, nothing has really recovered,' replied Heather with a melancholy sigh.

Marcie turned to Bella, who was the strongest of her three friends in so many ways. She was such a capable horse rider that there'd been talk at one point of Olympic success, but money worries and a father too fond of the bottle put paid to that dream. Still, she ran, what Marcie believed was, the successful livery and trekking centre. It was unusual for Marcie to see Bella's mood change and she was about to ask her why when Bella opened up.

'We're all struggling a bit, to be honest, Mars. All dreading the postie. I haven't even opened my emails in a week,' stated Bella. 'Work is drying up. Everyone is in financial dire straits whether it's the cost of hay and feed or the price of soft drinks and alcohol for Heather. We thought the North Coast 500 was going to bring in all this money, but for us it's only if tourists are on a detour. I'll be honest – and I don't think the girls would disagree – Strathkin's kinda on its last legs.'

Marcie looked at her friends as they nodded and groaned. She had no notion that things were that bad but, worse still, she had no idea how she could help. Once again, laughter had turned to silence.

There was a collective sigh, until Heather blurted out, 'Enough of the long faces.' She slid unceremoniously off the sofa onto the floor and settled with her feet tucked beneath her. The tension that had swelled up amongst them disappeared, and the conversation that followed was easy. They returned to reminiscing about their last get-together almost a year ago, then briefly touched on the real reason Marcie was home.

They giggled about reprimands they'd received from Lisanne, about wearing short skirts, drinking, boys (particularly farming boys), the correct way of courting and the marriage rituals. They laughed as they were taken back to their school days. Marcie fetched the obligatory Marks & Spencer snacks from the kitchen, which were devoured with gusto, as the fire turned to embers.

Their mirth was eventually interrupted by the piercing

*honk* of a car horn outside followed quickly by flashes from the headlights.

'Crikey, is that the time?' asked Bella, looking at her watch. 'Is that Ruaridh for you?' she went on with a swift glance to Marcie then Dina.

'Brodie,' was the response from Heather.

'Who's Brodie?' asked Marcie.

'Long story,' said Heather, leaning in and planting a kiss on her friend's cheek followed by a theatrical wink.

The friends gathered up their belongings and coats and made their way out to the hallway. Marcie opened the front door wide and they said their goodbyes, making promises of their next meet up as they headed out the door. Marcie waved and watched as they climbed noisily into a Land Rover parked on the driveway outside.

Silence filled the house and Marcie breathed out a long sigh. She picked up her phone, scrolled to her favourite Spotify jazz channel, and the dulcet tones of Jamie Cullum drifted into the kitchen. She began to gather glasses and plates but stopped herself. She was a dyed-in-the-wool disciplinarian for putting things away after a party so that she woke to a clean and tidy house. However, tonight, unusually, she decided to leave the wine and glasses where they were on the busy worktop. Her childhood home was messy and lived in, which somehow made it feel even more welcoming. She switched off the light, leaving only the glow of fairy lights draped over antlers above the fire.

Marcie looked back into the room as a smile danced across her lips. This house had a warmth that wrapped people up as they came in. It smelled like home, just the way she remembered from her childhood, and it had embraced her from the moment she entered its warm and soothing ambience. Years of love and laughter were engrained in the deep stone walls which sighed out their welcome. Next door, in the living room, the fire dissolved into embers of red and gold.

# THREE

Marcie woke next morning to a *ping*. Looking at the time on her phone, she could hardly believe it had gone 10 a.m. It had been years since she had slept so late and would have been several hours into her working day in London. The text message was from Callum.

> Morning lass, there's a treat outside.

Marcie rushed to the window and pulled back the heavy curtains. Her eyes lit up as light flooded into the room. A thick-set Highland pony was tethered to the fence outside, heartily tucking in to a tuft of grass. Her eyes widened like a child's. She pulled on clothes that had been abandoned the evening before and her old short riding boots. She was in such a rush that she didn't bother with her hat or a jacket. Instead, she rushed into the fresh morning air with a beaming smile, gathered up the reins and mounted the broad-backed beast. Within moments she was cantering and then galloping along the water's edge. All worries about being far away from her work and its daily traumas disappeared as the wind caught her loose hair.

Macie knew the route from her childhood, and the horse knew it well, too. When she was a child, she and her pony MillyMaloo used to ride the route most days after school, especially on cool summer mornings before her daily chores. In those days, she rode whenever she could, with friends or alone. When she and Ruaridh became a couple, they often took this route to the back of the estate through the thickets and forests to find a spot to explore the area, and each other. That morning, the warm sun on her back made Marcie slow the horse to a swaying walk as she took in the scenery. Her uncle had welcomed her back to Swanfield with his usual openness. His thoughtfulness at bringing her favourite horse to her touched her, and she felt her mouth form a smile of recognition and love and, despite his recent changes in mood, she was relieved to find he was the same old Uncle Callum. Their calls over recent months had made her worry about his health, knowing that he had cared single-handedly for her grandmother, while working every day. She shuddered at the thought of losing him, too.

Marcie took the pony slowly up to the high ridge as the horse tentatively picked its way through familiar terrain. They reached the top and stared down on the glen below with the mountains to the right. She wondered if this was the spot where, centuries before, her forebears had decided the valley was to be their abode. Strathkin Loch stretched out below with a drift of swans gathered near the tall reeds. She recalled Callum telling her that this was one of Lisanne's favourite places for a picnic when they were young. With old binoculars, Marcie and her grandmother used to sit near the viewpoint for hours and watch swans with their cygnets slip into the cool loch water.

'Knew I'd find you here,' came a voice from behind her. She knew its timbre, its tone, and her stomach gave that familiar little flip that she thought she'd lost forever. Even after all these years, even though she'd moved on, her heart beat just a little bit faster.

Marcie dismounted and walked over to Ruaridh who stood beside a beautiful blood bay with a white spray from his forehead to his nose. She let go of the reins and her pony immediately found a snack to sample. She resisted running up to embrace the tall, bearded man in front of her. But there was no need to resist; he enveloped her in a bear-like grip. She felt his rough beard on her skin and closed her eyes. He smelled the same, felt the same and hugged the same.

'I'm so sorry about Lisanne,' he said in almost a whisper, sounding solemn and, she could tell by his tone, sad. 'I saw her a couple of weeks ago. Dropped in for tea and cake. She looked great. I'd have said just a little tired.'

'She didn't really tell anyone,' responded Marcie, pulling away.

Released from his grip, she noticed he was fresh-faced and as outdoorsy and fit as ever.

'You look like a city girl!'

They both laughed. She was suddenly conscious that her face was streaked with last night's make-up, and she hadn't yet showered.

'Dina blamed you for the fact she couldn't get up this morning.' He stood in his normal wide-legged stance, hands shoved in pockets.

'We had a lot of catching up to do!' Marcie joked and blushed slightly.

'I saw some selfies. Your liver has a lot of catching up to do.' Surveying the majestic beauty of spring in the mountains, Ruaridh sighed. 'It's some view, isn't it? Bet you don't get that from your big city apartment?'

'It's a flat,' she corrected, 'and it's tiny and on a main road. Do you know there's a difference between a police car siren and an ambulance? I know them all. It's constant noise, noise, noise.'

Marcie followed his gaze to the stunning view as clouds cast their changing shadows over the loch.

'They'll be leaving soon, the swans,' she said, nodding at the white bevy below them. He stared at her, then he turned away, as if embarrassed to be caught in his own reverie.

'What...' they said simultaneously, then laughed.

'You first,' Ruaridh said politely, hand outstretched.

'What are my plans?' she asked him.

He smiled and winked at her cheekily. 'You've always been a mind reader.'

'I don't know. I had planned to stay until the funeral, sort the will, then leave. Callum will inherit everything so there's not much more for me here, to be honest.'

'Nothing could tempt you back?' he asked.

'I have another life,' Marcie stated.

'Another life or a better life?' Ruaridh enquired.

Marcie didn't respond to his question. Instead, she looked down to Swanfield. 'It looks so small from up here. I just don't know...'

She stopped as she saw a car pull up at the house. Adjusting her eyes, she realised it was a Hilux pick-up. Callum stepped out and made his way into the house.

'Callum's back. You'll be heading home then?' Ruaridh walked to his resting horse, pulled himself up effortlessly and settled into the saddle. 'I'll see you at the church, eh?'

Marcie smiled and nodded. Ruaridh smiled in return, turning the horse to the incline that would take him up over the ridge then down to the Balfour croft on the other side of the loch.

Once he was gone, Marcie took her pony and slowly made her way back to Swanfield.

*What was I doing?* she asked herself. *Stop acting like you're looking for a holiday romance. Dina's one of your best friends. You let him go.*

.  .  .

Once she was back at Swanfield, Marcie tied up the pony and
went inside to wash her hands. She picked up a book that was
sitting on the dresser and began to flick through it. Seconds
later, Callum appeared from the log store. He was carrying a
large bundle of logs destined for her fire.

'Just topping up in case you're planning to stay a bit.
They've been seasoning for a year or so, eucalyptus.' Callum
knew she loved the smell of fresh cut eucalyptus and dry
seasoned wood even more. It was a saved memory for her, the
smell of it burning when she climbed out of the school bus at
the low junction and made her way home to Swanfield. She
leaned on the counter and smiled as he made his way to the sink
and suddenly Marcie was wrapped up in his scent.

'You always smell of lemons, you know that?' Marcie
laughed. 'You've always been... *citrussy!*'

'Just because I'm away out here in the sticks doesn't mean I
can't take care of myself. Best gym in the world out there.' He
nodded to the hills and loch outside the window. He'd been a
daily loch swimmer for as long as Marcie could remember. The
season made no difference to him; he was always the first in for
their *Looney Dook* New Year's Day swim to bring in the new
year and wash away the last year's spirits – in more ways
than one.

'Mum took care of all the arrangements, you know. I really
hadn't anything to do. I called her lawyer, Richard MacInnes,
and he said he had what she called her 'Exit Letter' and that
everything had been paid for. She was a well-organised woman,
your grandmother. Probably where you get that spreadsheet
head of yours.'

They were quiet for a moment, clearly both lost in memories of Lisanne.

'What have you got there, lass?' Callum asked of the book Marcie was holding.

She opened at a page and pointed to the words before handing it to him.

'"Morning has Broken",' Marcie said without realising she'd spoken aloud, and she then sat down and hauled off her boots.

'What?' Callum asked.

'She used to play that song. "Morning has Broken". She loved it. She always said she was grateful for a new day. She loved every season, didn't she? Remember that April we were here for Easter, and she told me to stay a day longer because it was going to snow? Simon said, "it's April" and she said, "but it's the lambing snow..." It was a blizzard mid-morning. He thought she was a white witch!'

Callum handed Marcie back the notebook that contained old notes, recipes and favourite songs and Christmas carols. She held it close to her and leaned against the long kitchen table.

'When you live a country life you know the country ways. You lived here long enough to know that the lambs are born after the late snow. But for a long time, your mum and I thought we had a witch for a mum. She read the tealeaves, you know, and the cards. Talked about the "Curse of Strathkin" from the old soothsayers.'

'No?' gasped Marcie. 'What was all that about? Is it in here?' She held up the book.

At school, there had been gossip about the strange things that went on in the past. When her schoolfriends visited one of the village's derelict cottages on Halloween, they made a point of telling stories of ghouls and phantasms and the witches that had apparently been thrown alive into the loch. As they grew older and wiser, their visits to the bothies and run-down little cottages stopped. Though the houses they visited continued to decay, the stories they told drifted into folklore.

'I'm winding you up, lass!' Callum laughed.

Marcie snapped a tea towel at him and folded into heaps of laughter.

'Tea,' Uncle Callum ordered and thumbed her to fill the kettle for their first catch-up of the day. Shaking her head, Marcie reached up for the silver Carlton. No one spoke to her the way her uncle did. And she loved him for it.

# FOUR

The funeral wasn't nearly such a grim affair as Marcie had imagined. The small church was full. After the minister's plain Gospel exhortation, he didn't speak for too long. There was none of the wailing Marcie recalled from her own parents' service. But then, that had been such a shock. Her parents were still in their thirties when they died, and she was so young. All those years ago. 'Another family decimated on *the notorious A9*,' she remembered hearing attendees say as they waited for the two coffins to arrive. There'd been a heated debate between the minister and Lisanne about whether she, their only child, should attend the funeral. Silence only prevailed when Marcie marched into the kitchen at Swanfield and stated, 'I want to say goodbye to my mum and dad,' before she was swept up in an embrace by Uncle Callum.

But today was different. The weather was cold, crisp and April fresh. Lisanne was well-known and well-loved; there was no lack of people wanting to sing her praises. Callum's eulogy was graceful and engaging, telling the story of how his mother had come to the Highlands at twenty years old and turned a run-down farm into a thriving business. Soft light streamed from the high windows, casting shadows on his face as he spoke. He was older and greyer than Marcie remembered seeing him before. He seemed sadder than he had done over the preceding days, too. He glanced frequently over the congregation as if he were nervous, which confused Marcie. He wasn't a practised public speaker by any means, but he had grown up with these people and knew them well. Maybe that only made it worse, she wondered.

In closing, the minister gave his usual fire and brimstone sermon. Marcie glanced around furtively at the congregation who'd worshipped at this church their entire lives. The small church was packed, with more than a hundred standing outside to pay their respects. Although the service was short, Marcie wished she had Simon's hand to hold. Along with Callum, she'd decided not to have a 'meet and greet' outside the church at the end of the service but to invite mourners to Heather's hotel afterwards for some food.

Once there, Callum did most of the welcoming, to Marcie's relief. He listened intently to stories of old, while she tried to avoid flashbacks to her parents' funeral. Their wake was held at Swanfield, and she'd told Callum that she wanted Lisanne's to be held elsewhere. In the years after their death, Swanfield had been filled with laughter and fun, joy and good times, and she wanted to protect those memories from sadness. And if she could drop some money into Heather's meagre coffers, she was glad to help.

Marcie found herself at the window, looking out at the loch, with teacup in hand. She heard the rattling of a china cup and saucer and was surprised to see that her hand was shaking. Once again, her mind drifted to Simon. They'd agreed it would only be a quick visit and that his work, as he built up his new career, came first. But she still wished he was there soothing her.

A hand took the clattering teacup and saucer away, replacing it in her hand with a tumbler of warm whisky.

'I think you need this today of all days,' said Ruaridh as he placed her undrunk tea on the nearest low table. He gently guided her into the large tartan chair in front of the window and sat down opposite. She'd never seen him in a suit. It was dark blue, almost black, and his hair and beard had been trimmed.

'You've done really well,' Ruaridh said gently with a nod of encouragement. She wondered if this was how he talked to and encouraged his boys.

'Four boys,' she mumbled quietly.

'What?' he asked.

'I'm sorry, I'm miles away. Your boys...' She glanced out to the grass in front of the hotel where four blond-haired boys were running about. They were scolded by an elderly black-clad lady with a pursed mouth, and they stood to attention.

'Ah, my four angels.' He laughed, looking out. 'Devils. They're a handful but handy to have around a farm. Dina wants to keep going until I get my longed-for girl.' He smiled. 'But she's exhausted with this lot, so I think we're stopping at four.'

The oldest boy, tall and sporting a mop of unruly blond hair, looked up and waved, and his father waved back. Dax was born not long after his parents' French honeymoon. Dina had said the name meant 'Leader'. That was her only unusual choice as the next three were named Donald, David and Douglas.

Marcie smiled. A 'what if?' fleeted through her mind as she took a long drink from the amber liquid, making her wince.

'Gosh, there's no water in it!' she exclaimed as it burned her throat.

'You've been away too long!' Ruaridh scolded. 'Water in your whisky, tut, tut, tut.'

'I like a splash to open up the aroma,' Marcie explained. 'It's too harsh for me otherwise.'

'It's one of the best malts out there. That man of yours is taking you down a deadly path.' Ruaridh shook his head, and Marcie smiled as Heather joined them in the window nook.

'Well, that went as well as it could.' With a sigh, she put down her tea on the table next to Ruaridh. She nodded towards Marcie's glass, and her friend handed it over. Heather downed the whisky in one.

'Oof! I needed that. Funerals are so grim. So final.'

'Death usually is,' replied Ruaridh in his familiar, dry-witted way.

The three of them stifled their laughter.

'When I die, I'm being planted in the garden next to the stables up the road. Already discussed it with Bella. Willow coffin. No flowers. None of you are invited.' Heather leaned over and took Ruaridh's glass, replacing it with her own empty one. Ruaridh stared down at his new empty glass incredulously.

'Are all funerals like that, though?' Heather went on. 'I tend not to go, always say I'm busy back at the hotel. I forgot how desperately sad they are. Why are you wearing a pink tie?'

'It's my wedding tie,' replied Ruaridh. 'It's the only tie I have. Think it sent the minister into a tailspin.'

They all stifled another giggle. Next moment, they were joined by Callum. Relieved of his horror of speaking in public, his face had relaxed, and he leaned down to kiss Marcie's cheek.

'You're cold, my love. Let me get you something to warm you up.'

'I'm freezing, too, Callum,' Heather said, with a smile.

Callum winked and headed to the bar.

Heather watched him leave and turned back to her friends.

'He's a handsome guy for his age. Play your cards right, I could be your step auntie.' Heather gave Marcie a theatrical wink.

'How many have you had?' Ruaridh asked as Bella strolled

up hand in hand with a set of twin boys and the youngest, Douglas.

'Is this a party, Daddy?' asked six-year-old Douglas as he slid onto his father's knee and circled his arms around his neck.

Ruaridh kissed the boy's forehead. 'No, darling, we're just having a catch-up.'

When the wake was almost over, Marcie stood at the entrance to bid farewell to the mourners as early evening sun lit up the hotel. She found herself next to the family's long-time solicitor, Richard MacInnes.

'I'll catch up with you and your uncle this week. I know you'll be keen to get back down the road to London,' he told her. 'We can meet back here if you don't want to drag yourself all the way to Inverness.'

'I'm happy to come to see you.' That moment, she spotted Callum chatting to a blond-haired, handsome man who wore a pair of sunglasses which was incongruous in the Highland village.

'Someone thinks he's in Monte Carlo,' said Richard, mirroring what Marcie was thinking.

'Who is that?'

'Brodie. Brodie Nairn. Lives up at the back of Strathkin village.'

Brodie was an unusual name for these parts. It must be the same man who picked up the girls after their night at Swanfield, thought Marcie.

'Hmmm.' She turned as Ruaridh and Dina, surrounded by their four children, made their way to the large Land Rover parked at the side of the hotel. Ruaridh gave her a wave of goodbye as Dina approached her.

'When are you heading back?' Dina asked in her soft Highland tone.

'Maybe end of the week.' Marcie took in Dina's perfect hair and make-up, and her beautiful fawn cashmere Max Mara coat. *How can she look so stunning in this raw landscape?* They both turned as Ruaridh brought the vehicle around to park.

'Let's meet back here with the girls?' Dina suggested. 'Next few days then?'

'Sure,' agreed Marcie and they embraced. Ruaridh slid from his seat, with the boys squeezed in the back, and came round to open the door for Dina. Marcie watched as her friend gently touched his arm before climbing into the passenger seat. Ruaridh didn't look back, but Marcie raised her hand in goodbye.

Marcie and Callum stayed in the hotel for the next few hours. They nursed their drinks as more mourners came and went. Neither of them wanted to acknowledge how Lisanne's death would change their relationship. Marcie wanted to bring up what would happen to the house and the Swanfield estate, but with alcohol fuelling her thoughts, and with Callum's faraway gaze, she decided that today was not the best day to do so.

As evening fell, Bella came over with two large cardboard boxes and sat them on the table in front of Callum. He looked at her quizzically.

'An *encore* from Heather,' she stated. This was their made-up term for leftovers, which Lisanne always said sounded more appetising than 'yesterday's food'.

'Oh, I couldn't possibly,' said Callum, raising his hand in protest.

'Well, it's already been paid for,' Heather replied.

She collected glasses with a matter-of-fact expression before turning back to speak to Ally, her only bar staff.

Marcie and Callum looked at each other, raised their glasses, and both said in unison, 'An encore'. It was a final tribute to the woman who'd made them what they were, and it seemed a fitting end to what had started as a very grim day.

# FIVE

The next morning, the same broad-backed Highland pony was waiting for Marcie when she woke up, late yet again. As she crossed the gravel, she heard the familiar crunch of a horse on the stones behind her and saw her uncle meandering up the long driveway.

He held up a tartan bag, and Marcie grinned.

'You're up late!' he stated.

'I can't get out of bed these days,' she explained as she tightened up her saddle, squared up the stirrups and prepared to mount.

'Race you to the top of the hill,' challenged Callum.

He turned his charge and began to trot and then canter to the side of the house. The horse took the hedge border in its stride as he picked up speed. They both increased their pace to a steady gallop across the nearby field that took them down to the shore and along the beach that ran to the left side of the loch; the village was on the opposite side. Marcie was no match for Callum, who was born in the saddle and well-known in the village for his keen horsemanship. Eventually, she caught up and they cantered together along the shore until they came to a halt beside the old concrete jetty that had been abandoned when villagers left the area after fishing and farming began to fail.

'Top of the hill or here?' shouted Callum, who was now several feet in front of her, and she pointed to the jetty on the other side of the loch, facing the old worn pier.

By the time Marcie caught up with him, he'd already dismounted and tied his Highland pony, Roma, to a nearby fencepost. He made his way along the jetty to where a stack of large stones had been left years ago and now formed a makeshift seating area.

Callum unhitched the tartan bag from his shoulders and disgorged a picnic onto the concrete. He put a flask and grease-proof-wrapped sandwiches down on each corner of a red and white checked tea towel. It was clearly a rehash of yesterday's food from the wake but somehow this fact made the picnic even more welcoming. Heather had gone to some effort yesterday not to put out dainty finger food but to offer substantial, homely fare that reflected the woman herself. Marcie settled her pony, climbed up to the improvised picnic area and took off her gloves. On this warm spring morning, the sun crept above the mountain peaks and cast long shadows onto the loch.

They opened the sandwiches first, thick homemade slabs of bread, one with egg mayonnaise, the other with hand-cut home-boiled ham. Half of each one was swapped; a ritual Marcie and her uncle had performed for as long as she could remember. Callum reached into his top pocket and took out a pair of sunglasses, handing them to his niece who was squinting in the sun. They ate in silence for some time. No words were needed; they knew what each other was thinking. Would this be the last time they did this? When would Marcie next be back?

'You don't get these in London?' Uncle Callum asked with a smirk.

'What? Doorstep sandwiches?'

'Real food,' he replied, and she could see laughter in his eyes even behind his sunglasses. 'Country food, I like to call it. I remember going to one of those fancy, expensive restaurants in Edinburgh. I never knew you could cut vegetables so small.'

'Why do they always have the same fillings?' She opened her sandwich as if for a forensic examination.

Her uncle shrugged. 'Just always been like that. I think when your mother and I were born we went straight to solids and bypassed the milk stage.'

'It's "the Highland way",' they said together, mimicking Lisanne's favourite phrase.

'You must miss her...' Marcie started to say.

'Not sunk in yet, lass. Grief affects people in different ways. I'd rather lose one parent than two, though.' He took a long sip of milky sweet coffee direct from his ancient tartan flask, having given Marcie the plastic lid to use as a cup.

Marcie took a long breath. She knew it was time to say what was on her mind.

'I can't stay, Cal. There's nothing for me here. I've moved on.' Her voice was quiet, and she half-hoped that he hadn't heard her. Her words sounded so final and dismissive of his love for her. She thought of Bella, struggling with her trekking centre, and then of Heather, with a beautiful, whitewashed hotel that had hardly any visitors. What was to become of her beloved Strathkin? Its crofts were in danger of being bought as holiday homes to be enjoyed for a few weeks a year and left boarded up for the other eleven months. Was the village destined to become a place where locals had to move away for work in Inverness or Aberdeen, or even further afield?

'You escaped, you mean,' stated Callum. The ponies whinnied and snickered behind him.

'Roma!' he shouted with a whistle, and the pony shook its mane, then continued to mouth the rich grass. 'Florence,' he called to hers.

Marcie smiled at the light-coloured mare standing proudly, looking out to the water and soaking up the spring sun. 'She looks like a Florence. She's light, like Florence in the late summer. Golden and rich.'

'Wouldn't know,' Callum muttered.

Marcie noticed the upward intonation in his voice. Not a question. Not really an answer. Maybe a statement. Callum had been stuck here on the farm, the croft, the estate, call it what you will, for most of his life. Even her own mother had managed to escape, but Callum had been the homestayer. He'd never been allowed to spread his wings.

Marcie suddenly felt a stream of guilt flow through her. How could she be so dismissive of her home? The village bewitched anyone she brought to its enchanting landscape, but what if you craved more to stimulate your senses and had been denied that opportunity? What if being here was akin to a prison sentence with no chance of parole? She'd never thought of it like that. She always thought her uncle preferred to stay in Strathkin. But at the mention of Italy, his spirit seemed flattened, and to her that said it all. She vowed to make it up to him when they went to Inverness. She'd take him somewhere special, not to one of the new *fancy restaurants* (as he would call it) serving what he referred to as *Stepford vegetables*, but to The River House on the banks of the Ness, where the fish was fresh and the décor to his taste. And they could look out on the water, their favourite thing to do.

'Why not come down to London?' she suggested. 'We live near the British Museum. You'd love it.'

By the look on his face, she knew that she'd said the wrong thing.

'Do you know that place is full of things stolen from other countries?' Her uncle took her plastic cup, stood and jumped down onto the sand, crossing to the water's edge to rinse it out. A bevy of swans took off from the reed bed near the house and swooped low across the water. They watched intently, not speaking, until the birds disappeared. Marcie shook out the tea towel, shivering at her insensitivity. She had riled her uncle for some reason, and that upset her.

She hoped to change the mood to one of his favourite subjects. 'I'm planning on being back in June.'

'Oh, aye? I'd be concerned if you'd decided that wasn't in your diary anymore. Where do you think this time?'

'We could go mad,' Marcie began, 'and leave the mainland. Maybe try Orkney?'

Since the death of her parents, Callum had filled the gap of both mother and father, taking her on memorable days out and small trips across the Scottish Highlands. Every year, on the longest day, when the sun never set and the days remained bright well into the wee hours, they went camping, travelling from Cape Wrath to Smoo Cave, and from Dunnet Head to Thurso. They would sit on a blanket, watching the sun skirt the horizon, as Callum told her stories. She propped herself up on her elbows while looking out to the sea, the end of the world, in raptures at his tales. Despite her grandmother's death, she hoped the trips would continue – a shared tradition that she would pass down through her own family when that time came.

'Maybe.' He nodded. 'Aye, maybe Orkney.'

'We need to go and see Richard,' said Marcie, walking back up on to the jetty.

'There's no rush.' Callum fixed his eyes on a red kite as it swooped and circled on the thermals.

The remnants of their lunch were packed away and they mounted their ponies and trotted in a line along the shore.

'How are you settling into your old room?' Callum asked as the horses meandered slowly along the sand.

'It's so peaceful,' she said, and as if on cue, a yawn escaped from her mouth. She raised her hand to cover it.

'I was thinking of what we were talking about the other day,' she began. 'About the white witch stuff, you know.'

'Aye, lass?'

'Was there any truth in it?'

'If there was, your granny would have told you about it. Runs down the female line apparently, if it's true.'

'Would she have told Mum about it?'

'As I say, lass, if there's any truth in it, but it's died with them, eh? Sad to say.'

Some steps ahead, Callum raised his hands in a wave and pulled Roma around onto the machair, then he turned up to follow the road back to his croft, leaving Marcie with her thoughts. Maybe tomorrow she would have another word with him. She wasn't keen on going to see Richard to discuss the will alone, but perhaps that's what Callum wanted her to do and didn't have the heart to say to her. To break everything down into cold hard facts and the division of jewellery and property, it would be so final.

Marcie let the pony lead her back, a journey the mare knew well. She dismounted to take Florence to her stable at the back of Swanfield, deciding it was time for a long soak.

She went upstairs and into her room, catching the noise of distant laughter through the open window. On the other side of the water, the Balfour boys were outside their lochside croft, playing with their father while Dina sat on a blue-painted bench. They played some sort of game where the boys picked things up in the garden and took them back to their mother, intercepted by their father, who hauled each boy up over his strong shoulders as they emitted screams of delight. As the game ended, the boys ran down to the water's edge while Ruaridh walked back to Dina, bent down, placed both hands on either side of the blue bench and passionately kissed her. It was no quick peck; this was the kiss of a couple still very much in love. As he pulled away, Marcie watched as Dina placed her flat palm delicately on his cheek. Marcie gasped as she realised that she was intruding on a very intimate moment. She dashed behind the curtain, in case they looked up and saw her. Back against the wall, she momentarily closed her eyes. When she opened them again, the giggles and screams carried to her by the wind had gone. Looking back, she saw the Balfour brood had disappeared inside.

Marcie went to draw a bath and soon slid under warm scented water. *I can't stay here,* she thought. *I need to get back to my real life, and far away from my old one.*

# SIX

By breakfast time the next day, Marcie's mind was racing. She planned to call in to see her uncle straight away so they could go to Inverness together. As a lawyer, she knew the will reading wouldn't be like the kind of grand reveals seen in movies. The bulk of the inheritance would go to Callum, and she would receive some of the jewellery she'd played with absent-mindedly as a child, unaware of its true value. She tacked up Florence and started on a slow meander along the road, intending to ride for a short time and then return to her uncle's croft. Pulling the pony up a small bank, Marcie was taken aback as a large black Range Rover flew past her on the narrow road, and she struggled to keep Florence from bolting.

'What the actual!' she exclaimed, shocked at the driver's recklessness to speed on a single-track road. She almost shouted 'tourists!' then thought better of it. Her pony was already spooked. She slid off the animal to let her take a breather with a grass break.

It was almost thirty minutes later that she made it back to Sweet Briar. Stopping on the hill, she looked down into the yard where unexpectedly she saw the black Range Rover that had nearly driven her off the road. Marcie patted the side of her pony's neck, calming the beast, watching as two burly men dressed in moss-coloured Highland wear stepped from the back door of the house. They were followed by Callum and the blond man her lawyer had identified as Brodie, the same handsome young buck who had picked up the girls from their catchup night at the house. The four men were clearly involved in a deep discussion. After firm handshakes, the two well-dressed men climbed into the 4x4, reversed and, in a sea of gravel, roared out of the yard. Brodie nimbly lifted himself into the Hilux pick-up truck and chatted to Callum through the open window. Marcie watched Callum lean forwards as if whispering to the young man, then, as he always did, tapped his hand twice on the sidebar. The pick-up moved off and Callum waved before strolling back into the cottage.

It had been a strange sight. The two men were overdressed for the area, in what looked like new clothes. They reminded her of rich Americans who came to Scotland to shoot with clothes straight out of the wrapper, and a Schultz & Larsen rifle they could barely keep steady without the strong hand of a local ghillie.

Marcie walked with the pony into the yard as Callum came strolling out of the cottage, wearing a Cheshire cat grin that would have been hard to disguise.

'How are you enjoying this, lass?' asked Callum as he patted the pony firmly on the flanks.

'She's a real beauty.' Marcie smiled. 'But we were nearly run off the road by whoever was in the fancy car. Who were they?'

Callum continued patting the pony. 'Oh, they're friends of Brodie's. Just visiting.'

'I've not actually met him yet – what does he do?' she probed.

'He's a friend of Heather's. She brought him back from her

travels in the Far East or something. He's helping out on the croft. He's a fit young man. Gets a lot done. Allows me to spend time with you.' He smiled. 'Speaking of which, are you here for a bite of lunch?'

It was a strange conversation, but Marcie dismissed her misgivings, deciding to take him up on his offer of lunch at Sweet Briar.

As usual, the sandwiches were substantial and hearty. They danced around several subjects until Marcie decided to get to the point.

'When are you going to see Richard?' she asked. 'I was debating whether I should wait to decide on the future until after I've talked to Simon. But I'm not sure. I suppose while I'm here I really should go to Inverness for a chat. We had a tentative arrangement to meet so I'll confirm, if that's okay with you?'

'Well, it's entirely up to you,' Callum said swiftly.

'What are you going to do with the place?' she went on. 'Are you going to move back into Swanfield and tenant the croft or have you other ideas?'

'Och, who knows, my love, who knows?'

'Well, I suppose I did make a tentative arrangement to see Richard when I was here. So, I'll maybe go, just update my paperwork and stuff. I'll go tomorrow and fly back home to London at the end of the week. You are coming, I take it?' She waited for him to agree but it appeared no such agreement was forthcoming. Marcie didn't want to press him, so she said nothing, until Callum broke the silence.

'It's strange,' he stated, 'hearing you talk of somewhere else as home. This will always be your home as long as I'm here.'

'You should come down for a visit. It's always busy but there are some lovely parks and places to see. London is a wonderful place,' she said, trying again, as if it was a peace offering, and, once again, attempting to cajole him from his comfort zone.

'I don't need parks,' he said, nodding towards the window and the great outdoors.

'Do you ever get lonely?' Marcie asked quite unexpectedly.

'Too busy to get lonely, my love.' He stood, his hands in his pockets, and gazed out the window. 'You can be alone but not lonely. You can be in the busiest place in the world but be overtaken by melancholy.'

Something wasn't right but Marcie couldn't put her finger on what it was. In some ways, her uncle was still the old Callum he'd always been, but since she'd come back, he'd been more up and down and moodier than she'd ever seen him. Of course, he would be different given the sad circumstances, but Marcie felt sure something else was going on.

They settled into silence again. Marcie watched her uncle stare out at the wilderness beyond. She'd always loved listening to his stories throughout her childhood, the gravity of his voice lulling her to sleep. They shared a rich history, uncle and niece. But now something was missing. When he turned around, she noticed a single tear roll slowly down his cheek. Marcie loved him like her father and hated to see him so vulnerable. She wrapped her arms around his shoulders, breathing in the smell of his cologne, as his tears fell.

After some time, she slid from her uncle's grasp and headed outside to the driveway where the pony was grazing. She hauled herself up and galloped away. Tears that had been welling up inside her gushed out like a fountain. She let them blow away in the wind as she picked up speed, her hair blowing wildly. She was still crying when she circled back to the house, threw open the door and ran straight upstairs. She threw herself onto her bed and sobbed uncontrollably, as if a lifetime of tears had decided to finally escape.

# SEVEN

Marcie set off early in the cool spring morning air. It took almost an hour and three quarters to drive to the small city settled on the River Ness. Inverness had changed so much since her childhood. The rural lands surrounding it had been transformed by new housing estates; new roads brought an influx of people looking to escape the rat race. Marcie walked along the riverside where a host of new restaurants had sprung up offering global dishes that once would have been unthinkable so far north from what she and her friends used to laughingly call 'civilisation'. Marcie was struck by the vibrancy of this, her nearest city. Inverness looked, dare she think it, vaguely cosmopolitan and the very thought made her smile.

The solicitors' office was in an old converted Victorian villa on Huntly Street in the city centre. As senior partner, Richard MacInnes had the office on the first floor with a large oriel window overlooking the river. In the high-ceilinged room, a mantel clock ticked loudly atop a large fireplace, and a framed charcoal-drawn Landseer hung on the wall. The place had the air of a Victorian hunting lodge. Sitting in an old, battered and well-worn leather chair, Marcie was glancing at her watch when the door opened sharply, and Richard burst in followed by the heady smell of cigar.

'No, no, don't get up.' He waved to her as she lifted herself from the low chair.

He carried an old manila file, the kind she hadn't seen since her internship at a family solicitors in Golders Green ten years before.

'Yes, we still use these.' He laughed. 'Never got into this *invisible filing* as I like to call it – all in here. I'm not a luddite but I like *things*, Marcella. No idea what goes on in the gubbins in there.' He gestured to his slim-screened PC. 'I know I drive Margaret mad' – and as if on cue the genteel and fragrant Margaret came in with a tray containing two cups of watery black coffee and a small matching jug of milk. Margaret left discreetly, walking backwards to the door as if she was in the presence of royalty.

'Talking about driving, nice wheels.'

Marcie looked at him quizzically.

'Saw you park outside. Hire from the airport?'

'Yes. Only one four by four in so I took it.'

'Good idea. And good service the other day. Good turnout. Met a few people I hadn't seen in a few years. That's the thing nowadays, you suddenly wake up one morning and realise you no longer go to weddings, you just go to funerals. Thought she'd last for a good few more years myself. I suppose we none of us have any idea, well, any inclination about our time of departure. You didn't make it up in time?'

'Well, as you said, even though we know someone is ill we tend to carry on our own lives, don't we – not really wanting to know the truth, I suppose. I've been so focused on work. Now I realise my focus was in the wrong place.' Even while she was trying to justify her absence to her solicitor, he was muttering while looking for something and Marcie realised it was probably for the best to let Richard ramble on.

'What age are you now, Marcella? Thirty-something?' he asked, not looking up but instead continuing to search through the file for his missing piece of paper.

'Thirty-two.'

'Not married?'

'No. Not yet. We work at our own pace.'

Despite knowing Richard her entire life, Marcie thought this question was a bit too personal.

'Steven?' he queried, not looking up from his files.

'Simon.'

'Hmmm. Well, anyway...' He handed her a cup of the watery coffee, and said sharply, 'Down to business.'

Marcie took a sip and immediately put the cup back down. She reckoned there were no more than five grains of coffee in the brew. It was undrinkable.

'I'm not being nosy, you know, asking about your, well, personal circumstances.'

Marcie smiled, blushing slightly. 'It's okay, Richard. I'm a late starter. We're engaged so I'll keep you in mind when the invitations go out.' Richard laughed in his hearty way at her comment.

'Once we do this, we're going to have to get your new will sorted out. I'm not surprised Callum isn't here today. Huff, is it?'

Marcie wasn't sure where all this was going. Richard opened a drawer on the left-hand side of his huge mahogany desk bringing out a slim neat file, opening it with a flourish.

'Very methodical, was Lisanne. Very straightforward. So, let's cut to the chase. Swanfield, the croft, the farm, the tenanted crofts, basically everything, including the two rusting Massey Fergusons... you know, I remember them in a competition. Lisanne was the first to buy one. Talk of the town, it was. I remember...'

Marcie sat back in the chair, waiting patiently as he went

into one of his long-winded stories about days gone past. Richard caught himself.

'Sorry. Wife's always telling me about this. *Rambling Richard*, she calls me. I'll cut to the chase... again. Lisanne changed her will in January. Well, more like a codicil. All the jewellery – of which there are mostly sentimental pieces, I believe, apart from some key notable jewels kept in the safe here – were always left to you, but in January, she changed it so that all property comes to you, too.'

The ticking clock seemed to become louder in the stunned silence. 'What?' Marcie eventually managed. 'She left Swanfield to *me*?'

'Yes,' stated Richard firmly. 'Swanfield, the tenanted farms of Stratheyre, Lubnaig, Marchwood, Broomfield and the rest. All change.'

'But... but Callum is her son. The eldest boy. He inherits everything. It's like, well, the law,' she queried, taken aback.

'He did. But not now. I advised her to write a new will, but she just wanted to change the property part. I imagine a copy of the original will is at Swanfield, but I have the codicil here.' He held up the thin file. 'No issues with it. All above board. Came here to do it, *very* determined she was, too.'

'It can't be true. What on earth am I going to do with a Scottish estate?'

'Have you discussed this with Callum?'

Marcie, looking like a rabbit caught in the headlights, said, 'I asked him to come with me, but he didn't want to.'

'Well, you're certainly going to have to think about what you want to do, because there's a lot of money in that estate. You'll need to decide whether you want to sell up. Or keep part of it and start your own business, maybe. You could run your office from here. We have electricity now,' he joked.

'Good grief, I'd never sell Swanfield,' Marcie said, aghast, sinking back into the chair.

'Well, I think you and Callum will have a lot to talk about when you get back west.'

Richard opened the drawer on the right of his large ornate desk. He took two crystal glasses out followed by a bottle of Springbank from Campbeltown, twenty-five years old, a smooth and sought-after Scotch malt whisky. He poured two healthy measures and handed one to her. Marcie would normally refuse but she took it with a shaky hand. Pressing the glass to her lips, she inhaled the strong golden liquid. Standing, Marcie's legs felt as if they'd turned to jelly. She steadied herself and walked over to the window. A swing bridge carried people from the north to the south side of the river. The city had changed. Had she? Had Marcie changed enough to return to what had been, to her, *a sleepy backwater*? She searched for her mobile in her bag and dialled Simon's number, only for the call to go straight to voicemail.

'Shall we call it a day, Marcella? Let that news sink in and we can meet again when I've discussed the outcome with Callum? I don't imagine there will be much to discuss about the crofts. They'll largely remain unchanged, I suppose? It's a big estate to manage, mind you, although each of the crofters will still look after their own patch, I assume, probably about five hectares? Would I be right? I haven't gone into any great detail from the plans so far. But fairly substantial in their own right.'

'I believe they're all still tenanted. I know Stratheyre and Lubnaig and, I think, Broomfield have been in the same families for years, maybe a couple of acres each, but I've not really kept up to date. Maybe Marchwood is derelict or gone to seed, I think is the expression I've heard Callum use? Looking after the tenanted properties has never been on my list of things to do – it's just not been a priority for me. It was my impression that Callum would inherit as the only son so... my bad as they say.'

Marcie really had no explanation about the tenanted crofts on the Swanfield Estate and as her mind raced, Richard nodded, she hoped, in agreement. As she left the office, Richard accompanied her down the stairs, but as he talked all his words disappeared in a fog of confusion.

She sat on a wooden bench directly opposite Richard's office with an audible sigh. Everything was the same, but everything was so suddenly different.

Her eye was caught by a familiar figure striding across the bridge. It was the handsome figure of Brodie Nairn. He turned his head, locked eyes with her and walked straight up to where she was sitting.

'I thought that was you, Callum's niece. We haven't been formally introduced – I'm Brodie.' He held out a hand and she took it gracefully. His hands didn't feel like the rough hands of a farm worker but then again, didn't everyone wear gloves nowadays?

'Yes, we seem to keep missing each other. I saw you at the funeral. Thank you so much for coming along.'

He nodded. 'Well, I only met your grandmother a few times, but I felt I should pay my respects in the Scottish way.'

He had a hint of an accent... Scandinavian, Danish, maybe? His skin was so pale it was almost translucent, and he had a mop of unruly blond hair and piercing blue eyes. Blond, blue-eyed ice queens were rare in the Highlands where the progeny of the Spanish armada remained in a foothold. Only Heather had a similar look with natural blonde hair and pale eyes turning heads from her first day at school. Marcie's own green-grey eyes bucked the trend and her 'mousey' hair had long since been given a touch of sunshine by her expensive London hairdresser.

'Actually, I'm just going to grab a bite to eat before I collect some things and head back. Would you care to join me?' he asked, somewhat hurriedly.

Marcie was about to refuse him, but with her news she knew she'd feel better being with someone, and she needed a softer seat than the bench she had thrown herself on moments before.

They walked down Huntly Street and stopped at the curiously named Fat Pheasant where they were shown to a table overlooking the water.

Marcie asked him about his background, which he glossed over as if he was embarrassed by it. He revealed himself to be a university dropout, ending up where most dropouts do – in Bali. Then he'd drifted to Thailand where he went to *find himself* and instead found a Highland woman who looked exactly like him. They had a brief holiday romance and, after it ended, he'd found himself pining after her, which had brought him to Scotland. It was a curious tale, made the more curious by the fact that Marcie's friend Heather had never really mentioned it. Maybe her pride had set in, and a holiday romance was best left at that, or maybe she was too embarrassed to bring it up because of the age gap. Heather easily had several years on him.

They ate a delicious meal of monkfish with pancetta and fresh asparagus and afterwards shared a cheeseboard. Brodie was easy company and Marcie thought it must have been quite simple to fall in love with him. He had that loose Scandinavian air about him, slight stubble, hair just that little bit unkempt.

'Don't you mind the cold, working outside?' Marcie quizzed, hoping her question might lead Brodie to reveal more about himself. 'Or do you try to help Callum from getting lost in a paperwork mountain? Taking in the whole estate, it's over six thousand acres. It's pretty hefty.'

'I'm an outside worker. I'm used to the cold, and I love the outdoors. Any discomfort is worth it for such a spectacular setting.' He flashed a smile of perfectly straight white teeth. He was indeed very charming.

'How did you end up working for Callum?'

'Well, your very good friend Heather introduced us. It was

lucky that I was available, and he was looking for some help around the house.'

'The house?'

'Well, the farm, the *croft,* is it you say? My mistake.' Marcie found herself nodding in agreement rather than trying to explain the somewhat confusing Scottish legal system of crofting. Callum had several land workers under his command for different seasons: for tending the cattle and sheep, for instance; the arable area of the croft produced root vegetables and an orchard with autumnal plums and apples. Brodie seemed a strange choice to work on Callum's croft, Marcie thought. He seemed more a city slicker than a labourer on the soil. But, she supposed, as Callum got older, any young and fit worker could relieve him of some of the heavy farm work, and her uncle had mentioned that he was drowning in paperwork. Brodie told her he had started by quite literally doing the heavy lifting, then a bit of supervision of the seasonal workers and had graduated to helping with some of the paperwork. But he preferred being outdoors and they worked well together, Marcie realising that this personable young man could more than likely fit in anywhere.

They continued to chat round the houses as new friends do, both giving just a little away and tactically swerving anything too personal at this stage. Once they had finished eating, Marcie went to the ladies' bathroom and patted her face lightly with a cold damp tissue. She felt as if she had travelled to a different universe since leaving Swanfield that morning. She'd been listening to Brodie's voice, but only half paying attention; laughing in the right places, frowning at others, all while feeling she'd somehow drifted into another body and was looking down on herself in a strange half-light.

Did Callum really not know that Lisanne had changed her will? What would that conversation look like when it happened? Richard had asked whether Callum was 'in a huff'.

Was that why her uncle had chosen not to travel with her today? He'd waited all his life to inherit Swanfield, hadn't he? It was never *really* Marcie's intention to leave London and her successful – if stalled – career to return to Strathkin. But, then again, how many more promotions could she be bypassed for? Was it time to walk away? *NO*, the Highlands weren't where she belonged anymore. Seeing the girls had been wonderful but their strained faces told her that moving back here was not the stuff of fairy tales. The idyllic Highland lifestyles portrayed on the Hallmark channel were just that – pretend, not real life. Marcie pushed thoughts of difficult decision-making out of her head and returned to the restaurant where she picked up the bill and went back to their table. Brodie was already slipping into his Gant jacket. He protested at her generosity but accepted it graciously, and Marcie thought she could get to like this new interloper.

Outside, she bid him farewell, and Brodie headed to the local Farm and Household supplies shop. He wanted to pick up general 'beets and bobs', he explained in his strange tone, and Marcie went back to her car to make the long journey home.

*Did she just think that? Was Swanfield home?*

On the drive, Marcie decided that she wasn't ready to leave the career she *mostly* loved, which she had strived so desperately to get. While her heart was torn by the beauty that surrounded her, she had left the Highlands for a reason.

As soon as she reached the house, she dropped her coat over the chair in the wide hallway, curled up on the small two-seater sofa by the fire, opposite her grandmother's favourite chair, and telephoned Simon. She had a lot to update him on.

# EIGHT

To say Simon was shocked by Marcie's update would have been a misnomer. Her fiancé had left the law disillusioned and feeling let down by the rat race, but a return to farm life was not on his agenda. And yet, as a farmer's son from North Yorkshire, he was never a good fit with his legal colleagues in London. Like many before him, he'd fallen for the draw of the bright lights and had worked long tedious hours so that he and his flatmates could indulge in a lavish lifestyle. He'd found himself burned out by the age of twenty-nine. A friend offered him part-time work in a local wine bar and it suited him well. His father had worked in Italy as a young man, marrying the daughter of a Tuscan farmer on the way, before relocating her and her Italian traits to the rolling hills of God's own country and Simon had grown up with a foot in both camps. A strict Yorkshire upbringing with one parent and a love of the best food and wine with the other ensured Simon was surrounded by a liking for great Yorkshire produce, all washed down with the best imported grapes. In this new and less stressful career behind a different kind of bar, Simon had fallen into the chatty and welcoming world of being a favourite neighbourhood barman.

He was easy-going and affable, and profits turned swiftly, delighting the bar owners. He was soon promoted, and as the wealthy clientele grew, so did his reputation as one of the best bar managers in the business. He was settled and secure. He felt, at last, at home.

When he met Marcie, she, like him, was coming out of a period of singledom. They had been in the same chambers at that time, and he had seen her around the office, taken in by her feisty nature and whip-sharp brain. She was as smart and tenacious as he was quiet and studious. He was too intimidated to ask her out but watched her command attention in meetings and get-togethers after work. It was on one of those nights that they found themselves, unintentionally, the last ones standing. He suggested a trip to the zoo the next day as the weather was to be fine, not thinking she would accept, and then, when she had said *yes*, he spent the whole night awake, stomach churning, thinking of the day ahead.

When they walked and talked that afternoon as they trailed around the confines of London Zoo, they chatted about everything from wildlife to conservation and it was as if they had known one another for years. Their conversation was relaxed and open; later they found themselves lying side by side on Marcie's wool poncho that they used as a picnic rug, and Simon took her hand like it was the most natural thing to do in the world. Weeks later, he'd found a pink Post-it sticky note on the front page of his work notebook that simply said, 'I love you'. He folded it and placed it in the top pocket of his jacket over his heart, a heart that seemed to be bursting with joy. Even now, in a low mood he would take out the small square of pink paper and look at it. It wasn't long before they moved in together, and not long after that they were talking about marriage and children. But unkept promises of her promotion and of making partner had delayed their plans, and they hadn't talked about their future in a while.

As usual, Simon was full of questions. Like Marcie, he was keen to find out what Callum thought about this whole new scenario that neither had expected.

'What's behind it?' he asked for the umpteenth time as he interrupted her with questions to which she had no answers.

'I've absolutely no idea, Si. I came up here with firm plans, as you know, for a few days and now it's like someone has thrown a hand grenade into the middle of them.'

'Do you want me to come up?' he asked after a brief moment of silence, but she could hear the reluctance in his voice. She was the main decision maker, the one who took the chances, the one who would jump in feet first, and he was the exact opposite. But it meant they fitted each other, and Simon knew her well enough to know that if he suggested coming up, she would put him off, preferring to tidy up this part of their future life herself.

After the call, Marcie pulled together some cheese, fig jam, biscuits and grapes for an early supper. She poured herself a large glass of Protos Reserva, a heady Spanish Ribera del Duero, one of Simon's favourites, and sat at the kitchen table, music on low. It was early evening, and the spring light filled the large kitchen. She put a notebook and pen in front of her and sat staring at the blank page. As if she were preparing for a legal case, she wanted to compose the words she would say to Callum, so she didn't let her emotions take over, but her mind was a blank.

*Remain detached*, she told herself, and took a deep breath. She drank large gulps of wine until the glass sat empty in front of her, and she refilled it. She nibbled at some cheese, popped some grapes into her mouth then a bit of dry cracker. She picked up the pen and instead of concentrating, found herself doodling. Her mind turned to Brodie. Why had Heather not

told her about her holiday romance? Was it just embarrassment
– or something more?

The sound of wheels on gravel alerted her to her uncle's
return. She felt her heart beat a little faster as she thought about
how she was going to impart the news to Callum – would he be
heartbroken? Devastated? Relieved? Did he already know?
There came a heavy knock at the back door and the bearded
face of Ruaridh looked in. She felt relieved that it was only him,
and embarrassed of the flush in her face from the hastily gulped
wine.

'Home is the traveller from the big city?' He beamed, and
Marcie summoned a smile. After the events of that day, she
wanted to be swept up in his arms for a comforting hug.

'It's changed a bit,' she said, stumbling over her words. She
must have drunk more wine than she realised.

Ruaridh strolled over and picked up the bottle from the
counter next to her.

'Nice,' he said as he read the label. 'Of course, Simon is a bit
of a wine connoisseur, is he not? Too rich for my taste and
nearly fifteen per cent! Hope you got the paracetamol when you
were in "Bootsies".'

She chuckled at his reference to what she and her girlfriends used to call their favourite, and only, make-up store
when they were teenagers.

'Why not take that away with you and you can have it with
dinner? I've had enough as it is.' She lifted both hands to her
flushed cheeks.

'Passing off your hand-me-downs?' he joked as she turned
again to face the sink.

Marcie's mind, her body full of wine, started playing tricks
on her. She felt dizzy, overwhelmed. Why was Ruaridh here?
What did he want?

'How much *have* you had?' he joked, and she looked up
at him.

She reached over and took his hands, placing them on her hot face. For a moment, so close to him, her world stopped. His touch felt so familiar… so comforting, like old times. She closed her eyes, slowly, and leaned in.

But he leaned away.

'Whoa! Whoa! Marce,' she heard him say. 'I think that's the wine talking!'

Too embarrassed to speak, horrified by what she'd almost done, Marcie turned with shame towards the window, grasping the sink. It was then she caught sight of Callum outside. Their eyes briefly locked before he turned away and walked towards the small lane that led to Sweet Briar.

When she turned back to face Ruaridh his hands were up, palms facing her.

'I'm so, so sorry,' she said, burying her face in her hands. 'I don't know what came over me.'

'That *out of my league* expensive wine is what came over you, I think!' he said with an attempt at humour and a nod to the half-empty bottle. 'I'm here as your pal, *nothing else!*'

'I'm so embarrassed.' Her hands covered her face. She didn't want to ever remove them or catch his eye.

'My mum always said I was irresistible,' he joked, and she managed a pained laugh. 'Plus, Dina has always said she'd put *these* in a jar in the kitchen if I ever wandered, so, thanks for the offer, but I'm quite fond of 'em,' he added, indicating his crotch.

They both burst out laughing, and she felt her embarrassment lift slightly.

Ruaridh pushed his hands into his pockets and shook his head. 'Anyway, I was calling in to invite you to dinner. Don't know how long you plan on staying but there's a few pheasant in the freezer that we need to cook, and Dina wanted to know if you planned on dropping in before you head down the road. Plus, I think the boys are quite enamoured by the glamorous big city lady.'

'I don't know if I can show my face.' She reached for the bottle, planning to pour the rest of the wine down the sink.

'Well, you can rest assured, I won't be telling. No sense in upsetting anyone.' He winked, now standing in the centre of the room, a distance between them.

Marcie nodded sheepishly. 'Tell Dina thanks, I'd love to.'

'Great, say Friday? You can stay over in the new spare room. Looking at the way you're putting it away, I wouldn't trust you if I gave you a lift back.'

He headed to the door, taking the wine bottle from her grasp on the way.

'Waste not, want not,' he said and patted her firmly on the shoulders, like an old friend.

A second later he was outside, sliding into his Land Rover.

Marcie was in a bath by 8 p.m. and in bed soon afterwards, playing the evening's events over in her head. *What on earth had come over her?* Thinking about her actions still raised a flush to her cheeks. Despite this, she slept soundly, but she woke up before dawn with a vision of Callum's face through the window in her thoughts.

She ran over in her mind what she was going to say to him, about what he'd seen her do the evening before, and about Swanfield.

# NINE

Marcie wasn't surprised when she walked around to Sweet Briar the next morning and found it empty. Mornings were either busy with deliveries, visits around the estate, drop ins to the tenant farmers and, if at home, what appeared to be never-ending paperwork. As usual, the door was unlocked and so she went into the kitchen. She looked for a pen to write a note but didn't find any lying around. In the living room she could smell the aroma of last night's fire still in the air but the woodburner had already been cleaned and a new fire set for that evening. She sat down on the window seat and watched a red kite drift on the thermals, eyes scanning the grass below before it melted into rocks and sand on the loch side. She picked up a cushion to place behind her back and a brochure fell to the floor. Marcie bent to pick it up and noticed there was a yellow Post-it sticky note attached to the front with a scribble that read 'Page 34' and a heart drawn with a red pen. On automatic pilot, she flicked through the glossy magazine to the noted page and was met with a picture of a stunning white sand beach with gentle lapping waves in the Indian Ocean. It was the kind of beach she had seen on the island of Harris on a long-ago holiday, though she imagined the temperature at this destination would be several degrees warmer. Was Callum finally getting away to a long dreamed of holiday? And was she about to snatch that dream away from him? Callum had spent his entire life tending to Swanfield after the early death of his father, and his mother had become used to her only son being the one to work the land. Now his longed-for retirement gift to himself would not be within his grasp. Marcie rolled the magazine up and slid off the deep windowsill, replacing it carefully where it had fallen from behind the cushion. She would call back later or maybe tomorrow – leave a bit of space between them after his long stare at her through the window. But you couldn't really hide in Strathkin, not for long anyway. Besides, they had to resolve their issues otherwise they would invariably raise their head in some way.

A thought occurred to her as she walked back to the house. What if her uncle was in now? Not *the* house, *MY* house. So instead of heading in, she took herself up to the high ridge, without the aid of her four-legged friend, and sat on an old flat stone known locally as the 'tabletop', looking down over the village and the loch. Black smoke from an early morning fire wove a thin black line from the Balfour's croft. The strong wind brought her an occasional squeal of one of the boys as they raced around the large garden with the family dog. It was like an advert of the perfect Highland family upbringing. The image stirred a longing in her, and she made her mind up to call Simon early again tonight. She'd seek his impartial advice before she spoke to Callum. Would she tell him about what she'd almost done the night before? Closing her eyes, she lay down on the stone; it was warm from the sun. She imagined herself in the Balfour croft, and a dog by the range, the familiar sound of someone chopping wood outside. The warm smell of baking filled the air, and this scene of seemingly domestic bliss made her smile benignly. She woke herself up from the daydream saying, 'NO!' What had made her think like that, transporting herself into the life of one of her closest friends, wiping her out of the picture? She yelled 'NO!' again, this time almost shouting out loud at the same time an even louder noise came from down the hill, the sound of motorbikes.

'Excuse me, please?'

At first, Marcie thought the accented voice belonged to Brodie, but as she adjusted her eyes to the light, she realised she was looking at a man dressed entirely head to toe in leather, with sunglasses firmly affixed to his young face. She sat up suddenly, hearing further chatter behind him. Two similarly dressed young men struggled up the scree, laughing loudly at their efforts.

'We're looking for a photograph... like a selfie of us.'

She held her palm over her eyes as they adjusted to the sunlight. She struggled to her feet and the first man reached out a hand to help her up.

'We are so sorry to have wakened you.'

'Hmmm?' was all she could muster in response. 'Oh, not a problem, I just drifted off for a moment there.'

'We are from Germany and work as doctors in Glasgow.' He gave a nod to one of his other friends. 'When you must catch up on the sleep, the best thing is to take the power nap. If you cannot find us, we will usually be on top of a WC in the quietest hospital ward.' They all smiled, clearly remembering the times they had managed to escape the pressures of work for some quiet respite. They had certainly brightened Marcie's day.

Handing her their camera, they lined up for a photograph, playfully pushing and shoving each other near to the edge of the high ridge. The man, who introduced himself as Rudy, tried to explain how to use the camera. Instead, Marcie grabbed her own phone from her back pocket and took a photograph. She gave her phone to Rudy who immediately sent it to his own phone and held it up for the other two to see.

'Where are you guys climbing? How long for?' Marcie asked as she watched Rudy deftly and smoothly run his camera around the scenery, taking photographs.

'First we do Beinn Dearg and then Beinn Alligin but last is Liathach... it has two Munros and it is apparently quite the challenge, but we have a week and after the other two, I think we will be good.' His English was almost perfect, Marcie marvelled. 'We will be coming back here in some days,' he said with the easy confidence of youth.

'Are you camping?' asked Marcie.

'Why, of course,' was the nonchalant reply supplemented with a shrug of the shoulder and a glance to the laden bikes below them.

'You see that white building down there?' She pointed to The Strathkin Inn, which was clearly visible from their vantage point on the high ridge, a light plume of smoke drifting upwards from the chimney stack.

'Why, yes, of course I see it.' He nodded.

'Then why not book in here for coming back? There's a ceilidh this Saturday, a Scottish dance – I'm sure you guys would enjoy it. They have baths, too, in the room so you can have a good soak after your climbing.' He looked at her curiously. 'A long lie in the bath, relax your muscles after your climb?' she explained, and he smiled.

'Ah, a long soaking, I see, I see.' He nodded. Smiling and drawing his hand through his hair he further went on, 'We are staying in a bothy last night so...' He gave a shrug as if to apologise if she found them a little fruity.

'So, what do you think?' she asked encouragingly. 'Should I book you in?'

Rudy looked to his two friends, and they were nodding and shrugging their shoulders at the same time.

'Yes, yes, we will stay here.' He smiled at her. 'You will stay here, too?'

'Yes, oh yes, I'll be here,' she agreed and was delighted with herself for managing to secure a booking for her friend in what seemed to be a quiet time for Strathkin despite being the start of the holiday season.

With a swift look at their watches, they bid Marcie farewell and scrambled down the hill to where their bikes were propped up, heavily laden with camping gear. The three doctors roared their way into the clear day, dipping down along the loch side. She watched as they gathered speed, keen as they were to get to the north of Torridon beyond Strathkin, to begin their ascent of the three peaks that dominated the skyline in this Highland outdoors playground.

Marcie descended from the high ridge. She decided to herself that she couldn't go to the Balfours on Friday, join in their domestic bliss. She would only embarrass herself further. *Was she still in love with Ruaridh, or was she simply in love with the thought of being in love with him, of a life of homeliness here in the rugged western Highlands?* Of course, she was seeing it at its best, just before summer. She had been caught up in the enchantment of Strathkin. There were also dreich, dark, long winters with incessant rain battering against the windows and a wind that would have you struggling to stay on your feet; not to forget snowstorms that would close the road for days. She'd heard tales of the emergency services having to bring in supplies by air after days of not so splendid isolation. This was not her life, not anymore, she tried to convince herself. Her life was one of high heels and make-up, of Friday night cocktails and laughs in the karaoke bar later. Of hardworking men and women like her living a glamourous cosmopolitan but sometimes lonely life. Wasn't it? She was conflicted.

She had been a prosecuting lawyer, a defending lawyer, her company taking in the whole gambit of legal challenges. She loved family law, domestic law but was now working in commercial law which she found challenging but fulfilling. She appreciated the fact that she now ran a team of women, all feisty like her, soft when needed, but certainly not pliable, and she was absolutely delighted that not one of them had joined the golf club where she knew her boss conducted most of his business. If she were to move to Swanfield, what would that entail? Certainly, it would be less stress from one corner but possibly a different kind of stress in another. How would she tell her team, and, in particular, the young girl she'd only just hired, who was from a disadvantaged background. Marcie had been mentoring her with such great success, which gave her a feeling of utter joy.

Could she work from home as she very often did, but from *THIS* home?

However, it wasn't her decision alone to make. She was the decision maker in the relationship, and she was fairly sure that whatever she decided, Simon would agree. But while she thought of what *she* could do, what would *he* do? It was different managing a popular London pub and eatery to upping sticks to what most would term the middle of nowhere and try to make a go of it. His sometimes fragile mental health made Marcie think that she had to handle this decision and future planning of their lives very carefully. Very carefully indeed.

She headed up to the Inn to speak to Heather, planning that she wouldn't tell her the whole story of the codicil and her dilemma, till she'd talked to Callum. Sometimes, too, Heather could be a little indiscreet, so Marcie thought she would keep that piece of information to herself. She also wanted to find out about the enigma that was Brodie Nairn, who'd followed her friend halfway around the world but hadn't yet revealed the whole story. He seemed kind and helpful, and he was certainly very pleasant company at lunch, despite her mind being elsewhere.

By the time she reached the welcoming foyer of The

Strathkin Inn, it was early afternoon. At that time in London, she'd be going to find her lunch at Pret or at one of the local bars. Though dying out, lunchtime drinking was still seen as the norm around the busy Leadenhall Market area, though she had never been part of that crowd, or at least not often. Here, though, it was different; even though it was the start of the tourist season, after the late Easter holidays, the pub was empty. Marcie had expected to see at least a few elderly locals propping up the bar. But no. The fire remained unlit, and the hotel looked entirely vacant. A grandfather clock in the foyer ticked down to the pub's opening hours.

As she entered the bar area, Marcie shouted, 'Hello?' to the bar and beyond, the store, the side office, the kitchen. She took herself over to a table by the window and looked down to the loch side and across to Swanfield.

'What time is this to show up looking for lunch?'

Marcie turned around to see Heather appear from behind the bar to join her at the table. In the daylight, the room looked shabbier than it had done at her grandmother's funeral. The lovely comfortable tartan reader chair was frayed around the edges, and the rug it sat on looked almost threadbare. Her friend, too, looked rather unkempt. She had a vague smell of smoke hovering over her, and her red eyes and heavy lids betrayed her lack of a restful sleep.

'I've got good news!' Marcie said to avoid what may have been an awkward conversation.

'You've won the EuroMillions and you're my new investor?' asked Heather, only half joking.

''Fraid not, but it's still good news,' said Marcie, with the hope that at least a few hundred pounds of revenue may keep the wolf from the door at least for this month. 'I've got you a booking for Saturday night, after the ceilidh. Three guys from Glasgow, well, Germany.'

'You're talking in riddles, Mars, please explain.'

Marcie explained her meeting with the German doctors and their trip to tackle the three Beinns. Rather than looking pleased, her friend let out a long yawn.

'Late night?' asked Marcie, leaning back in her threadbare chair.

'Poker night,' replied Heather, stifling another yawn.

'On a Wednesday?'

'Got to take business when you can get it,' said Heather matter-of-factly. 'I'm exhausted, Mars. I wasn't joking when I said I was avoiding the postie.'

Right on cue the little red van pulled up at the gate. Heather slid down on the chair to make herself small and invisible from the road.

The postman stopped halfway up the path, pulled some envelopes from their elastic band prison and then continued. He rapped on the door sharply and strolled back down the path to the van and on to his next stop, the neighbouring trekking centre.

'You can come up now – he's gone to Bella's,' said Marcie, with a nod to the van pulling away from the hotel.

'I don't have a flipping penny in the bank, Mars. I'm on my knees, literally and figuratively, if you must know.'

Her friend investigated the middle distance, and Marcie could see tears well in her eyes.

'I'm so sorry, Heather, really,' Marcie comforted her, reaching over to lay her hand on top of Heather's. 'I don't know what to say. I didn't think it was *this* bad.'

'I spent a lot of money on refurbishing the rooms after all the staycation crowd brought in the ready cash, but it only carried on for one year. After that they all started to go back to Majorca or Bulgaria or the *bally* Caribbean. Instead of banking that money, I paid out and cleared the debts and now it's worse than ever. I only get one-night stayers looking for a picnic lunch, or a couple of people driving the North Coast 500. I can't charge big city prices so I'm barely breaking even in my room occupancy. Unless there's a reason for a local family to celebrate or commiserate then *this...*' She stood up and waved her hand around the empty space. '*THIS* is *MY* daily grind.'

She threw herself back down on the chair, and Marcie saw the toll the stress was taking on her friend. Her skin was dull and the sparkle in her eyes had been replaced with tears.

'What can I do?' asked Marcie gently.

'What can *you* do? I'd ask you to set fire to the place, but I've had to stop paying my exorbitant insurance. I had another plan but that's just gone down the Swanee; anyway, I need *another* plan, pronto.' She suddenly shot bolt upright. 'Lunch?'

'Only if I'm paying,' insisted Marcie.

'Well, you're not getting a freebie, *rich bitch*,' Heather said as she made her way through the bar and into the kitchen beyond. It was a throwaway comment that Marcie didn't think twice about, knowing that her friend was going through a difficult time. Inheritance aside, it was clear their monetary lives were on different trajectories.

Marcie enjoyed a lunch of warmish soup and a toasted ham sandwich that looked vaguely familiar from the funeral tea some days ago. She thought maybe it had been frozen – an encore presentation indeed. Even so, she was glad of the food after her trek around the loch and up the hill. Thankfully, their conversation turned into light-hearted gossip about their early years and soon their laughter filled the empty room.

Marcie decided not to bring up the subject of Brodie and his following her to Scotland. The subject would have to wait for another day, as she got the vibe from Heather that any real conversation was off limits while she went through this hostelry trauma.

Once she'd finished eating, Marcie got up, stretched and patted her full stomach.

'I'm nipping in to see Bella next, fancy a walk?' she suggested.

'Nah, I'm thinking of a lie down. I don't think I'm going to get an unexpected coach load,' replied Heather, looking to the empty car park at the side of the hotel. 'See if Bella can drive you back, or you'll be sore tomorrow.'

Marcie nodded. She glanced out the window and noticed that Callum's croft across the loch had no smoke coming from the chimney. He must still be out, so an early night was on the cards, she planned. 'Don't suppose you've seen Callum?'

'I knew he was going to the mart in Dingwall but nah, not seen him,' answered Heather, referring to the weekly cattle auction market in one of the local towns a hundred miles away.

Marcie placed a twenty-pound note in the empty tips jar and stepped back out into the clear day. It was only a short walk from the Inn to the trekking centre.

As she approached, a distant horse's snicker told her that her friend would be in.

To her relief, the mood at Strathkin Trekking Centre was far more amiable than the desperate state of the Inn. Bella was out in the stable yard near the shore brushing down her own horse, Pebbles, with a radio blaring from the office beyond. The majority of the twelve liveried stables were occupied, and a girl in her early twenties was just beginning to lead out a party of two on well-groomed and keen Highland ponies for an afternoon trek in the local hills. A well-trodden path, mostly created by Bella's father years ago, took the paying guests on a meander through spectacular scenery and allowed them a stop on a viewing platform, far up from the road that looked down to the loch and the mountains beyond. The pair clip-clopped their way out of the yard with a wave from Bella and started a slow

low climb along a track at the back of the house, disappearing into the trees and out of sight.

Bella's father had laid out the track not long after he built the stables, designing it for a gentle meander through the forest. He had used old, unwanted Massey Ferguson tyres from Lisanne and planted them with wild geranium and heather, including wild blueberry so that the horses would stop and have a forage at the picturesque areas of the trek, and the guests would be amazed that the ponies not only knew their way but would casually stop at the most picture-perfect places. Invariably, the treks ran over the two or three hours the guests had paid for. Bella had told her that, luckily, all her recent guests had been returnees from previous times, though her income was still very little, with no real tourists to speak of. Like Heather, sadly, business was tough, getting tougher. Bella's meagre inheritance had dwindled as month after month passed by with no clientele. She told Marcie she had offered livery to local farmers so the horses stabled around her no longer belonged to her; in fact, her pony was the only one now stabled that she could claim as being truly hers.

Although dressed casually, Marcie knew her city clothes were incongruous in the middle of this old but spotlessly clean stable yard. Bella's blue gilet was covered in horsehair as she ran her currycomb over Pebble's flanks.

'Yo!' she shouted from still some metres away. Her friend turned, raising her sunglasses, her jodhpurs covered in mud, unlike her well-worn riding boots that were polished to a shine.

'Hey!' returned her friend with a broad smile, throwing the comb down into a bucket that rested at her feet. 'I've been looking for an excuse to stop. Just found it.' She took off her thin gloves, then patted the neck of her favourite charge. 'What brings you round here – didn't see the car?'

Marcie stretched and found her thighs beginning to ache.

'It's okay till I stop,' she said, rubbing the back of her legs and the outside of her thighs.

'You'll be sore tomorrow, city girl!'

'It's all that bracken on the machair – if it was straight and flat it would be no problem.' She looked over the loch to Swanfield. As the crow flies it would be a short jaunt, but the trip up to the high ridge was beginning to take its toll on her slender, but office bound legs.

'I stopped in to visit with Heather.'

'Oh aye?' replied Bella, beginning a walk to the office.

'I didn't realise it was quite so bad.'

'The drinking?'

'Well,' started Marcie, 'I was going to say the business. I didn't realise, well, I didn't imagine it would be as bad.'

'Took on too much – we told her, me and D. When she was busy, try to bank what you can, we said. The winters aren't what they used to be, so we all have a tough time over the quiet season, but she carried on with her refurbishment. Spent the lot. Now she's trying to keep the wolf from the door and she's on the run. And I mean *on the run*.'

'What do you mean?'

'Booked an expensive holiday last January and basically buggered off to Southeast Asia.'

'Why didn't this come up the other night?' quizzed Marcie.

'Embarrassment. Do you know about Brodie? Lovesick puppy arrives on the door, and she takes him in – another one drinking whatever profit they're making. Threw him out when he started fiddling with the till and, well, Dina said he must be rattling 'cause all that's in that till is pennies.'

They went to the office, and Bella turned down the local radio which was tuned to Radio Loch Broom, or Loch broom cupboard as they joked when they were younger due to the audience being small, low and local. It became somewhat of a joke in Strathkin until the Ullapool residents found out and started calling Strathkin its little sister, *Toy-town.* Even today, the local rivalry remained.

'Where did she pick him up?' asked Marcie, not mentioning that she had met Brodie in Inverness, albeit accidentally. She needed to know more about this new man in town from her friends. Only when she had collected *evidence,* as she liked to call it, would she then gather her friends together to disclose their meeting. It was at the forefront of her mind, however, that there might be absolutely nothing suspicious going on and she didn't want to look a fool for jumping to all sorts of conclusions.

'Thailand,' said Bella, raising her eyes to the ceiling. 'Went there to "find himself", ha!' she added with air quotes and a disgruntled look on her face.

'Jealous?' asked Marcie to lighten the mood. 'He is a bit cute.'

Bella laughed slightly. 'Yeah. Maybe I've just been around the horses too long,' she qualified, and they both smiled as the tension lifted.

Strong tea was made, and they moved to sit on the old bench outside the office in the courtyard.

'I can't believe he's working with Callum. Brodie, I mean,' said Marcie.

'Hmm,' replied her friend, blowing on her tea.

'I'm just wondering...' began Marcie.

'Yaaas?' quizzed Bella, seeing Marcie's inquiring mind tick over.

'Oh, I suppose it's nothing, but I just think, what is he doing here? He's nice enough, certainly lovely to look at, but he's come a long way from home to work here on the croft.'

'Heather said early doors he was running away from something. Never really expanded on it. You think he's a *chancer*? Hustler? What in the name of the wee man is he going to hustle out of herself? She doesn't have two pennies to rub together.'

'Hmm,' qualified Marcie, and they sat in silence for some moments, concentrating on their strong tea. 'Just coming all this way to end up as a land labourer. Sounds strange to me, but he seems pleasant enough and he seems to be helping Callum out. Maybe I'm just too protective of Cal.' They sat in silence for a moment longer.

'You are. He's settled well into the community. Cal is more upbeat with Brodie around. Win-win.'

Out of the blue, Marcie asked, 'What was the name of that guy you got off with?'

'*Got off with*?' Bella looked at Marcie over the top of her sunglasses. '*Got off with*? Narrow it down a bit, eh?'

'The guy at the dinner that time. Remember, over at Strath Aullt, after that shoot we were working at?'

'That German guy? Wolfgang or Wolfie or something, why?'

'I met some German guys on the high ridge. Off climbing up the Beinns. I told them to stop at Heather's on the way back, come to the ceilidh. They're all a bit cute, doctors.'

Bella looked at her in surprise, drawing away to peer at her side on.

'Oh, not me, of course, I'm spoken for. I meant for *you*, but just because you're on a diet doesn't mean you can't look at the menu,' she joked, and they both burst out laughing at the very thought.

Marcie watched keenly as Bella whirled her tea around in her chipped mug. She couldn't tell either of her friends about the inheritance just yet. Here they were, both struggling, both with failing businesses due to no fault of their own. Here she was, not even living in the Highlands nor with any real intention to move back, being gifted, for want of a better word, an endowment that could end all their sleepless nights and stop more furrowed lines being drawn on their still-young faces. Bella took Marcie's cup and emptied out the cold tea.

'She used to read the leaves, you know, your grandmother,' said Bella. 'She was really spiritual.'

'Why am I just finding out about these things now?' asked Marcie. 'Callum said that the other day. I never knew.'

'White witch. You must remember all those stories she told about curses and stuff in Strathkin? Things to do with the Kelpies in the water? Ancient folk tales of mysticism and legends?' Bella asked with dramatic hand gestures.

Marcie shook her head in disbelief. 'All those spooky stories about strange Scottish water horses, phantasms in the loch? Nah, not my scene. Made up nonsense.'

Bella stood up, then stretched her arms behind her to clasp her hands and open her chest.

'Maybe I should jack it all in and come to London. Got a sofa bed?' she asked, changing the subject.

'I asked Callum down for a few days, but he's not interested. I mean, I love it here, Bells, I really do, but how could you spend your entire life here and not want to go anywhere else?'

'Maybe once you bugger off, he'll sell up and jump on the first plane out.'

For a moment this possibility danced around in Marcie's head. Maybe this was why he was avoiding her. She was reminded of the brochure she found at Sweet Briar. Maybe it wasn't a holiday, after all. Maybe it was a complete getaway. If so, his plan would be turned around when he found out he hadn't inherited his family pile as expected. But why wasn't he opening up about any of this? Since her parents' death they had shared everything, so why would he not want to sit and chat about what was clearly on his mind? She was very aware that she was doing exactly what she would normally encourage others not to do, but her mind was conflicted.

Marcie was still pondering this as Bella gave her a lift back to save her tired legs from the long walk, and they bid farewell in the drive of Swanfield. Marcie looked up at the large, impressive home, built in the 1880s with red sandstone quarried from Caithness in the northeast. It was an impressive building by any standing, starting life as a hunting lodge with a few bedrooms, and then added to throughout the years to end up as the focal point of the village, with the cottage of Sweet Briar next door frequently used as staff quarters or for visitors. Its days as a bolt hole for the landed gentry as they hunted and shot their way around the Highlands had long gone when it was changed into a family home. The only reminder of previous times were the various mounted stag heads that still hung on the walls around the large hall and staircase. Marcie had loved to hear old stories about visitors to the house when she was a child, but had come to detest the animal trophies that had led to nightmares. After his first visit to Swanfield, Simon had presented Marcie with a Highland cow's head mounted on a plaque – a jokey felt-covered toy that was immediately banished to the spare room. She had appreciated the sentiment and the thought behind it, but it was never recovered from its box and never spoken of again.

She turned around as she viewed the still snow-capped mountains and the ridges that lay beyond, reaching down to the loch with its craggy coastline and clear icy water. Breathtaking as they were, she knew the danger that lurked in their quiet still-ness. She stretched out her shoulders and went into the warm embrace of the house, looking forward to another early night, cosied up in her bed, and bringing Simon up to speed with that day's goings on in her increasingly long phone calls.

# TEN

Callum sat looking at the empty grate for an age. The house was cool now but there was no point in him building a fire when there was no one to share it with. The previous day, Brodie had gone to collect supplies at the Farm and Household Store in Inverness. He should have come back to see to the feed and hay that morning but there had been no sign of him.

Earlier, Callum had seen his niece at the top of the high ridge speaking to some bikers. He'd watched as the bikers roared off, hearing the noise of their powerful motorbikes reverberate around the mountains. He bemoaned the few tourists who passed through their beautiful homeland these days. They brought much-needed money to some other parts of the Highlands, but had mostly passed Strathkin by, which both saddened and gladdened him. He didn't want the village to change. Marcie must have noticed that his mood was up and down these days. He was conflicted about the life he wanted, and he only wished he could tell her why.

To make sure she was okay, he followed her trail in the distance as she made her way across the hill to The Strathkin Inn and to Heather. When he saw her go into the hotel, he walked through his garden to the back door of Swanfield. He looked around, pleased that his niece was as tidy as he was, and made his way to the lounge. He moved some cushions around the window seat, lifting them up, searching. Where was it? Had Marcie found it, and if so, would she have read it? Or had he left it in his own home?

An image came into his head again of soft gentle sand underfoot, like the white sands of Morar, only warm. He longed for the sun on his back. He wanted cocktails at sundown.

He looked across to the hotel past the Balfour croft. It was such a clear day, cloudless now, that he wondered if they could see lights on in Sweet Briar as clearly as he could see their houses. The village was alive with gossip, and church on Sunday was awash with whispered low voices and furtive looks between friends and parishioners. If someone was late taking laundry in on a Saturday and it unexpectedly fell to Sunday, they would be on the sharp end of some gossip, such was the hold of the church still in this part of the western Highlands. What on earth were *they* doing that it had to stretch so far into the *Lord's Day*? Babies to soothe, drunkards to put to bed, it made no difference. Gossip was currency and some people salivated at the very thought. What would they think if they had seen what he had so clearly witnessed the night before?

For years, everyone in Strathkin believed a Mosse and Balfour wedding would be the event of the decade, bringing two well-established families together to keep the names alive and a foothold in the area. He saw the way his niece's eyes danced when Ruaridh's name was mentioned. But he knew deep down she was no marriage wrecker. He remembered the stern warning from Lisanne when his own indiscretion became known all those years ago in their tight Swanfield circle. The family involved disappeared into the night, a marriage in crisis. A small farm closed up while gossiping villagers nudged and pointed. He wanted to leave then but was persuaded that he had to live out his life where he was always intended to be, except now under the more watchful eye of his mother and all the scrutiny that small village life brings.

He decided to go back to Sweet Briar; he didn't want Marcie thinking he was still freely coming and going when she wasn't there. It would only be for a few more days and then he would be ready to gradually move his own personal possessions back into his childhood home.

He left through the back door. Reaching into his pocket for a bunch of keys, he quietly locked the door behind him. He made his way to his own house and found the brochure peeking out from behind a cushion. He sighed and smiled. His mind was beginning to play tricks on him. He sat down on the window seat. He opened his book of daily tasks, looking at lists that seemed to get longer and longer, and his mind drifted to a future far, far away from the confines of Swanfield.

# ELEVEN

Since arriving back at Swanfield, Marcie had slept more than she had done in months, years maybe. With such total quietness – save the occasional hoot from an owl – Swanfield was so unalike their little Bloomsbury flat. Single glazed, it absorbed every noise that came from the busy Southampton Row below: ambulances, police cars, motorbikes, the screech of tyres as enraged drivers fought with delivery drivers on bikes – life in all its forms was everywhere and all around them. It all became part of the background of city living, and after a while the noise blended into a low buzz that was simply always there but almost unnoticed.

The Highlands were so different.

From her first night back, she had slipped into her old queen-sized bed with sheets and a blanket overlaid with a hand-made crocheted shawl, the heaviness of it providing comfort and solace. Here she had never had to resort to the tiny blue tablets prescribed by her GP to aid her sleep when her work was overwhelming and a restful night remained elusive.

The only problem, she surmised, was that she was sleeping too late. But tonight, she *was* restless. She tossed and turned past midnight. When she finally drifted off, she woke with a start, hearing something outside that wasn't familiar. She crept out of bed and to the window, pulling slowly on the heavy lined curtains, straining to see in the dark.

The loch was glistening under a high moon. Something caught her eye to the right of the house. It was a vehicle, dark, black maybe, lights off, creeping up the drive slowly, past the side, around to the back, gravel, pebble and shingle cracking under broad, heavy tyres. Marcie felt her heartbeat quicken and leaned against the wall, stock still, knowing that the back door to the utility and boot room, then kitchen, was unlocked.

'Flip!' Marcie left her bedroom on tiptoe and quickly inched her way into the guest bedroom at the back of the house, looking out as a car pulled up to Sweet Briar. Callum's words rang in her ear, telling her about recent break-ins, something virtually unheard of in this little enclave. Doors to neighbours and friends were never locked, and the freedom to roam without a care in the world was something she relished as a child. But at this moment, she cursed herself for being so reckless. The world had changed. Had Strathkin changed, too? At least Jamie MacKay was on the ball.

She tried to catch sight of a prowler but a car door opening and then quietly closing was all she could hear as she strained to look out into the black.

She slipped back to her room and picked up her phone, releasing it from its charging cable. She quickly dialled Callum's number. The phone was switched off.

'Oh no!' she said quietly under her breath as her mind raced.

Should she call 999? How long would it take for the police to get from Ullapool? An hour? More? She edged her way back to her bedroom window and looked over to Lochside Croft. Lights were still on. She scrolled through her *Contacts*, not knowing who she should call at this time of night.

Suddenly, Swanfield seemed very far away from people, places, help.

She was trying and failing to get her mind to make a quick decision when she heard another noise. The thought struck her that someone was inside the house. She leaned against the bedroom wall trying to regulate her breathing when the noise came again. It was the sound of a car door opening, then softly closing.

The fact that whoever had made the sound was outside gave her respite for a moment. She peered at the car as, to her relief, it pulled away. She recognised even at this distance that it was the car that had almost run her off the road some days before. In the driver's seat, she saw the unmistakable outline of Brodie Nairn.

Marcie leaned back against the wall, her breathing slowly returning to normal. A thin line of perspiration rested at the base of her spine as she sighed with relief.

'What do I do now?' she asked herself, having almost been scared half to death over something that was probably nothing.

Brodie had more likely than not left something at Sweet Briar and was coming back to collect it. But why do so at midnight, in the pitch dark, with no lights on his car?

It made no sense, and yet it was the only explanation she could offer herself at this time of night. She would have to wait until the morning to ask Callum. For now, she would try to get some sleep. But first, she had to make sure the doors were locked.

She skulked downstairs, walked into the kitchen, turned on all the lights, and made her way to the back door, only to find it was already locked. She looked on the key hook for the key and there it was with a large key ring attached. Marcie didn't recall locking the door. She tried the door again, checked the front door to make sure it was secure, and then made her way back upstairs. On her way, she flicked on the outside light, deciding to leave the lights on for peace of mind and as a warning to anyone out there that they would be seen.

It took an age to get to sleep but finally she drifted off only to be wakened by her phone ringing. It was Simon, explaining that he couldn't get time off work at the bar, encouraging her to make her mind up to head south sooner rather than later now that they had their future to decide upon. She joked that she wasn't being held hostage against her will and promised that she would start packing. She didn't tell Simon about the night's events, knowing that she couldn't leave Swanfield until she found out why the mysterious Brodie Nairn was skulking about so late.

The rest of the morning was uneventful. She found herself checking the back door several times, before sitting at the large kitchen table pondering long and hard about what the day would bring. Her acceptance to dinner at the Balfours had been playing on her mind. She thought up excuse after excuse for not going, realising every single one of them was as weak as yesterday's tea. Ultimately, she decided that to not go would appear churlish and somewhat suspicious.

By late afternoon, the clothes pile on the floor was getting bigger and bigger, just like the evening her girlfriends came over. Her cool city clothes had remained mostly in her case save for her black velvet shift that she had worn to Lisanne's funeral. Eventually, she settled on white jeans tucked into low black patent heeled boots and a camisole covered by a lace sweater that would keep the chill at bay if they drifted out into the garden. Next, she put on light make-up and let her hair fall down to her shoulders. She picked up a bottle of wine from the utility room along with the box of chocolates and ground coffee she had bought as a gift.

When she was ready, she looked out the window across to Sweet Briar. No smoke drew up from the stack and there were no cars, so Callum was clearly still out and about. He must be working; after all, a visit to the far part of the Estate was an all-day affair. While she was not too worried – after all, her uncle had his own life here – they still needed to resolve their differences before she made her way home to Simon. She also wanted to find out about the goings on the previous evening. She strolled out to the front of the house, carefully locking the carved wooden front door behind her.

Just as she arrived at the entrance to the driveway, Ruaridh pulled up in his Land Rover and jumped out.

'The boys will love this!' he called, beaming.

Marcie realised her outfit looked out of place – smart casual city yes, country dining, maybe not. She spotted the children across the water and waved enthusiastically as a genuine smile crept across her lips. Sliding into the passenger seat, she saw that the vehicle was littered with children's toys, books, empty yoghurt pots and the evidence of sticky little hands.

'Sorry, we virtually live in here. Family chauffeur.' Ruaridh shrugged and swung the Land Rover around on the single-track road, up on to the verge and back onto the road.

'I nearly didn't come,' she blurted out, almost unintentionally.

'Why?' he asked, somewhat taken aback, turning to look at her quizzically.

'Well, the other night,' she confessed, shaking her head, blushing at the thought.

'Ach, don't worry about that, I've forgotten it already!' he joked, jostling her arm which made her feel even more embarrassed.

. . .

It took only moments for them to arrive at Lochside Croft. She got out of the Land Rover just as the sound of screaming children became lounder and louder as three blond boys jumped and skipped their way up to the garden gate, with the youngest, Douglas, standing on the wooden gate, forcing it to swing open to allow her to enter.

Marcie could barely understand the children as they all chatted to her together. Douglas took her hand and led her down to the loch.

'Daddy and I were looking for fishes,' he explained, pointing a mctre or so out and looking up to her for approval.

'Did you find any?' she asked, leaning down to his height.

'No, but Daddy said there was a big one in the freezer, and we had to take it out secretly and show Mummy to make her squeal.' He smiled up at her, all gapped teeth and a blond mop of hair. His grin was infectious.

She lifted him and pointed across the loch. 'Do you see that house over there?'

'The castle?' asked the little boy.

Marcie laughed. 'It's not a castle, it's just a big house – that's where I live.'

'Did your mummy die?' asked Douglas, matter-of-factly, taking a piece of her hair and wrapping it around his fingers.

'No, it was my grandmother. She passed away.'

'Did we go to her leaving party? My papa says when it's time for him to go he's having a leaving party, but I don't know where he's going after that,' he stated, now holding his hands out in a quizzical way.

She ran her hand across his soft cheek and let him slide down her body, his bare feet disappearing into soft sand and shingle. He pulled her by the hand up onto the lawn, where his two brothers were running circles around the grass with arms outstretched like little human aircraft. Beyond them, Dina sat with her arm around Dax, her oldest, on the pale blue bench, the colour a replica of the lintels and doors on this charming cottage. She held up a glass with clear fizzy liquid and lemon.

'Cocktail hour at the Balfours – it's G&T tonight.' Dina beamed, and Marcie wandered up to join her.

Dax smiled and asked politely if she would like a drink, his soft Highland lilt a charming distraction from his chaotic brothers as they tore around the garden.

'That would be lovely,' she agreed and sat down next to her friend on the bench, sighing deeply.

'I forgot how gorgeous it is from this side,' she said, looking back over the loch to Swanfield.

'It's perfect,' said Dina, and she pushed her sunglasses up higher on her face. 'I can't ever imagine leaving. It's idyllic.' She gave a sigh of contentment and they both sat for a few moments surveying the scene as a red kite danced above them, gliding in the light breeze, while the children made their way to the shore picking at rocks, and peace was restored.

'When are *you* going back?' asked Dina, turning slightly towards her friend.

'Supposed to be Sunday.'

'Supposed to be?' quizzed Dina.

'It will be Sunday,' qualified Marcie. 'I have some things to sort out down the road.'

'Everything okay with you and Simon?' quizzed Dina suspiciously.

'Oh, gosh, yes, everything is great. It's just that, well, I need to, oh gawd, I don't know where to start.' She sighed, leaning back against the harled white wall behind her.

Dax appeared with her early evening drink, carrying it carefully in both hands. He walked at a snail's pace towards her, not wincing at the pebbles and shale path under his bare feet, his tongue resting on his lips in full concentration.

She took the drink tenderly from him and clinked her glass against Dina's. It was deliciously refreshing, and she took a hearty gulp.

'Okay, you two lovelies, you want something to eat now or are you dismembering the male race one by one?' roared Ruaridh as he came out to join them, a bottle of beer in hand.

The boys, on seeing their father, ran and skipped hurriedly up the lawn from the loch side. He held his beer bottle up high so that it didn't interfere with their cuddle-bombing. The youngsters screamed and yelped as they attacked their father with leg grabbing and hand pulling, and he yelled at them to stop in a veiled attempt at anger which simply seemed to make them more boisterous.

'I think it's the spring in the air, the longer nights, it makes them mad,' explained Dina, shaking her head as she watched her husband being attacked on all sides. 'Him included.'

Marcie smiled. Ruaridh had adapted to the role of father with ease. From a family of only boys whose first words were 'tractor', it was simply history repeating.

'Do you ever think back to school?' asked Dina. 'Could you have imagined this?'

'Not in the slightest,' said Marcie as she ducked to miss a foam ball that had headed her way.

Ness, the family dog, lying in the shade, joined in the fun with an occasional woof. It seemed to Marcie a picture of perfect domestic bliss that Dina fitted with so well. The most beautiful girl in the class, maybe the school, the girl who could have left all of this behind and gone anywhere, had been married at twenty and a mother at twenty-one and was likely to live out her days at Lochside Croft.

Marcie looked beyond the fake fighting and over to Swan-field. It was always a welcoming sight to her, but it looked stark and empty tonight. She knew the only sound from inside would be the large clock on the mantel, idly ticking away the minutes and years.

Ruaridh broke away from the fighting three and came back over. Dina smiled up at him while Dax stood beneath the lintel of the half-open door, silently watching his brothers and the group on his bench.

'He's the quiet one,' Ruaridh said with a nod to the oldest brother of the four, 'always thinking, always planning. He's definitely...' He and his wife looked at each other with a smile rising on their faces. 'Dina *with a dick!*' they said together quietly and naughtily. After a second of recognition, all three burst out laughing. Marcie looked over to the blond boy languidly leaning on the blue doorway, hand behind his back, squinting in the sun as it shone upon his face, his sparkling eyes and blond hair – there was no doubt that he was Dina's first born. The curve of his cheek, the dimple on the chin; he could have been Dina at the same age.

Inside, the kitchen table was as noisy as she expected as the children all in turn vied for her attention to tell her stories about school and fishing and learning to ski and boating on the loch and then swoon with amazement that she was related to Callum and lived in the big city of London.

'We can see into your house when the lights are on,' said Douglas, giggling, looking at his other brothers round the table for support and their input.

'Stop it. That's rude,' scolded his older brother in the soft Highland brogue of Strathkin, and a look of apology and silence reigned for the briefest of moments.

The dinner was a beautiful pheasant dish, shot the previous season by Ruaridh on a rare day off with friends on the hill, and it was braised with wine, garlic and plenty of onions in a heady mix that made it feel more of an autumnal dish than early spring. It was the best thing Marcie had eaten since she arrived, followed by a homemade pavlova with red berries from the freezer that had been frozen moments after picking last season. Plenty of wine was flowing but Dina had her hand over her glass. She signalled to Ruaridh that the serious drinking and a proper ceilidh could only start once the young boys were safely in their beds, and that it was his turn to provide the turndown service as they jokingly called bedtime.

'Do you remember that trip we had to see the ship?' asked Ruaridh. 'Where was it, Dundee or Glasgow? And they gave us cheese sandwiches on white plastic bread and a packet of crisps?'

Marcie laughed. With an entire Highland larder surrounding them, their packed lunches had been made up from whatever had been shot or caught nearby. They'd looked incredulous when handed white bread and a slice of processed cheese.

'Remember old Mr McLeod who taught art and creative studies?' asked Dina.

'Old *Two Suits*?' asked Ruaridh, leaning down to lift another plate that was handed to him from a lineup of boys. The youngest stood on a plastic step over the sink, collecting coloured picnic tumblers that had been used as their water glasses.

'Yes, one day black, next day blue, next day black, next day blue and remember that day on the twelfth of August he came in in tweeds? I think we all got detention!'

'He was...' Dina began then looked round to make sure the boys were all busy.

Marcie leaned across the table. 'What?' she quizzed.

'*Arrested*,' said Dina, making a tunnel with her hands over her mouth. 'Couple of months ago. Up near the Altan Dubh. Near the picnic spot.'

'Seriously?'

'He was a creepy bugger,' said Ruaridh, leaning over Marcie to pick up the breadbasket that was filled with bread middles and crusts. Some of the boys liked the crispy outside, and the others preferred the soft middle to wipe up the juices off their plate.

'Shhh!' warned Dina with a nod to the line that was slowing down. The boys knew that as this part of the evening was finished, they would be hauled off to bed with no bath tonight, as the Saturday football five-a-side had been cancelled for the second week in a row. Instead, in the morning they would be heading up the hill with their father for a bracing walk or yomp.

Ruaridh disappeared upstairs with the children with the promise of coming back down to share stories of what had happened in the village in the last year since her previous visit. There were whoops of delight from the boys that their father was putting them to bed – meaning their naughtiness could remain unchecked a little longer until Ruaridh brought the storybook out to bring the youngsters' evening to a conclusion. The two friends cleared what was left on the table, cling-wrapping what could be saved for a lunch or supper the next day. With no supermarket or local shop nearby, people were resilient in repurposing food and leftovers, and the next day's picnic would contain at least some of what had been left at the table.

'Do you remember my purple sandwiches?' Marcie laughed later on as they began to empty the dishwasher of the first quick wash.

'Gawd! The beetroot sandwiches!' laughed Dina, joining in.

'Beetroot on white bread? I was clearly less sophisticated in those days,' said Marcie with a shake of her head.

'It wasn't white bread, it was a *Swanfield Tin Sandwich Loaf*,' said Dina, trying as best she could to mimic Lisanne's accent.

They laughed the laugh of true friends who had a shared history of childhood memories, and Marcie leaned back against the large American-style fridge freezer, recalling Ruaridh reminiscing about his first trip to London. He had found it mesmerising, he told her. During his last visit with Dina for their tenth anniversary, he had felt the shine had been taken off and the couple realised city living was not for them.

The large open kitchen was essential for their big family; the wood burner at the end of the room was at one point the only heating in the house. Ruaridh often told stories to his boys about growing up there, when he and his brothers had shared a bed. In the winter, the condensation ran down the inside of the windows, and the inside of the cottage was almost as cold as the unforgiving landscape that lay beyond their front door. He would joke with the boys that this was back in the black and white days, and they would howl with laughter. Now this house was open and welcoming with two large tan leather sofas sitting either side of the wood burner and a homemade table separating them and the two armchairs that faced the fireplace. It was comfortable and messy with toys but had a warmth even on the coldest day.

Marcie went over to pick up Dina's wine glass to refill it, pouring as she walked.

'You've not finished your G&T, slow coach, or your wine,' said Marcie as she returned to the table to retrieve the tall tumbler, still half full.

'It's just tonic, if you could fill it up with some ice from the freezer.'

Marcie walked over to the freezer, but when she turned, she saw her friend leaning with her back to the sink with a huge wide grin on her face.

'What's made you so...?' started Marcie and saw her friend's right hand rest on her still-flat stomach.

'You're not?' she gasped.

'Sure am!' Dina grinned, a smile as wide as she'd ever seen.

'O.M.G!'

'Ssh!' warned Dina with her finger covering her lips. 'No one knows yet, not even Ruaridh, and...' She made a point of peeking up the stairs where howls and squeals of laughter could be heard above them. She cupped her hand around her mouth. 'It's a girl,' she whispered, loud enough for her friend to hear.

Marcie grinned and rushed over to hug her. Dina lifted her finger to her lips again. 'I don't want to say anything just now. You know we're waiting on that forestry contract and I'm not sure it's going to come through, so if it doesn't, I've decided that's the perfect time to tell him – keep spirits up. It's a constant worry, truth be told. We've lost two contracts to some of the bigger companies and I'm not sure I want Ruaridh working with all that logging equipment, but we need to keep our options open. It's a hard graft catering for six hungry mouths and another one on the way means we *really* need to keep the wolf from the door. It's not easy.' Dina sighed but she had a look of perfect contentment on her face as her eyes drifted to the chaos beyond the stairs.

'Better top this up then and not give the game away.' Marcie filled her friend's glass to near the top with tonic water and refreshed the ice and lemon so that it looked like a properly refreshed gin and tonic.

With the table cleared they went over to the three sofas at the far end of the room and sat down. Dina lifted her long legs onto a handmade driftwood table that was scattered with half-burned candles, and children's detritus like coloured tumblers, books and crayons.

'I've always said this is a home, not a house,' sighed Marcie. 'Sometimes our place in London looks so spartan, like a show home. Simon says it looks like it's been taken over by forensics.' Dina gave out a little giggle. 'And Swanfield, oh Dina, I'd love you to get a hold of it. It's like a museum. It's like one of those houses you go and visit that has been frozen in time. I love it, I do, but look at your beautiful curtains...'

'Handmade.'

'I know. The heavy drapes in Swanfield, they were handmade, too, but I think it was by Queen Victoria's seamstress! They're ancient!'

They laughed as they heard Ruaridh's heavy footsteps. He ducked slightly as he came down the stairs. Only the faintest giggle could now be heard from the rooms upstairs.

'Are you okay in the office, Mars, I meant to ask?' said Ruaridh and pointed to the extension beyond the utility room. 'Had it built when I thought I was going to be a big shot exporter, but we all know what happened there, eh? Bit of a guest room now.'

The local fishing had all but dried up – literally – though the original plan for the room was a granny annexe for Ruaridh's grandmother, but she had died long before the building was finished. It had since then become a storeroom, an office, and, with a mini kitchen and shower-room, it took overflow guests or the occasional tourist who wanted to do some loch fishing with Ruaridh as their ghillie and guide.

The office/bedroom was decorated with muted Ross hunting tartan, with a high-end tourist in mind looking for a touch of stag and antler. However, tourists were few and far between in Strathkin, and the room sometimes looked like a museum piece. According to Dina, the boys had been pestering all winter to make it into a playroom, only for their father to unceremoniously toss them out into the wind and snow and tell them to come back when they were hungry.

Marcie had always loved Dina's artistic flare. Dina could make a doorstop out of driftwood or rustle up a supper with some string and a glass of water, and she knew already she would sleep like a log in the cosy tartan enclave.

Ruaridh sat on the sofa directly opposite Dina with a wink as he picked up his refreshed bottle of beer and gave a great sigh. 'Ooft, they're a handful,' he said while gulping down the golden liquid.

'I told you,' said Dina with a shake of the head, 'they have spring fever.'

'Nah, it's the big city guest, they're all in love with you. Douglas is *totally* in love with you, says you smell lovely. At least, I think that's what he said. I mean, when will his new teeth grow in? It's like having a conversation with someone in a nursing home. I'm always covered in dribble and spit,' he joked as he made a point of wiping down the front of his checked shirt.

'Ruaridh!' scolded Dina and another wink was exchanged.

Marcie sat up, slipped off her boots and tucked her feet beneath her, sinking into the big comfortable sofa, suddenly feeling very tired. She stifled a yawn.

'I'm always like this here, it's the fresh air. It's so clear and clean. I can't keep awake,' she said and covered her mouth with her hand as she yawned again, no longer able to hide her waves of tiredness.

'Wow, you sucked all the air out of the room there, Mars,' scolded Ruaridh, and she laughed, looking at him.

*You are going to be smiling like the cat that caught the cream tomorrow*, she thought. Her eyes drifted to Dina who gave a slight nod, knowing exactly what her friend was thinking. Despite her moment of madness (as she had come to call it) in the kitchen of Swanfield, she looked at these two people in front of her and realised that theirs was an enduring love. Marcie knew deep down that the best thing she had done was to leave Strathkin and seek her own fulfilment elsewhere. Marcie loved her past, but her future only had one man in it, and she wanted what these two had with her own true love.

Marcie slept soundly until she was disturbed somewhere in the early hours by what she believed were whispered words and people trying, and failing, to talk quietly. Not used to being in a house full of children, she rolled over under the warm duvet and drifted off into another strange dream where walls were crumbling around her, and she watched as items were stolen from Swanfield. She tossed and turned as if she was in the grip of something and woke with a start to look at the face of a young toothless boy by the side of her bed. He made her yelp in surprise.

'Did I wake you? Are you awake now?' he asked as only children do with his toothless lisp.

Marcie struggled to pull herself up on the pillows, pushing her shoulders back. The young boy looked at her, captivated by this new stranger in their tight little family group.

*What a beautiful boy he'll grow into someday*, she thought, *and what a marvellous big brother he will be.*

'Can we go down to the water?' he asked her while sucking heartily on the ear of his Jellycat.

'Ah,' she pondered.

'Mummy's not up yet and it's really quiet.'

She looked at her watch on the bedside table. It had just gone six. She looked down at her nightwear – a black jersey nightgown, which wasn't exactly suitable attire for wandering outside, then caught the sight of a thick, heavy dressing gown hooked on the back of the door.

'Okay,' she relented and slipped out of bed, her feet cold against the bare wooden floor. She put on the dressing gown.

He took her hand, leading her to the back door of the little annexe, and she tiptoed along the pebbles around to the front of the house until her feet hit the soft morning dew on the lawn that led down to the loch side and its shingle, shale and sandy beach.

The day was clear, bright for the time of year this far north, with the clouds wakening over the hill. Marcie knew that the sun would fight its way through them to create another glorious spring day.

'Look!' said Douglas, excitedly pointing into the distance, and it took a moment for her to adjust her sight to see something far away over the mountains, raising her hand over her eyes to shield the bright sunshine.

'A wellycoppa!' said Douglas to her then handed her his cuddly toy, leaning down to let his hand float in the water. Marcie, confused for the briefest of moments, could suddenly hear a rotor blade in the distance as she squinted her eyes to see, with her hand covering her brows, but already the machine had dipped down and out of sight.

'What a scene of domestic bliss!' shouted someone behind her, and she turned to see Dina at the top window, with a grin at the scene before her.

'Can you swim?' Marcie suddenly asked her new young friend with a sudden thought of concern.

He nodded without looking up but stretched his hand behind him so that she could take hold of it. She sat down on the grass as the young boy looked closely at a piece of broken shell, picked it up, investigated it then discarded it.

'Aren't you cold, Douglas?' she asked, suddenly feeling the chill of her cold feet on wet grass. She knew that Dina would probably already be in the kitchen finding her favourite Arabica coffee and warming up a cafetière.

He shook his head, totally engrossed in his search for the perfect piece of stone or pebble.

Suddenly a roar startled them both, and Douglas jumped out of the water and straight in for a comforting hug. The helicopter swooped low over the house and straight along the loch at a distance of only several hundred feet. Marcie could feel the blast from the rotor blades above as Douglas clung closer to her and the deafening noise encircled them. She found herself instinctively covering his young ears before he started releasing himself gingerly. They were looking at the ripples of the water on the loch that were now washing up to their feet like waves.

'Whoa!' gasped Marcie as she watched the chopper make its way down the loch and then up as it glided slowly over the mountain range beyond.

'*WHOA!*' repeated Douglas loudly into her face, so close that she could smell the sweet morning milky breath of him. 'That was *fast!*' he said with huge wide blue eyes and then turned tail and ran up the grass, shouting to his brothers at the top of his voice.

By the time Marcie made it up to the door, Dina was just coming out with two mugs – one with freshly made coffee and the other with a piping hot chocolate. She indicated to the bench with a nod, and Marcie tiptoed over the shale and shingle towards her. Dina dug straight into her deep dressing gown pocket and pulled out a pair of slippers.

'This isn't my first rodeo.' She laughed to Marcie, who slipped the warm slippers over her feet and then rested them on the ground. She took the coffee gratefully from Dina.

'Did you see that?' said Marcie with a sip of the warm milky coffee. 'I'm sure he parted my hair, he was that low!'

'Mountain rescue,' explained Dina, 'up over the hill. It's usually either that or they're practising. It's a rescue today. They know the boys usually shout and wave at them – we saw them last year and they came up to the head of the loch and did a bow when we told them it was Donald's birthday. You know the way helicopters do – like they're saying a little hello?'

Marcie shrugged. 'The only helicopter I see in London is the air ambulance or the occasional police helicopter if there's a demo or something on.' She took another sip of coffee and marvelled at the silence of the Highlands, the peace, the solitude. Her busy life in London seemed a lifetime away. Her regular light sleeping had changed and she felt more rested, something she had taken for granted when she lived here all those years ago.

'I'm sorry if we woke you early.'

'Early?' asked Marcie, cupping her coffee in her hands.

'Ruaridh got a call from the Mountain Rescue Team Leader asking if he'd go out.'

'I didn't know he'd joined up,' said Marcie, her eyes drifting to where the helicopter had been headed down the loch.

'You know what he's like. Ruaridh always thinks the world is a better place with him in it.'

Ruaridh Balfour certainly knew what he was capable of. He was the boy most likely to succeed in anything he did. He was always cocksure, and his school posse thought he was the veritable bee's knees and Ruaridh's high opinion of himself certainly didn't disappoint.

The women sat in silence for a moment looking at the stillness of the loch and the restored serenity around them. The boys were not yet awake, save for Douglas, and only the occasional birdsong interrupted their moment of peace.

'What did he say when you told him?' asked Marcie.

'Hmm?' quizzed Dina.

'That you're expecting?'

'Oh, we never got to the big reveal. Bloody phone call in the middle of the night. I'll save it. Plus, we need to hear about this contract first. Listen, why don't you come back over later? Or we could always come to you?' Dina said with more of a hint than a question.

'Why not? I can go down to the store and we can have something outside. It's nice enough. I've seen loads of salmon in the freezer, and I can nip up to Strathdon or to the farm shop at The Aizle for extras.'

Dina nodded with confirmation, and Marcie thought how excited the boys would be to see their house from the other side of the loch. She would be happy to let Dina and Ruaridh have some alone time by taking away the noise and the chaos. She had enjoyed being with them the night before, observing their coordinated parenting like they were born to it, and a tingle ran through her to think that she and Simon would one day be as relaxed and comfortable as parents, a role these two seemed to have settled into with ease.

'Could I cope with your boys on a sleepover?' she asked her friend.

'Actually, they're no bother, they mostly entertain themselves. I could keep watch from here,' said Dina with a look over to Swanfield, sitting stoic on the opposite side of the loch.

They both laughed and part of Marcie mused, *what have I done? what have I unleashed?* and the other part of her understood that giving Ruaridh and Dina some 'me' time was the right thing to do. Together they could enjoy the quietness of this wonderful secret they would share.

They went back into the cottage, and Marcie made her way to the annexe to quickly shower, pinning her hair up and deciding that a make-up free day was in order. Some cold water and a bracing loch walk would certainly wake her skin up.

Marcie joined the Balfour breakfast table. Without their father to wind them up, the boys seemed calmer while Dina floated effortlessly between sink and table with cereals and juice. Dax was helping his mother in his own quiet way. Once again, Marcie thought the boy was her friend's twin; they looked alike, sounded alike and Dax took his lead from his mother in a calm and ordered way.

With plates and dishes loaded in the dishwasher and an agreement to take the boys across to Swanfield late afternoon (too early to tell them as they would have been insufferable all day), Marcie stored what little she had brought back into her tote and went out to the front of Lochside Croft.

Douglas was once again back in his favourite spot at the edge of the loch, no longer in pyjamas but in shorts and a long-sleeved neoprene top.

'Are you going home, lady?' he asked in a small voice, squinting to look up at her.

'Yes. I have to head home now,' she replied, walking down to where he was hunched at the loch side.

'Are you going over there?' He pointed with short arms but a determined attitude.

'Yes. Do you want to come over later?' she offered.

'Stranger danger,' he said with the short-term memory of children engaged in so many different activities and in whose young lives adults came and went with such frequency. His shoulders turned and leaned down again to search for his elusive pebble or stone. Marcie shrugged and hoisted up her tote.

She had only walked a couple of steps when her phone rang in her bag. By the time she fetched it, it had rung off with no caller ID. It rang again, and Marcie was reluctant to pick up thinking it was some sort of scam. It was only when she heard the house phone at Lochside Croft ringing that her interest was pricked. It was an odd time of the morning for people to be looking for you, so she turned and walked quickly back up to the cottage, keeping one eye on Douglas at the water's edge. She heard a noise like a shout or a scream and felt her pace quicken slightly in the few steps it took her to get to the front of the house. Dina appeared at the open door, her hands up to her face. Her ashen face turned to a look of abject terror.

'It's the Liathach,' she said. 'Something terrible has happened on the mountain.'

'What? What is it?' asked Marcie, her voice raised several octaves.

'There's been an accident. Ruaridh left in the middle of the night, but...' she began. 'They've gone missing.'

'Who, Ruaridh?'

'The team. They're out of radio contact.'

'Well, maybe they're still searching for the people missing in the crags, I mean, I mean...' Marcie began to search for an answer, but words were going round and round in her head.

'They want us to meet at the village hall,' said Dina, stricken.

Biting her lip, Marcie watched as Dina ran her hand across her stomach. The sounds of the children drifted downstairs. The women looked at each other, and Marcie didn't know what to say or do. Throughout their lives, even on the few occasions it happened, a full-scale mountain rescue was always something to fear. Marcie felt a creeping sense of unease. In the past, men from the village had failed to return from rescue missions, and sons and daughters had been left without fathers. Experience and knowledge were no match for the mountain, which could both sustain life and take it away in the blink of an eye.

'I'll call Heather,' said Marcie. 'She's just up the road – she can come and look after the children.'

'No, call Bella,' said Dina. 'Heather's probably still got a lock-in.' She pulled herself to her feet and ran up the stairs.

'Hey, guys, let's get a shizzle on – Auntie Bella is taking you up to see the ponies,' called Dina quickly.

Ten minutes later, the boys came back down, none the wiser, dressed quickly in last night's clothes on the orders of their mother, just as Bella arrived at the back door, clearly out of breath and with the same fearful look as Marcie and Dina.

'I've heard them since early – the search and rescue heli-copters,' said their wide-eyed friend, speaking in a low voice and throwing off her jacket onto the empty chair. She made her way around each boy in turn, grabbing them close and kissing them furiously on the tops of the head. It was clearly a normal ritual as not one of them complained.

'I'm so grateful, so grateful,' said Dina to Bella, a look of thanks from friend to friend. They grasped one another's hands in a sign of solid friendship.

'Well, don't you be long at the shops. We're going to go up to the stables after a second breakfast and we're going to have a wee bit of a treat, aren't we, boys?' said Bella loudly, in an effort to divert their gaze from their mother's fearful face.

They nodded in unison, clearly oblivious to what was going on. Only Dax looked slightly suspicious at this early morning girls' club in their kitchen. It had barely gone 7 a.m. and Marcie thought his young brain would be trying to figure out what in this scene was not right, not realising it was the absence of his father.

# TWELVE

When they got to the village hall, they were met by an empty
police van and a regular police car, both with blue lights flashing. No one was outside the hall or in the vestibule, but as soon
as they entered the main hall, they found a scene straight out of
a TV drama. Groups of people were huddled together talking in
quiet tones; a centre table was down the middle of the large
space. Maps were spread out held flat by large lamps. The man
looking at the largest map was talking about grid references
while a colleague leaned over it pointing to Beinns and valleys.

Piles of ordnance survey maps were strewn across the long
table, and the distorted sound of radios crackled and echoed in
the high roof space. Marcie looked at the kitchen area where a
group of policemen, including Jamie MacKay, their local police
officer and schoolfriend, was talking to a sergeant she didn't
recognise and a woman beside them looking closely at a map,
passing a compass between them. Ruthie Gillespie, the local
postmistress, made tea wearing a WRVS tabard. Marcie
wondered how she was going to describe this to Simon later; she
never thought she would ever get caught up in such a scene.
People with looks of panic and fear gathered around. Marcie

realised that everyone in the village had come together to comfort and soothe each other. She approached people who clung to her, but she didn't have words to share. She felt numb to what was going on around her, thinking of what might lay ahead. She hugged a woman who was standing near her, hands shaking holding a teacup and saucer and tried to comfort the woman of her grief when she herself had no idea of how to deal with her own emotions.

The local Mountain Rescue Team was a mainstay of Strathkin. At least two ceilidhs were held in the village every year to support them for as far back as Marcie could remember. At one point, every man in the village had either been part of the volunteer MRT or a co-ordinator for fundraising and charity events. She remembered these events from her childhood; the fun and laughter and drinking and dancing that had become part of her social life as she got older. Mostly, she remembered the quiet table full of mostly silent, stoic, grey-faced men who had suffered from the stress that invariably accompanies a tragic accident out on the hills, be it in the middle of a cold snow-covered mountain on a beautiful spring day.

The two uniformed men dressed in blue in the middle of the room held up radios to their ears. Marcie realised they were from the Royal Air Force, possibly co-ordinating one of the helicopters they had seen this morning.

The one that flew over Lochside Croft earlier was the bright yellow search and rescue helicopter that would normally drop off MRT members and pick up casualties. For the moment, there was no roar of blades, and the people in the hall went about their business quietly and in a professional controlled manner. This situation was clearly something they had trained for. Orders were given in hushed tones, and people scurrying about were light on their heavy booted feet.

The quiet was suddenly broken when someone shouted, 'SIT REP.' One of the uniform-clad men with an earpiece stood up on the small stage where ceilidh bands had officiated over dances and birthdays, bringing people together to celebrate in a whirling skittish. Now a solemn silence fell over the hall. The sergeant and Jamie came out of the kitchen, appearing anxious to hear the latest situation report. Their eyes fell upon Dina as the sergeant nodded and said 'carry on' to the man on the stage.

'The three climbers were last seen at the far peak of Liathach by a climber on his way back down yesterday. They had tented nearby but when the climber returned last night from a walk, he noticed the tent still there and it had not been entered since his departure. We've now discovered a notebook with the route and a contact number for where they were staying tonight – the hotel here – but the manager reported them overdue. It was dark by nine and although he said they looked like experienced climbers with appropriate mountain gear, there's been no sign. Their mobile number is not contactable. Strathkin MRT were called out in the early hours and contact was lost with them about 0245 hours. The MRT Land Rover is at the base of the mountain range in a shaded area and Rescue 137 dropped off – it's empty so they're clearly on the crags but no answer from radio, no contact now for' – he stopped to look at his watch – 'just over five, nearly six hours.'

Marcie looked around, searching huddled groups of people for Callum's familiar face but he wasn't there. The police officer on stage began to talk about achieving specific goals and outcomes, carefully avoiding the gaze of the two women standing at the back of the hall. He spoke methodically, like he had been trained for these specific tasks, with an emotionless detached voice, looking at no one in particular.

Beside her, Marcie noticed Dina's legs buckle. A woman from the village who was vaguely familiar, wearing the red and white tabard with RED CROSS emblazoned across it, pulled a chair over and sat Dina down. She disappeared and returned moments later with a piping hot cup of tea, leaning down to speak with Dina.

'They're very experienced on the hills, they've been climbing since they were wee boys. Ruaridh will be fine – he knows what he's doing,' she reassured with the smile of a skilled comforter.

Marcie saw Jamie heading to the door to check his phone and decided to approach him.

'Hey, Marce,' he responded but she saw concern creep across his face. He took her arm and led her to the door. 'You guys, you and Dina, really shouldn't be in here. I've had a bit of grief from the boss who's up from Inverness. Keep yer heads down, eh?' he suggested.

'What's happened?' asked Marcie.

'You heard the Lieutenant from RAF Lossiemouth. It was a wee bit challenging up there yesterday near the top – still a lot of snow and ice up there, it's only April, mind. Word is' – he took her arm and led her into the vestibule – 'another climber thought he heard something and when he looked up the hill, he thinks he saw someone, or something, falling.'

'Oh, God.' Her hand shot across her mouth as Jamie leaned in close.

'There may be more than one casualty, to be honest. We're still trying to find out – seems like the climbers were all roped together. One of the guys is up at the car park interviewing the witness now. Hey, you don't know anyone here who speaks German, do you?'

It went over Marcie's head for the briefest of seconds before she made the connection and grabbed Jamie's arm. 'German?'

'Yeah, there's some indication they might be German, probably young, too, judging by the amount of Haribo and Pringles they had in their tent. Listen, I really shouldn't be telling you that,' he said with a concerned expression.

Marcie pulled out her phone from her pocket and searched

through her pictures, her hands shaking. 'Jamie, I think this is them. I met them the other day. They were doing the three mountains and finishing up over there on Liathach. I met them up at the high ridge, they're working in the Central Belt,' she blurted out suddenly. 'I think they're all in their twenties, they're young, they're doctors.'

She held up the picture she had taken of the three smiling young men. She was lost for words as they looked at the phone together. Jamie grabbed it without a word and hurriedly rushed back in to find his sergeant. People looked up from their maps and aerial pictures. A palpable buzz started as a slow hum. Suddenly people in the kitchen area were looking over the sergeant's shoulders to get a glimpse of the photograph on Marcie's phone.

Overwhelmed, Marcie rushed out into the fresh spring morning. Feeling like she was going to be sick, she walked quickly to the end of the car park where the grass fell away to the loch beyond.

She saw the boys in the far distance down at the shore near the trekking centre, and noticed a boy who she presumed was Douglas leaning down at the water's edge, a tiny figure. Would he still have a father in his life at the day's end? That moment, a red and white Coastguard helicopter swooped low over the village hall and headed back out to the far mountains, interrupting her thoughts. When she looked up again the four boys were all out, waving at the helicopter with yelps of joy. A vision of Ruaridh flashed through her mind.

*Please don't let him be a casualty*, her internal voice pleaded. Her thoughts were on Dina and their family. They needed him. The thought of ending the day without Ruaridh Balfour in the world made Marcie's stomach churn. This man had been in her life since they were children. She couldn't imagine a world without him in it. His ebullient laughter, caring nature, his irrepressible cheekiness, his thoughtfulness and kindness to strangers as well as to villagers. She knew in her heart that any romantic life with Ruaridh was long since over. Now more than ever she felt terrible for her drunken almost-kiss. Marcie shuddered at the thought of something happening to him. And were the three young men she had met lost alongside him? The prospect seemed so sudden, so cruel.

Returning to the village hall, Marcie sat at a table with coffee long gone cold. Her head was in her hands, trying to block out the noise. *Not those three lovely doctors,* she thought; so young, so chatty, smiley, so excited to be on their first climb in a country they had come to love. *Surely not them.*

When she looked up from her position at the back of the hall, she saw the tall, fair-haired figure of Brodie Nairn standing with the woman in the Red Cross tabard. She looked at him with a beatific expression as if he were an angel who'd come to comfort them. Marcie was distracted by watching the pair until Dina returned, having run home to fetch some blankets. She casually threw one over Marcie and patted her shoulders, then sat down heavily. It was clear she had been crying; she looked frightened, suddenly older than her years.

'Anything?' she asked quietly.

Marcie shook her head, rubbing Dina's back to comfort her. Marcie nodded to a woman who was offering cups of warm soup. Both women cupped the soup in their hands while staring ahead in silence.

It was a clear fresh spring day, not the depths of winter. That made the shocking turn of events all the more difficult to accept.

**STRATHKIN MOUNTAIN RESCUE**
*any hour – any day – any weather*

Dina's eyes drifted over the poster pinned to the notice-board behind them.

'I didn't know he had joined till recently,' she stated. 'He takes the boys hillwalking and caving, climbing. Anything outdoors. Anything he deems *fun*, I consider *vaguely dangerous*. You know what he's like.' Marcie nodded, staring into the middle distance. 'We did a fundraiser here last year, and he joined up. I was busy making cupcakes and he was signing up to be a hero.' She smiled. 'They meet once a month, to train...' Dina drifted off, seemingly in a kind of trance.

The sound of heavy rotor blades cut through the low chatter and through the windows Marcie saw a helicopter swoop low. Everyone fell silent, then the helicopter drifted off back up to the mountain range. The silence stayed. No one was dropped off. No one emerged heroic from beneath its whirling blades. Nothing.

Marcie watched from a distance as Brodie worked the room, offering words of encouragement, making cups of tea. He seemed keen to care for those like Dina with vacant or fearful expressions on their faces. But to her surprise, there was no sign of Callum. He had spent many years in the MRT and was nowhere to be seen. She had called, putting aside their estrangement. It had gone to voicemail. Marcie knew, over long fireside talks, of the trauma that some of the members had gone through, but it was strange that as founding member her uncle wasn't here.

The hours stretched on as daylight and nighttime blended into one. The next day soon arrived with no news and darkness descended once again. There was a suggestion that relatives and friends should find a new place to wait, but it was firmly rejected. This was a small village, and everyone belonged together, to share joy and tragedy. There was also talk of a press conference. There was chatter about the media descending on the village in their droves, but the tight cocoon of people in the hall closed in around each other, protective and comforting. And then it started. The rumours.

*Someone had spoken to someone. Somebody had overheard. Shouldn't say this, but...*

The hall's main door blew open and Lachie Bateman, the Mountain Rescue Team Leader, marched in, his presence sending a chill around everyone in the room. His earpiece was firmly fixed, his hand covering it to keep it in place, and he carried a crackling radio, making his way straight to the group of policemen in the side office, off the kitchen. Marcie watched as they huddled close together while he updated them, watching nervously as their faces grew grey the longer he spoke. He ran his hand through his thick white hair, looking strained. Someone started writing something down, and Marcie could feel concerned eyes glance to where they were sitting. Lachie caught Marcie's gaze, then his eyes moved to Dina. Marcie glanced at her friend, who rested face down on the table on her crossed arms and was breathing in and out loudly.

A police officer approached Ruthie Gillespie, the postmistress, who was still busy dispensing tea and sympathy and whose husband was, like Ruaridh, a keen volunteer. The policeman was accompanied by a female police family liaison officer, and as she placed her arm around Ruthie's shoulders, she guided her to the small room off the kitchen that had been designated as a rest room.

The wail that followed sounded like a wounded animal.

People looked up and around, and a small gasp was released from a group of people who had been standing with Ruthie just moments before. Hands covered mouths, silent tears ran down ruddy cheeks. Geordie Gillespie was a leader, a mountain guide, a husband to Ruthie and a father of two. *What would happen to the family now?* thought Marcie, eyes wide at this unfolding scene of horror.

Moments passed and then another female police officer accompanied a tearful woman she didn't recognise through to the small rest area. Then the face of a police officer was opposite Dina.

Dina reached out her hand, and Marcie grabbed it.

The police officer cleared her throat.

'Mrs Balfour?'

At first, Dina couldn't speak. Her beautiful face crumpled. 'Yes?' she whispered, almost inaudible. Dina pulled herself up, and Marcie reached out to steady herself and her friend.

'I can't go in there. I can't go,' she whispered, as if saying it louder would somehow break a spell.

Marcie looked at Lachie's pained face as he stood in the doorway. Once more, Marcie felt her friend's legs buckle beneath her.

'I feel sick.' Dina turned to her and gripped her hand tightly. 'I can't go in...'

Dina struggled to stay upright. Suddenly Lachie's arms were around her, leading her forward.

He led them both into the room, where he placed Dina very gently in one of the two chairs sitting side by side at a low table. A policewoman waited for them, holding a piece of paper.

'Can I confirm that you are Dina Starling Marshall Balfour, wife of Ruaridh Balfour?'

'Dina?' said Lachie, when there was no reply. He kneeled to face her, taking her small trembling hand in his. 'We've got Ruaridh – he's badly injured but still with us.'

'Dear God!' cried Dina as tears rolled down her flushed cheeks. Lachie embraced her in a bear hug. It looked to Marcie as if her friend's body had become liquid as she sobbed.

'Where is he?' asked Marcie.

'The survivors are being airlifted to Inverness, to Raigmore Hospital.'

'Survivors?' she pressed.

Lachie nodded, and Marcie caught his tear-filled eyes.

'We've lost three climbers and two members of our team,' he

said, his voice breaking. 'The boys you met. The German doctors.' He shook his head incredulously. An ex-RAF pilot, he had retrained as a paramedic and now co-ordinated all rescues in the area.

Marcie's tears fell as she and Dina held on to each other. Such loss of life was hard to comprehend: how could a fun-filled day out end in such tragedy? Ruthie Gillespie would now have to carve out the rest of her life without her gentle husband Geordie. Marcie didn't know the other woman, but she couldn't have been much older than she was, and she, too, was now a widow at such a young age. An unseen tragedy had befallen their beautiful village.

But Ruaridh Balfour was coming back, very much alive.

Dina clung to Marcie, sobbing with relief, and she embraced her friend tightly.

As Marcie comforted Dina, she wished Simon was there. She wanted him to wrap his arms around her, to receive his comfort. She realised now how much she missed him, how much she craved his embrace, how much she loved him as they were surrounded by an overwhelming sadness.

Whatever stupid thoughts she'd had about Ruaridh since her arrival for Lisanne's funeral, she realised they were childish and bathed in the past. It had been so easy to become caught up in the minutiae of peoples' lives here, a life she had left. At times, she had felt she was being drawn into her previous life and had had to bring herself back down to earth. *You will live this with them*, she thought, *and then you will leave and will go back to your own very different world. This snapshot in time is not real. Excitement followed by horror is not Strathkin.* And Ruaridh's heroic return would be a defining moment for her, too. *My life isn't here*, she realised. *My life here is no more. My future is with Simon far, far away from here.*

It took several days for the thundering helicopters to disappear and for life to return to normal. In the village, Marcie often passed people she didn't recognise: parents, brothers, relatives of those who had lost their lives, and she tried to acknowledge their grief the best she could, with a nod and a smile or compassionate glance.

Callum's phone was going to voicemail. Texts unanswered. She knew the trauma of survivor's guilt from when he was previously a well thought of member of the MRT – Lachie Bateman's right-hand man. Whilst she was concerned more than worried; she had convinced herself that he had simply shut down, and needed thinking time. It had happened before. Night terrors and trauma and then finally acceptance that he couldn't save everyone when he was called out time after time after time. Eventually he had retreated into his own shell to contemplate events and would isolate himself from the world outside. When he left the close-knit team of selfless men and women, he said he would never go back, such was the deep wounds and scars these rescues with no positive outcome caused.

Marcie felt this what was going through his mind now – something as dramatic as this happening so soon after the death of Lisanne.

From her bedroom window that looked out across Strathkin Loch, she watched as her friend's Land Rover, driven by Dina's father-in-law, pulled up to the cottage across the water. A crouched figure was helped out of the car followed by the sounds of excited children's screams. It was Ruaridh's arrival home from the hospital in Inverness.

The children crowded round him, and only Dax stood slightly aside as he surveyed the scene, seeing his father's strength suddenly sapped. He watched intently as the crouched-over, broad man, shoulders covered by a shawl, made his way towards the house. Ruaridh was helped inside, and Marcie closed the curtains, allowing the family privacy.

She thought about the secret Dina had shared with her.

How happy Ruaridh would be, and how joyful that the tragic loss of life was somehow balanced by bringing a longed-for girl into their boisterous family. She imagined his expression when Dina told him. Emotions bubbled out of her on this early spring evening, a fresh cool wind circling the loch, kicking up white salty foam, and she cried for the umpteenth time in this same week. She still had so much to talk over with both Simon and her boss, Henry, who was expecting her back in the office in the next few days. Were her tears only for Ruaridh and Dina, or were these selfish tears, mourning the loss of her old life? A life based around Swanfield, her glorious childhood home. She planned to say goodbye in the next few days, as soon as she'd spoken to her uncle.

# THIRTEEN

The conversation with Henry, her boss, the next day did not go as well as Marcie expected. The story of six people killed on the Scottish hills hardly featured on his daily news feed. News of whatever magnitude that far north was, as Henry told her, provincial, and only those involved were interested. It was a top of the news leader for one afternoon and dropped off the headlines by early evening. No one, he stated, was concerned in the slightest. He was keen to have Marcie back, but she knew she had to leave nothing unfinished before she stepped on a plane. They agreed longer bereavement leave; Marcie promised to work harder on her return. She put the phone down after their call and stared at the scene outside her window. Still and majestic mountains bathed in morning sun surrounded her. How different from her London view. She felt it again – that incessant pulling back and forth of her emotions.

From their daily phone calls, Marcie could tell that even Simon was becoming restless. She knew she was putting off the conversations they needed to have about their future. She was desperate for him to come to visit Swanfield, but he said no, assuring her that leaving Swanfield was like a sticking plaster.

*Come down here,* was his response. *Only then can we decide about whether to invest our money in Swanfield or to put the estate on the market. Maybe then we can talk about how it would benefit us and our future.* But Marcie knew, none of that was possible without first having a frank and open conversation with Callum. And he still seemed to be avoiding her. Whatever happened, Marcie was determined not to end up like her mother, who always said she was forced to give up the career she worked so hard to build up. To avoid the same fate, she needed a plan.

Her head in her hands, Marcie was alerted to the sound of raised voices outside. She made her way through to the kitchen and realised that the shouting was coming from Sweet Briar next door. She stepped out through the back door and saw Callum and Jamie MacKay, the local police officer, involved in a heated discussion.

She tried to listen in, then scolded herself. She was behaving like a local village gossip. If she wasn't spying on the Balfours, she was listening to her uncle have a blazing row with a man in uniform, who at the drop of a hat could relieve him of his liberty. She went back inside, trying to close the door quietly, but that moment a gust of wind from her open windows took the door away from her and it flew shut with such a heavy bang that it reverberated around the house and out into the back yard. Peeking from behind the pulled back curtains she saw both men stop mid flow to look back at Swanfield. Soon after, they parted company. To her surprise, Jamie turned and headed in her direction.

'Flip!' Marcie said to herself. She pressed against a larder door next to the window to make herself small and invisible. There was crunching on gravel as someone came to the window, looked in, then left.

Next moment, she heard tyres screeching and the heavy police vehicle pulled away from Sweet Briar. By the time she got back through to the dining room, the police 4x4 vehicle was long gone.

Marcie waited a good half an hour before plucking up the courage to go next door to tease out from Callum what had just happened and where he had been. She knocked the door with a *rat-a-tat* and pushed it open to be faced with Callum, cloth in hand, polishing his shotgun, with cartridges on the kitchen table. She gasped and Callum turned, shut and raised the gun he was holding so that it was only feet away from her. There was a moment of silence until Callum snapped open the gun with a crack and let it fall over his elbow.

'Marcie!' he said, almost scolding her, but there was a look of distress on his face.

'Oh, sorry!' she managed to say, her heart beating so loudly she was sure he could hear it. A sudden fear had come over her.

'I'm so sorry, lass, I'm so sorry...' pleaded Callum as he put down the gun and made his way over to her. 'Are ye okay?'

'For Pete's sake, Callum, shouldn't that be in the gun room?'

'Oh, I'm so sorry.' He genuinely looked worried at what might have just happened. 'I was a bit spooked, to be honest. Jamie was here, you know, Constable MacKay, and he was reminding me of the break-ins I told you about, so I was just getting prepared.'

'You're not flipping James Bond in *Skyfall*! If something happens here no one is going to arrive in a helicopter to save you – or us,' she qualified.

'Bu—' he started.

'Put that away!' she ordered. She was shocked at the way she was speaking to her uncle, but the thought of what could have happened frightened her to her core.

Her uncle seemed both surprised and jolted back to life at her directness. He walked around the table and hugged her, but even so, she felt a change in him. It wasn't the warm embrace from her uncle she would cling to when anything was wrong in her life. The hug was stiff, distant. Since the funeral, there had been a shift in their relationship, and Marcie could clearly sense it. But she couldn't think why. Had witnessing her indiscretion with Ruaridh caused his sudden coldness?

'We need to talk, Callum – we've all missed you the last few days here,' she began. 'What's going on, Cal?' Her tone took on a gentler resonance, which she hoped would extinguish the coldness that had crept in between them.

'Och, it's just the thought of you going away, I think, not knowing when you'll be back. It's been a joy, lass, having you so nearby, but things have to get back on an even keel at some point,' he said with a sigh.

'I can't just rush away and leave you, not until we—'

Their conversation was interrupted by the crunch of gravel outside, and through the window Marcie saw Callum's Hilux pick-up truck. Moments later, the lithe figure of Brodie slid out from the driver's seat, before collecting boxes from the rear and dropping them at the back door. Callum went out to greet him, and Marcie was sure she witnessed something exchanged between them. It was the same type of facial expression she would sometimes give to Simon – a warning to stay quiet, to say nothing. As if they were keeping a secret from her.

'Ah, hello!' greeted Brodie, hoisting a large bag out of the back of the truck and placing it down at the back door. So, he *does* do manual work, Marcie thought, although she was unsure if retrieving half a dozen bags from the back of a truck truly counted as farm labour.

'Brodie, hi,' Marcie said. 'I'm sure everyone would want to thank you for your help in the hall recently. Those poor German boys. I was just thinking about you – I can't remember where you said you were from? Was it Germany? No, Denmark?' She smiled at him.

'Me? I am a citizen of the world!' joked Brodie, placing the last bag of peat pellets on the side of the wall near the back door, then wiping his hands on a cloth hanging from his trouser pocket.

'May I?' He indicated to Callum that he needed to wash his hands.

'Be my guest,' replied Callum and opened the door wide so that Brodie could squeeze in past.

The young man made his way straight to the sink, picked up a bar of soap and started to wash his hands, taking his time as he did so. For a time, a strange silence befell the room. Marcie felt as if she was interrupting some silent dialogue between the two men.

'Listen, guys,' she said awkwardly, 'I've got stuff to do so I'll catch you later. Can you make sure that gun is locked away?' She gave a warning look to Callum before retreating through the back door and over to Swanfield.

She was both baffled and intrigued by Brodie, how he avoided her questions about his background, and his unfamiliar, almost mid-American, Scandi accent. Something told her it was fake. But why put on a fake accent? What was he trying to hide?

Or was she simply trying to find a scapegoat for her uncle's standoffish behaviour? Was her forensic brain trying to join two and two together and making five? What had happened to put an end to her fatherly relationship with Callum? Where were the usual horseback rides together and their gossipy picnics? Marcie was perplexed. Something – or someone – was driving a wedge between their cosy loving relationship. It might be that her uncle had learned about her inheriting Swanfield. But something told her it was Brodie who had come between them. She couldn't pinpoint why she was becoming so suspicious of him. He seemed to be such a stalwart of the village, judging by his behaviour after the hiking accident, and everyone spoke so highly of him. But there was something eating away at Marcie about this newcomer. She liked a puzzle. She liked to exercise her brain. And it was her opinion, and it would seem *only* her opinion, that there was something just not quite right about Brodie and his backstory.

Marcie decided to take a quick drive around the loch to see if it could help release some of her built-up animosity. She would stop in to see Heather, too. She had been comforting on the phone during the tragic mountain accident, and Marcie wanted to thank her for her compassion. And it would give her an opportunity to drop in Brodie's name, try to find out a little more, try to press her friend to give up any more information she had on the man who had so suddenly appeared in all of their lives. Was he, as her uncle seemed to think, an unexpected blessing with his hard-working and compassionate attitude to everyone he seemed to meet or was there something more – something that only she could see. She had a forensic brain and an inquisitive mind. Surely she couldn't be wrong on both counts. There really was only one way to find out. An interrogation of the most subtle kind.

She found her friend in the rear yard joking and jostling with a delivery man who was wheeling a keg into the back of the bar area. She waved happily when she saw Marcie pull up.

'Hey! Whassap?' she asked, pulling her into a warm hug.

'Your mood has changed since I saw you last – did a big cheque arrive in the post?' joked Marcie.

'Na, but who knows, tomorrow is another day. Fancy a drink?'

They made their way into the rear kitchen and through to the lounge bar at the front. An elderly man was sitting with a copy of the *Press and Journal* looking quizzically at the crossword. Heather nodded for Marcie to follow her through to the large sofas in a small sun lounge at the front of the Inn.

'So, what can I do you for?'

'Just a lemonade, thanks.'

Heather returned soon after with two drinks, placing both glasses on the coffee table, and sat on the large tweed sofa, releasing a puff of dust.

'So...' Marcie began, not sure where to start.

Heather frowned. 'Well, this sounds as if it's going to be painful...'

'Brodie Nairn.'

'As I thought,' said Heather, her eyes raising skywards. 'I wondered when he would come up again.'

'What's his deal?'

'In... what way?' asked Heather tentatively.

'He followed you back from Thailand and now he's working with Callum. I'm kind of at a loss as to know what kind of work he's doing. I don't know what it is about him that makes me suspicious. He's too...'

'Good looking?'

'I don't know – it's like he's too perfect for Strathkin.'

'Look, he turned up here like a lovesick puppy. I wasn't that glad to see him either, especially not when I found out his real age.'

'Which is...?'

'Twenty-six,' admitted Heather. 'It was a holiday fling, and boy, I needed it. He wanted to know where I was from and he said he'd never seen snow, he'd love to come visit, but I never in a minute thought he'd turn up!'

'Never seen snow? Seriously? He's meant to be Danish or Swedish or something, you think they have long, hot summers that last for four seasons?'

Heather shrugged. 'I dunno, I thought he was Australian to begin with.'

'Australian? For Pete's sake, Heather! Everybody loves him but I think he's causing a rift between me and Callum. Cal's been so distant since I got back. It's like Brodie is meant to be helping take work off him, but somehow, he's taking up all his time.'

'Ooh,' said Heather, sitting back, 'jealous much?'

Marcie persisted. 'Jamie MacKay was around this morning, apparently saying there had been break-ins in the area. What if he's got something to do with it?'

'Really? I speak with Jamie often and he never mentioned that to me. Besides, if Brodie was here to rob us, you think he'd have done it already then buggered off and not hung about.' They sat in silence for a moment. 'Look,' Heather went on. 'Maybe you're just thinking that this is one of your last times up here with Swanfield as your home and you're anxious, looking for problems. Brodie is fine, seriously, and Jamie Mac, well, leave him to patrol his land like a sheriff.'

Marcie looked for the words to make Heather understand her concerns but could find none.

'Seriously, what's your beef with him, Mars?' asked Heather with a raise of her brows. 'He's harmless. Let me tell you, he's been a hit at the last few ceilidhs. Danced Ruthie Gillespie off her feet. Oh, how is Ruthie, by the way? I went down to the post office and saw the funeral notice in the window.'

The village was still coming to terms with the tragic events on the mountains. A solemn veil been had cast over the community, with people still speaking in hushed tones in the street.

'She's as well as can be expected, I guess.'

'Look, on a brighter note, you asked me why I was so upbeat? Well, out of the dark comes the light, isn't that what Lisanne always said? I suppose I'd better tell you. Those German families that stayed here, they're all coming back all over the summer, all of them. They booked dinner, bed and breakfast all up front. I know it was a real tragedy and everything, but it's got me out of a bit of a bind. That's probably considered crass and all, Mars, but, well, gotta take good news where we can find it.'

Marcie didn't quite know how to respond. She was pleased for her friend, but also thought it was too crass to celebrate such tragedy.

'Listen, I'm going to do a bit of a ceilidh for the Mountain Rescue Team, raise some funds, goodness knows they need it now. Geordie was their star fundraiser,' Heather said, referring to Ruthie's husband. 'We could combine it with your leaving do. When *are* you heading south?'

'Once I can drag Callum away and sit him down for a chat.' Absentmindedly, Marcie twisted round one of her large sparkling diamond earrings.

Heather laughed. 'Any time you want to drop *them* down the back of my sofa, feel free. They would get me out of the red and back into the black.'

Marce smiled bashfully. 'These were the earrings Lisanne gave me for my twenty-first. I know there is a lot of jewellery described in the will, you know she was somewhat of a collector of old antique pieces, but all of that is with Richard in the safe. I just felt I had to wear these. It's been such a long time since I had them on.'

'Oh, right, and I got left an old bit of coal,' laughed Heather half-heartedly.

'I inherited Swanfield,' blurted out Marcie and, as soon as the words left her lips, she regretted it. It had been hard keeping such a big secret to herself for so many days.

'Wha...?' started her friend, blinking.

'Lisanne changed the will. Well, there was a codicil, that's when a—'

'I know what a codicil is,' Heather snapped, her mood suddenly changing. 'I don't need an overpaid fancy lawyer to explain it to me.'

'Whoa...' said Marcie, holding her hands up. 'It's not like I asked for it.'

'You've been left Swanfield. You couldn't be jammier,

Marcie. And what did Callum say to that?' asked Heather, in a tone Marcie hadn't known her use before.

'We haven't discussed it. I can't get him in one place long enough to sit down with him.'

A strange expression crept across Heather's face, then she stood, looked out the window of the Inn and across to the imposing house, its red sandstone glistening in the bright April sun.

'So, he doesn't know? He'll be flipping livid,' said Heather, almost speaking to herself, quietly under her breath. 'Or maybe that's why he's acting so strangely.'

Marcie was kicking herself for revealing this piece of news. Heather was indiscreet when it suited her, or after a few too many, and this piece of information was something that she should have discussed with her four friends together before letting one of them in on the secret. They'd held each other's secrets for almost thirty years, sharing hopes and dreams, in a sisterhood that spanned sadness and tears in equal measure. Marcie watched as her friend started rubbing the little red cord that ringed its way around her wrist. Marcie touched her own red thread as if in sympathy – their friendship bracelets still binding them together.

'So,' Heather said hotly. 'Callum doesn't know that he's been done over?'

Marcie reddened. 'What do you mean "done over"? It was as much a surprise to me as it will be to him.'

'Hmm,' mused her friend, 'and you'll be off, I take it. Up sticks and leave us all here?'

'Leave you all here? You *live* here,' stated Marcie, annoyed at how her friend was taking what would have been welcome news if the shoe was on the other foot.

'So, I suppose you *do* want your leaving party here?' questioned Heather, somewhat sarcastically.

'I'm not planning on leaving, well, not right now. I have extended leave from work.'

'But Callum doesn't know,' whispered Heather again under her breath, mulling over the words, still staring out the window. Her eyes were fixed on Sweet Briar across the loch.

'Don't say anything,' pleaded Marcie, 'not just yet, *please.*'

Her friend didn't respond right away. Marcie noticed her shoulders rise and fall as if in anger while staring out at the loch. Marcie, meanwhile, was furious with herself. She thought if anyone other than Callum needed to know that information, it was probably Dina and Ruaridh. After the tragedy that had almost befallen them, any piece of news, no matter how good or bad, would have balanced out the secret Dina had shared the night Marcie stayed at the Balfours, before the awful catastrophe unfolded.

'I'm heading out, Heather,' she said. 'Thanks for the lemonade.'

As she headed towards the door, Heather said nothing. She remained rooted to the spot, eyes fixed across the water. Marcie knew that her old friend was seething, only she didn't know why.

# FOURTEEN

The sleepover at Swanfield had been firmly off the agenda following the incident on the mountains. Now Ruaridh was home, Marcie felt that having the boys over would be a chance for Dina to have some quiet time with her recovering husband. The four Balfour boys, meanwhile, had begun to badger their mum about staying in the big – and, in their mind, haunted – house across the water.

With strict instructions from Dina not to fill them up on Haribo, Marcie made a trip to the village general store for supplies. She had a basket full of hummus and crackers and chips and dips before saying to herself, *this isn't a girls' night – these are four boys under twelve. What am I thinking?*

Strathkin General Stores was a cornucopia of delights, selling everything from chocolate to coal, locally made fudge to fresh fish and confectionery. There was a vast range of wine and liquor in the back of the shop, and a large handwritten sign on the front door that for the last forty years had read:

Closed Wensday

She filled her basket with as many mini chocolate bars as she could fit, and every flavour of crisps on offer, until the basket became unmanageable, and she hauled it onto the counter.

'Planning a trip up the hill?' Roddy McLeod, the store owner, asked as he scanned chocolate bar after chocolate bar and the banned sugar-filled jellies at the bottom.

'Poison,' he muttered to himself, lips pursed, as the small jelly sweets were piled up next to the already high, calorific pile.

'I'm having a sleepover with the Balfour boys,' she said cheerfully.

'Oh aye,' he said. 'Ruaridh bringing his boys over to the big house?' It was hard to keep a secret in a small village, and it was well known that they had been an item in the long and now very distant past. 'And how is the bold boy doing after that fall up in the hill?'

It was typical of the villagers to play down anything that befell them, unless they could make mischief out of it. It was openly talked about how two of the villagers' lives had been lost due to, in their opinion, the ineptitude of 'the tourists'. Those from 'the abroad', she had overheard somebody say just days before, as if some secret foreign powers were sending people over to dispose of Strathkin villagers one by one, and to drag them into the twenty-first century against their will.

'He's getting better every day, so I hear.'

'Aye,' sighed Roddy in a knowing, yet unknowing, acknowledgement.

She threw rather than packed everything in an old jute Fortnum & Mason bag, which received another disapproving tut from the shopkeeper, and loaded the car.

On the short journey home, Marcie noticed clouds forming high above the mountains. Violent dark skies were drifting down over the hills, an unwelcome sight.

Marcie had planned a treasure hunt in the garden with the

children, a game she had loved as a child. She remembered her first stolen kiss under a rowan tree, something her grandmother had told her was bad luck, and she wondered what memories these children would make in this little hamlet in the years to come as they grew into young men.

Marcie looked over to Sweet Briar and saw Callum high above the house working on the fields at the back; their long overdue conversation was about to come to a head. She was still angry at herself for spilling her news to her friend without discussing it first with her uncle, but there was no point in going over and over it in her mind. It wasn't going to change the outcome.

As her car drew up over the brow of the hill, she saw there was someone else with Callum. A female figure. She slowed down, and creeping closer, she realised that the woman was Heather, engaged in an animated conversation with Callum.

She put her foot down and drove straight back to Swanfield, taking the car round the back. She abandoned her shopping and made her way inside, raced up the broad staircase, leaving the back door ajar. She made her way quickly to the room at the back where she had spent most of the morning building a tent for the boys with various brush poles and sheets. She pulled back the curtain slightly and watched her friend talk with Callum. *Surely, she wouldn't betray her confidence?* thought Marcie. Though the window was open, the wind, now becoming even more blustery, was carrying their words into the air and dissolving them in the breeze.

'Never put you down as a Peeping Tom.'

The unmistakable voice of Ruaridh behind made her jump, and the window banged shut. Although she now couldn't see, Marcie was sure that Heather and Callum would have looked around inquisitively.

'I was looking at the sheep,' Marcie answered quickly.

Ruaridh walked over to the window. 'I see no *sheeps*,' he said, laughing to himself at his own play on words.

Marcie scanned the field, but it was now empty.

'I'm fine, by the way,' Ruaridh said, noticing her lack of concern about his recent escape.

Ruaridh was paler, and his beard had been neatly trimmed, unlike his previous Viking-like appearance. He had a heavy gash across the bridge of his nose that was clearly healing, the remnants of a black eye and several scrapes and scratches. His hands showed a series of rope burns which looked sore and red.

'How are you doing?' Marcie asked, concerned, while surveying his injuries.

'Och, getting there. Not something I'd want to repeat. Ever,' he stated, playing down the experience, standing back, hands firmly in pockets. 'You realise it'll be you and Dina up here come ten o'clock while they create havoc downstairs?' he suggested, surveying the tents.

'Is Dina coming then?' Marcie asked, relieved that she wasn't going to deal with a troop of overexcited children on her own.

'Yup. She's going to pop over – have a big night out at Swan- field. Result though – you'll probably have only three holy terrors. Dax is a wee bit clingy now so I'm not sure he'll come along. We can have some "man time". I've already got in some cigars and a bottle of Jack Daniel's and we're planning a night of poker before we turn on the babestation,' he joked, with his usual theatrical wink.

'Is that still a thing?' she queried, laughing.

'I really have no idea. I heard some guys at the lifeboat station talking about it but then that was probably ten years ago so upshot is, dunno, not a clue.' He shrugged heavily, following her out of the room.

Halfway down the stairs, a wave of what she felt was relief overcame Marcie. She stopped suddenly and threw her arms unexpectedly around Ruaridh. She half expected him to push her away like before, but this time he embraced her in return. He leaned down and gave a fatherly kiss on the top of her head.

'I'm so glad you're okay.' She said it softly as almost a comfort to herself.

'I know, Mars,' was all he quietly said before moving her arms away and releasing her firmly from his grasp. 'Seriously, though, Dina said we couldn't leave you with them,' he added, changing the subject as they carried on to the kitchen.

Ruaridh reached into Marcie's overstuffed shopping bag on the table and opened a packet of Monster Munch corn snacks, took one, examined the packet then made a face verging on disgust as he sucked his cheeks in. The packet was returned to the worktop.

'Pickled onion,' he muttered under his breath. 'I'll drop them off about six? Don't get them up too early. I'm having trouble getting myself up in the morning. Plus, Dina needs a bit of a rest. She's tired. Sore back. They're more than a handful. So, really, good luck!'

Marcie raised her eyes to the ceiling.

Dina did look exhausted with the stress and worry of the previous days, and Marcie wondered whether Ruaridh was having trouble sleeping because of the trauma. Callum had told her once about having nightmares for months before he finally left the Mountain Rescue Team. 'Survivor's Guilt', Callum had called it.

Ruaridh didn't mention the exciting news Dina had shared with her the night of their dinner. Maybe Dina hadn't told him yet, wanting to wait until he was stronger.

'Ruaridh...' Marcie began.

'Yaaas,' he replied, on his way to the door.

'Do you think Heather is okay?' she probed out of the blue. 'She seems to have a lot on her plate?'

He paused, looking at her oddly, clearly taken aback. 'Ooft.

That's a bit of a strange question. Not something you should be asking my wife? *A lot*, meaning? Everyone is busy in their own way.'

'Just getting a different perspective.'

'On one of your best friends? Why?' he quizzed. 'I mean, seriously, Mars?'

'I know,' she agreed, looking out the kitchen window. All she needed now was Callum to appear to set tongues wagging.

'Think it's something you'd better take up with D,' Ruaridh said, frowning.

'And what do you think about Brodie?' Marcie knew her tone had given away her doubts about him.

'The Brodster? What have you got against him? Nice guy, helps Callum out. Well liked in the village as far as I know. Well, certainly amongst the ladies.' He shrugged. 'Not heard a bad word against him, to be honest.' As if to move the subject on, he pointed to a cardboard box on the table that used to contain apples, which was now piled high with old ice cream tubs filled with wrapped homemade goodies.

'Our contribution for later – sausage rolls, pizza, flapjacks, brownies, sandwiches, bottles of flavoured water, but you'll probably end up passing that through to Cal; once the boys set their eyes on your haul, this'll be ignored,' he joked and headed to the door. He paused, turned back and grabbed the open packet of Monster Munch.

'Well, they're open now.' He winked at her and closed the door quietly behind him.

# FIFTEEN

Marcie was expecting to have good fun with the boys, and she wasn't disappointed. Ruaridh had dropped off Dina and the three boys exactly at 6 p.m. as discussed. Dax, as agreed, stayed with his father across the water. The twins and Douglas were already in onesie pyjamas, and as soon as they entered, all three raced up the broad stairs to the landing, then tumbled back downstairs in a whirl of dinosaur and tiger print. They ran out at pace to the front drive where they waved furiously across the water at the two left behind at Lochside Croft.

Dina held up a bottle of Viognier. 'Respite,' she said and handed the fridge-cold bottle to Marcie as they made their way into the kitchen. 'I really appreciate this,' said Dina, 'it's so good to get a change of scene. I've just been playing the whole thing over and over in my head. I needed to get out of the house.' She glanced back just as the boys, arms out like aircraft wings, flew into the kitchen, round the table and back out into the hall.

'I can't sleep,' she went on as Marcie handed her a glass of Appletiser, a soft drink, the colour of which would make it look like wine in her glass.

'Ah, so sorry to hear that,' said Marcie. 'I'm glad to give you a wee break, take some time out.' They went into the living room and sat in front of the television. 'I'm afraid it's only "council telly" here,' apologised Marcie.

'They've got all sorts of stuff with them. I wouldn't worry, once they've been fed and settled, they'll have forgotten about high tech – you've still got a DVD player?'

'Yeah, think so. I think it's in the side of the TV.'

'I've brought a few things,' said Dina, digging in the box.

'*Paddington*' – she held up one – '*Jungle Cruise*, oh and another, of course, *Brave*.'

'Nice selection, but you could have brought *Magic Mike*.'

Dina leaned down into the box and brought out that exact DVD and smiled wickedly. 'Let's hope they go to bed early!' She grinned and chinked her glass against her friend's. '*Cheers!*'

As Dina promised, once food had been scoffed, drinks demolished and sweet treats munched, calmness descended. Dina curled up on the sofa with the twins, Donald and David, entwined around her, dozing softly. Marcie found herself on the two-seater sofa with Douglas cuddled up beside her, arms wrapped around one of hers, breathing softly while she inhaled the soft sweet smell of the freshly washed child. The blustery wind outside was gaining momentum and every so often the open curtains would softly move forward as air crept in from the gaps in the old wooden sash windows.

The TV volume was switched low, and she glanced over as she saw Dina's eyes, like hers, start to close as a long yawn escaped from her. Something caught her eye through the window, but Marcie struggled in the half-light to see what it was. She moved in her seat slightly, and Douglas gave a long sigh, eyes opening a little to gaze up at her, then closing once more. She squinted to see better and saw that a car was slowly making its way to the front of the house. She was sure, even in this low light, that it was the same black Range Rover Brodie had driven days before. Once again, its lights were switched off and the car crept along the gravel, the noise almost covered by the gathering wind.

Marcie sat up, pulling Douglas closer into her, and saw a second vehicle turn into the long wide drive, headlights switched off. She grabbed the remote and switched off the TV, and her guests all moved slightly, then settled. With Swanfield now in darkness, the drivers of the vehicles would think its occupants were out or in bed at this late hour.

The wind began to moan louder as it came in through the window gaps. Tonight, there was hardly any moonlight to shimmer on the loch and light up the land, and certainly not enough for Marcie to see who was driving the cars as they snaked past the side of the house and round the back.

Marcie released herself from the young boy's grip. She slid very slowly and quietly off the sofa and began to tiptoe her way out.

'Marcie?' queried Dina in a voice no louder than a whisper.

Marcie lifted her index finger to her mouth with a silent 'Ssh.'

Dina, thinking her friend was simply escaping to go to the toilet, closed her eyes and drifted off into the half sleep of a mother of four.

Now out of the living room, Marcie crept along the hallway and up the stairs. She made it up to the back bedroom which gave her a clearer view into the yard at the back of Sweet Briar.

It didn't surprise Marcie that it was Brodie she saw making his way into the back of the cottage. She missed whoever came out of the second car as the driver's seat looked empty. Maybe her uncle was hosting a high-stakes poker game for men of the village in the small Highland cottage? Whatever was going on, Marcie was determined to find out.

# SIXTEEN

Callum stood on the high ridge, a place he had come to since childhood. A place he had taken his niece to the day after her parents tragically died. He remembered that they had sat together in silence, an unpacked and uneaten picnic beside them, listening to the rustle of the wind in the trees watched by birds high above, as a lustrous sea eagle skimmed the loch, leaving tremors in its wake.

A melancholy wave blew over him recalling his own mother, Lisanne, and the last few months they shared together before her death. Conversations with his mother had grown strained during that time, and he thought of all the things he wanted to say to her but now couldn't: words to resolve their issues, their differences. He wanted so much to talk to her about his life and the path he had chosen. But he couldn't find the words. Now he never would.

He was so conflicted. His beliefs were tearing him apart, eating him up from the inside out. He looked down on this vast scene that lay before him; the mountains and their inviting horror and their peaks, tempting you in only to unceremoniously spit you out.

His hand went to his hip as a searing pain ran through it. He had stared death in the face when he was a climber, as a member of the MRT. The crumpled faces of death still haunted him in the night, more so lately, as he was terrorised by ghosts of his past. Callum was aware of the emotions, that grief and anger would take over the days and months to come. In the days and weeks and months that followed, there would be an edginess in Strathkin until the next catastrophe took place. There always was one lurking on the other side of the mountain. Experts called what he'd experienced Post Traumatic Stress Disorder now, but, in his day, he had been told to man up and buy another bottle.

When he'd come back from Inverness, he'd gone up to Broomfield, the small cottage near the estate boundary. That was when he heard the first helicopter. He wanted to stay in retreat until the search and rescue was over. He wanted to clear his mind of the images that still haunted him. Callum's Bible was his only solace in the few nights he was away – that and the tempting holiday brochure that he'd been keeping secret.

He'd told Brodie that if anyone was looking for him, to say he'd stayed in Dingwall after visiting the mart, but it turned out no one had asked after him. Well, except for his niece.

Marcie had arrived at the right time; her youthful vigorous determination and girlish smile still struck him deep in his heart, and he was so glad that she had stayed just that little bit longer this time. But there were dark undercurrents afoot in the village, so he had taken to locking her door with his own key, just in case.

The fact that Jamie MacKay had dropped in to warn him must mean he knew there was something not right in this sleepy little backwater, too. Jamie was too good for this place, as witnessed only a few years before when some highly ineffectual drug dealers came to rent one of the empty cottages on the Strathdon Estate. Their extravagant Mercedes was highly incongruous on the remote, single-track roads. Arrests were made and villagers and guests to the Inn were heartily regaled with amusing stories of these high-flying crooks who tried to pull the wool over the eyes of the crafty people of Strathkin and failed. Like the islanders in *Whisky Galore*, everyone seemed to be involved in the capture of this group of inept villains, and even old Ronnie Reeves, eighty-nine if he was a day, told of his part in the biggest drugs haul this far north of, well, Loch Broom.

The smile of recall danced over Callum's lips for a moment. But this memory was only a distraction, he thought to himself, as a long sigh escaped from him. Looking down, he kicked a piece of broken stone in the scree and watched as it tumbled down, further and further, then hit a large rock and smashed into several pieces, before disappearing into the water by the shore.

'How easy it would be?' Callum pondered. He could close his eyes. Just one step, and, if he timed it right, he could hit that large grey rock and be unconscious before the slope of the hill dragged him down to certain death. He briefly speculated about the climbers whose lives had been so tragically taken, and what their last thoughts might have been. They had been so young.

*Spirited and lively*, he considered them when they met outside the general store. They'd swapped stories about the hills and had been so grateful when Callum handed over half a dozen bottles of water. They'd lifted them straight into their panniers, grateful to have water after Roddy had closed the general store early for the day.

The thought of being at the village hall, pacing, waiting, wondering, would have brought back too many recent memories of people lost and dead on the hill – haunted dreams of his own time leading the MRT. He couldn't face it.

Callum had read that your life flashed before your eyes in the moments before your death. How brief that showreel would be for him, having never left Strathkin. What had he achieved, accomplished, won, lost? Not much in his sixty-odd years.

And that's why he'd convinced himself he was doing the right thing. But where had that got him? Lisanne would have said he had got himself into a *right pickle* but that was nowhere near how bad the situation had become. When he had called Richard in Inverness, he'd been asked to speak to Marcie first. It was then Callum knew his worst fears had been realised. His mother had clearly decided to vent her hateful side at her only son, having found out his secret. Now that would have serious implications for his beautiful niece and everyone who had shared his life in this little hamlet. *How could Lisanne have been so cruel?* After he had so carefully looked after her in her final months. Taken such good care of her. Now he would be a laughing-stock in the village, once the news got out.

Callum knew he would have to sit down with Marcie, the new chatelaine of Swanfield, and they would have to move forward together. But for now, he wanted to avoid the conversation. His health wasn't up to it. Instead, he would lay low. If he could avoid both Brodie and Marcie, it would give him thinking time to plan a way forward out of the mire he now found himself in and allow him time to make plans for what was left of his future.

He reached into his back pocket, unfolded the envelope but didn't open the letter. He was tempted to use it as kindling later. He stared at it for a long time before folding the paper neatly and slipping it back into his pocket. It was news he didn't want to hear.

*Today wasn't the day*, he decided, and took up his crook, stretched and winced at his aching hip, playing over in his mind the words that had been said to him at the hospital, and began the walk back to the bothy.

# SEVENTEEN

Marcie hated Zoom, FaceTime, Teams, Google Meet. She disliked all the new technology that meant you couldn't go five minutes without your peace being invaded by someone who wanted to know your every spit and cough since their previous contact. Over the last couple of days, her chats with Simon felt as formal as meetings, with the only thing missing being an agenda, and they had been cut short by the patchy internet at Swanfield. She knew she would get a much better signal on her phone if she went down to the Inn, but she was now in Heather-avoidance mode. She didn't know what to say to her now that she suspected her friend had betrayed her confidence.

Marcie knew she should have shared her news with Dina and sought advice on how to deal with Callum. But now she was sure Callum was trying even harder to avoid her, and that Heather had bleated her secret.

Marcie was sifting through her wardrobe for things she wanted to take back to London – whenever that happened – when a slamming car door made her jump. Once again, she saw Brodie outside her uncle's home – and he wasn't alone. He was with a burly, middle-aged man who grabbed him by the shoulders and kissed him on one cheek then the other.

Careful that no one could see her, Marcie pulled the window up as silently as she could. She struggled to hear, not because they were speaking quietly – they were loud and boisterous – but because she couldn't understand the language. She often joked that Danish was so close to Scottish that sometimes when watching a Danish TV drama, she forgot to watch the subtitles. But this language was different. Was it a Balkan language? Croatian? Serbian? Russian?

It was Russian. She'd heard enough Russian speakers on the television to identify the pattern of the language. That answered her question, she thought. Australian, Danish, Scandi, Brodie was none of these but was, in fact, a Russian.

Looking closer, she recognised the older man as one of the men who had nearly run her and her pony off the road previously. Like before, he wore new-looking clothes and highly polished brogues. She could smell his cigar smoke as it drifted up through the window. The two men laughed and joked for some time before the stranger threw the cigar to the ground, not bothering to stub it out, grabbed Brodie in a friendly embrace and made his way to the car. He was gone with a crunching of gravel and a screech of expensive tyres.

Brodie bent down, picked up the cigar in a gloved hand and with the wet cloth he had been carrying, nipped the lit end off to render it safe near the dry grass. He walked over to the black bin designated *ASHES* and dropped it in, taking off his gloves and wiping his hands on the cloth.

He began to make his way into the back door of Sweet Briar but not before stopping and taking a long glance up to the window where Marcie rushed out of sight. Her back was against the wall next to the curtain, her breathing laboured. She'd had a lucky escape, or so she hoped. The goings on next door were getting more mysterious by the day. Where was Callum?

# EIGHTEEN

'So,' said Simon over her FaceTime on the iPad, 'you think Strathkin is being overridden by the Russian mafia, albeit in one's and two's?'

'I know you think it's funny,' she sighed. 'But I have absolutely no idea what's going on here.'

'Mars, I don't find it funny. I just think you've been watching too many of those bingey crime dramas. I mean, it is awfully remote up there. I think people's imaginations must be ripe.'

'There's no point in talking to you when you're in one of these moods,' she complained, raising a cup of tea to her mouth and blowing on it.

'One of what moods?' He laughed. 'I just think you're making a mountain out of a mole hill. It's Strathkin, for goodness' sake, it's not the bloody Costa del Moscow.'

'It might not be,' she conceded, 'but I still can't track down Callum. He's gone walkabout again. Apparently, he went to the mart in Dingwall, came back, and went away. I'm telling you, Si, he's booking a holiday to the Maldives, and I need to tell him he can't.'

'He doesn't even have a passport, Mars. I know that 'cause when I was last up – three years ago, was it? – he told me. He didn't even have a photo driving licence. Seriously, you need to track him down, have a long chat like you used to have, and get your backside on a plane south, back to reality.'

Marcie knew Simon was right but what he recommended was easier said than done. When they finished their chat, Marcie was none the wiser about what was going on in her uncle's life. What's more, she was unsure about what was going on in her own.

Maybe Brodie was just a regular guy looking to make a living – but who were these strange friends of his that kept turning up? Maybe he and Heather were up to some trick or so. Her friend was quite open about sinking in debt, and maybe they were working together on some scam. The sensible side of Marcie's brain said *how could you think such a thing?* But the suspicious side said *how else could you explain their behaviour?*

'Slimy charmer,' she said aloud as she stopped on the landing. Brodie was a charmer, there was no doubt about that, but there was also an underlying menace, an underlying *something* that she couldn't put her finger on. Drugs? Was that it? Was he involved in drugs, bringing them up the A9 to sell here in Strathkin?

Maybe Simon was right, he normally was. Perhaps she'd spent too much time curtain twitching and not enough time thinking about going home; she had started to pack but had found every excuse to stop, like an invisible bind was keeping her from returning to London and to her life of what she was now thinking was casual mundanity compared to *sleepy* Strathkin.

Marcie remembered, as a child, laughing with her girls about how the village thrived on gossip and how every snippet was traded like shiny baubles. Now, here she was doing exactly what she complained about all those years ago. Myths and legends, witchcraft and stories. Strathkin was alive with it, and maybe she was just getting caught up.

Marcie decided, on the spur of the moment, that enough was enough. She headed through the kitchen and utility to the back door.

'Flip's sake!' she said aloud as the normally open door was once again locked tight. She plucked down the key, unlocked the door, marched across the yard and up the path to Sweet Briar, and rapped on the door loudly. There was no answer. She tried the handle, and the door was locked so she rapped again, this time more loudly as if she were the police on a dawn raid.

'Are you in a hurry?' came a voice behind her, and Marcie turned to see Brodie.

His appearance caught her by surprise, and she stumbled over her words. 'Oh, I was...'

'Yes?' he asked without a smile.

'Do you know when Callum will be back?' she queried.

He pulled the rag from his pocket and wiped his hand slowly, his icy blue eyes not leaving hers. 'I am not his keeper.'

'I just need to pin him down. To talk to him.' Marcie realised that she was doing something that she would never do in her legal life – offer up information, giving her opposition an in.

Brodie remained silent. He was taller than she recalled – or was it that she suddenly felt very vulnerable, smaller and an easy target?

'Anything else?' he asked.

Marcie found his demeanour vaguely menacing – far from the charm she'd experienced before – and didn't know how to respond. 'Who was he?' she eventually asked.

'Who?'

'The man that was here just now. In the black Range Rover.'

He made a quizzical face, then shrugged his shoulders nonchalantly. 'He came to speak to Callum, who is not here.'

'Where *is* he?' Marcie insisted.

Brodie shrugged again and looked around the yard with a sigh. He slung the rag over his shoulder and casually put his hands in his pockets. Even up close, his pale skin was flawless, resting over a perfect bone structure. At once, she found him unnerving and menacingly handsome.

'How would Callum know a man like that?'

'A man like what? A man who drives an expensive car?' asked Brodie.

They were going round in circles. Marcie was becoming as frustrated as Brodie appeared.

They stood, like deer about to face off at rutting, neither wanting to give in. There was no wind or bird call to break the silence.

She looked at him, chin raised, as if to face an adversary in court, but his ice-blue eyes looked deep into her and her words seemed to disappear. She looked away to break his gaze, up to the hills, and bit the inside of her cheek.

Marcie turned and walked away. Some would think she stormed off in a fit of pique, but as she turned, tears welled up in her eyes. All of a sudden, she was in a situation that was alien to her and she didn't know where to turn. The stalwart of her life, her uncle, was gone and she had been usurped by this young interloper.

She looked round to see an empty space where Brodie had been standing only moments before. There was no sound of a door closing, nothing. It was like he, too, had magically disappeared into thin air. Or so Marcie wished.

# NINETEEN

Marcie was frustrated as she looked at the screen.

No social media presence. Not one.

*How was that possible in a guy of that age?* she thought. There was not a trace of *this* Brodie Nairn, Strathkin's *own* Brodie Nairn, on any platform from Facebook to Instagram, Snapchat to X or Telegram. Marcie sat in front of her laptop, her finger tracing a line around her lips, deep in thought. *Who are you?* Someone who charmed and smiled his way into the lives of the people of this welcoming village? A man who'd driven a wedge between a kind man and his niece?

Or was he as good and genuine as everyone thought? Was Marcie simply jealous? Jealous of the relationship he now seemed to have with Callum, or the sway he held over her best friends?

Marcie's legal brain started doing what it always did – looking at the argument from both sides. Maybe he really *was* the best thing to happen to Strathkin in a long time. Callum had certainly been more upbeat with an extra hand around the croft, and the girls, well, she was convinced Heather still circled around Brodie's orbit. If someone had no social media footprint currently, Marcie had only two opinions – their age was a barrier, or they were hiding from something and wanted to appear *under the radar*. She had seen Brodie with a phone, so what was the deal? she thought to herself. Marcie needed to speak to a more neutral witness. She sent a text to an old friend, grabbed her car keys and left the house.

She soon found herself sitting in The Aizle, a large sprawling restaurant and gift shop off the main road that led from Strathkin to Inverness. It had started off as a stop for lorry drivers taking their refrigerated haul of fish south, and then it was extended and built on as tourism in the area took off. Now it sold everything from casual Highland wear to fake antlers and stag-themed trinkets.

It wasn't a place that the locals would normally take a day trip to, so hopefully she wouldn't become a topic of discussion for Roddy McLeod at the village store. To anyone passing, she looked like one of the many single people sitting around the café, laptop in front of them, working away with free Wi-Fi and access to good coffee. Through the large window, she looked for the police car parked across two spaces in the car park. She smiled. It didn't matter how many years Jamie had been in the police, she thought; if you're a rebel, you're a rebel.

Jamie MacKay always took pride in his uniform and today it looked shiny and new. Jamie caught her eye, waved, and came over.

'Well, don't you look amazing!' she said, smiling as he noisily pulled out the seat opposite her and sat down.

'Who'd have thought it, eh?' He returned her smile, clearly recalling his patchy youth and his frequent skirmishes with the law. Coming from what was commonly known as the wrong side of the tracks – even by Strathkin standards – gave him a distinct advantage when he slipped into his uniform. Why steal a car with the chance of getting caught when you can be paid to drive fast cars well above the speed limit? If you wanted an adrenaline rush, he often said, join the police.

'It was a lovely service,' he blurted out as if to break the ice.

'Yes, I know – at least it wasn't all the usual *death and salvation is coming to us all*,' replied Marcie, running her finger along the rim of the cup in front of her. After some more small talk, Marcie filled him in on her suspicions about Brodie.

'It's not normal,' explained Marcie. '*Everyone* has some sort of profile. Seriously, if you're not on one platform, you're on another.'

'Mars. Come on. I have no idea what you're talking about. I closed my Facebook page years ago when all the girls I fancied at school got married and most of the guys I knew were *still* arseholes, so even *I* don't have a presence anymore. And as for platforms? There's virtually no signal up here anyway, so, why would he bother?' explained the police officer. 'Maybe if you're trying to do business or stalk somebody, I can see the attraction but...' Jamie shrugged. 'To all intents and purposes, he's a nice guy. I've not heard anyone say a bad thing about him. People move around all the time, Mars. I can't stop a guy working here 'cause you've taken a dislike to him.'

'It's not a dislike, as such.'

'So, what's your problem?' Jamie took a sip of coffee. 'What does Ruaridh think of him?'

'He thinks he's okay. Good at helping Cal around the croft. He seemed to comfort everyone during the accident.'

Jamie tapped the table. 'I think you need to take a step back. He's helping Cal. He's well liked in the village – you clearly don't like the guy so you're looking for some excuse for me to have a word.' He waited a moment then turned. 'I've known you a long time, Mars, so I'm going to be blunt. Just because Lisanne isn't here anymore doesn't mean you rule the roost. Lisanne was a formidable woman, as you know, but even *she* didn't get to decide who got to stay in Strathkin just 'cause she took a dislike to them. Ask my inspector, believe me, she tried.'

Marcie knew what her grandmother could be like: a loving, kind and generous grandmother but also intimidating, formidable. 'So, who are the guys in the big fancy cars? They keep turning up at the house. I told you one nearly ran me and Florence off the road?'

He cocked his head. '*Florence*? Cal's horse? Did it almost hit you? You've always had a vivid imagination.'

Marcie flushed. She knew this wasn't going to go much further. She was hoping to get Jamie on her side, but it was obvious he was a no taker.

Once they'd finished their coffees, they walked out together. A clop of hooves nearby made them look around as Bella came walking past on one of her Highland ponies.

'Caught at last!' She laughed and pulled the pony up, sliding herself out of the saddle and leading the horse to the side of the road to have a nose in the grass.

She smiled, slipping her leather gloves off and walking over to them. 'What's up, muchachos?'

'This and that,' said Jamie with a smile, taking his aviator sunglasses out of the side of his body armour, and placing them over his nose.

'He thinks he's in a Tarantino movie,' said Bella with a laugh.

'I shall leave you ladies,' he responded with a slight shake of the head. 'I'm certainly not in *From Russia with Love*,' he stated with a glance to Marcie. He strolled casually over to his marked police 4x4 and drove off, heading out of the small car park and along the side of the loch back to Ullapool.

'Well, that was rather cosy. What was it all about?' Bella asked as she wandered over to the bench beneath the main window of the café.

'Hmm,' said Marcie with no explanation.

'Are you inviting Jamie to your leaving do?'

Marcie sighed. 'What *leaving do*? You lot are just trying to get rid of me.'

'Heather told me you're planning to bail?'

'I don't live here, Bells, I'm not *bailing*.'

'Lighten up, it's just an expression. No need to get heavy about it. We all know you've got to go back sometime. Now that you've sorted things out here, I suppose there's nothing else for you.'

Marcie's mood worsened. 'I've not sorted anything out. Have you seen Callum?' she quizzed.

'Not a peep.'

'Well, I'm not going anywhere until I sit down and decide the future with him. If there is a future.'

'Who stole your scone?' her friend asked with a nudge, a casual expression that made Marcie reluctantly smile.

'Callum didn't inherit Swanfield,' she said quickly.

Bella leaned her head back in the spring sunshine, letting the warming rays hit her pale face. 'Yeah, right. Who did then?'

*Here we go again,* Marcie thought. 'Me.'

Bella sat bolt upright.

'You're joking?'

'No.'

Bella unclipped her riding helmet, pulled out her scrunchie and ruffled her hair, letting it fall over her shoulders as she took in the news.

'Flip's sake.' She looked across the landscape. 'What did he say? I mean, it's his life's work.'

'I'm not sure he knows yet.'

'What do you mean, *not sure he knows*? It's his house, is it not? I mean, when Lisanne died, rule of thumb it goes to the eldest son, and with your mum and dad, well...'

They both sat for a moment in silence.

'Please don't say anything,' Marcie said. 'Until I've spoken to him.'

'Not a word,' Bella agreed, running her fingers across her lips in a gesture of zipping them shut. 'So, Callum...'

'He's not around. Went to the mart in Dingwall and I've not heard from him since. I don't think he's been to see Richard MacInnes 'cause I'm pretty sure Richard would have called me.'

'So, what you gonna do?' asked Bella as she played with the numbers on her phone. 'Sell up, or move back?'

'Really? I have no idea,' said Marcie with a shrug. She stood up and walked across the road to where Bella's pony was feasting on its roadside picnic, patted its neck and looked up to the cloud-dappled sky. Marcie wasn't being evasive with her friend. She still had no idea what she was going to do.

## TWENTY

Marcie didn't want to wander too far from Swanfield in case Callum turned up. She made her way to the village shop for some groceries, only to find that it was closed for a funeral. There was a note on the door telling villagers to take what they wanted, and an honesty box had been placed on the counter. The note also reminded patrons to double check the fridge and freezer doors were well closed if they needed an urgent ice cream or a Findus crispy pancake. Marcie couldn't imagine anyone venturing in for the dusty bottle of Old Inverness whisky that had sat on the shelf behind the counter for as long as she could remember. She stood outside the shop, delved into her bag for her phone and held it up, hoping she would get a signal. She didn't.

Marcie drove back to the Balfour croft where she found Dina and Ruaridh on a tartan rug spread out on their front lawn with tea and scones. Douglas was playing at the water's edge; the other boys were at school.

'Can you smell these all the way across there?' laughed Ruaridh, not bothering to get up from his prone position, holding up the plate of scones. Dina smiled and pointed to a folding chair near the bench at the window. Marcie collected it, opened it up and sat by the edge of the rug.

'There's plenty of tea in the pot. I'll get Douglas to get you a cup,' she said, but Marcie stopped her before she could call on the boy.

'I'm fine. Seriously. Had one a while ago. I remember the secret here is not to drink loads of tea in case you get caught short on the road.' She laughed.

'Never had a problem with that myself. Cheers then!' said Ruaridh, holding up his mug and slurping loudly. Dina caught Marcie's eye and raised her own in a silent statement of *men!*

Marcie noticed that Ruaridh now had almost no sign of a black eye, and his hands seemed to be healing from the rope burns. The cut across his nose was now nothing but a dark scab, and she wondered if it would leave a deep scar.

'I was down at the shop, but the honesty sign is on the door.'

'Aye, funeral for the Duffer,' stated Ruaridh. 'It was this morning, we went to the church but not the afters.'

'Alister MacDuff,' explained Dina, 'passed away around the same time as Lisanne. They waited for the family to come up from the central belt.'

'Drank himself into an early grave,' qualified Ruaridh, slurping his tea loudly so that it attracted the attention of his youngest son from the water's edge. The boy gave a childish giggle at his father's noisy drinking. Ruaridh raised his pinkie finger as he drank.

'Funny, but I never thought he was a drinker,' said Dina. 'Never away from the church when it was here, and when Elsie passed away, he used to still go every Sunday over to Strath Aullt. You know the Free Presbyterian Church here closed? A few years ago, now.'

As people and villagers dwindled so did the places of worship and schooling. Children were now having to travel a distance in the local school bus, along with parishioners who still attended either the local Free Presbyterian Church or the Free Church, while the last of the Roman Catholics and Episcopalians had either given up going or made a weekly pilgrimage over the hill to the chapels beyond.

'He was one of those guys that always looked old, though, didn't he? I thought he was a teetotaller myself but that was a long time ago,' stated Marcie as her eyes drifted to the water.

'Aye, when you two were young lassies, so that wasn't yesterday!' said Ruaridh then stood up quickly. 'I'll be off before I get scalded,' he joked and made his way down to the pebble shore to join Douglas.

'How's he doing?' asked Marcie when Ruaridh was with his son at the water's edge.

'He had a bit of a nightmare last night for the first time. I'll be honest, Mars, I haven't asked him about it. You know Ruaridh, he's the strong silent type, but can also be very open. I know he'll talk about it when he's ready. I can't stop thinking of those boys you met, though. Not knowing it was probably their last day on Earth.' Dina instinctively put her hand to her belly, not yet swollen, and bit her lip.

Marcie watched as Ruaridh bent down to whisper something in his son's ear. The young boy swung and raced up to Marcie with a handful of shells.

'Marcie, lady! Look! I've got you a *pwesent*.' She laughed at his pronunciation and examined the shells and pebbles he offered her in his tiny open hand. His parents watched this sweet interaction.

'Ruaridh and I were wondering what's going to happen to old Alister's cottage.'

'Hmm?' asked Marcie, looking up.

'Well, it was a tied cottage, was it not? Part of Swanfield. Part of the estate. Sure, Elsie used to clean for Lisanne back in the day while Callum and Alister and the rest worked the beasts,' said Ruaridh, walking back up to the grass picnic.

Marcie looked puzzled. 'To be honest, I don't know. Was it?'

'Pretty sure it was,' he went on. 'So wa... what was that other one? I get them mixed up.'

He nudged Dina with his bare foot that still had pieces of seaweed attached to it.

'Lubnaig... or Stratheyre?' Dina suggested.

'Oh yes, both those cottages were tenanted. When did old Angus Fraser die? That wasn't that long ago now, was it? And Cailean Whatshisname who came up from Perthshire?'

'They're all Swanfield, are they not?' asked Dina. 'Right up to Broomfield until it joins Strath Aullt?'

Douglas started to count out tiny shells and pebbles into Marcie's still-open palm. He struggled after counting to eight and went back to one.

'Alister and Elsie – they were at Kintyre Cottage,' determined Ruaridh. 'Angus was at Lubnaig. It was Cailean who was at Stratheyre.'

'McAskill! That was Cailean. He was a cousin of Elsie, or was that Angus? I'm sure they were related.'

'To be honest, I don't really know.' Marcie shrugged, embarrassed that she hadn't taken more notice of both her family estate and also what Richard MacInnes had clearly explained, or tried to explain, while she sat in his office in shock.

'I'd only seen Angus Fraser out on his boat the day before, too. Looked as fit as a flea, losing his hair, mind you,' stated Ruaridh, standing tall, shaking his head and shoving his hands in his pockets.

In the near distance, a loud honking noise echoed round the stillness of the glen. Ruaridh stretched out his hand to Dina to help her to her feet.

'School bus. Let the madness begin. Want to stay for tea?' Dina asked as she wiped crumbs from her dress.

Marcie looked down to Douglas's wide blue eyes and smile of anticipation.

'Why not?' she agreed, smiling.

'It's beans on toast tonight,' stated Douglas with glee. *Right now, that beats sole a la meunière at Kettner's,* thought Marcie, and she leaned down to shake out the picnic blanket and follow her friends into Lochside Croft.

# TWENTY-ONE

Later, Marcie sat at the kitchen table in Swanfield with her laptop open. She wasn't getting very far, as the house's limited Wi-Fi wasn't playing ball. But she knew her search was a long shot. Sometimes the old ways, the traditional ways, are the best, she concluded after her search came to nothing.

A pile of newspapers for kindling lay in a basket by the fire. Seeing them triggered a memory as she pulled the basket towards her and the smell of burned coals drifted out. She could hear her grandmother's voice as she explained and showed her how to tear the big broadsheet newspaper in two and carefully fold the pages over, roll them, then tie a huge knot in it before placing it at the base of the grate, then piling wood kindling on top followed by just a couple of dry and seasoned logs. An old-fashioned set of bellows sat next to the fire. Marcie brushed her fingers over the brass embossed edge.

She pulled out the first copy of the *Press and Journal* and scoured its pages. Nothing. Then another. Still nothing. Then another one. She was almost near the bottom of the pile when she found it. A death notice. The newspapers were out of date order, and some were missing, but there was his name:

*Alistair McDuff. Suddenly at home at Kintyre Cottage. No flowers please.*

The date of his death was noted as three days before Lisanne.

Marcie went through to the vestibule at the back where another stack of newspapers was piled up precariously on a wooden box. It took a few searches but there they were.

*Angus Fraser. Suddenly at home at Lubnaig Cottage. No flowers please.*

*Cailean McAskill. Suddenly at home at Stratheyre Cottage. No flowers please.*

*Elsie Fraser...*

Her forensic legal brain was fired up. She sat at the table with the pages ripped out and in date order. Was it madness to think what she was thinking? So many sudden deaths over such a short space of time couldn't be a coincidence.

The next morning, Marcie went to talk to Bella at the trekking centre.

'It's hardly *Midsomer Murders*, Mars!' joked her friend, referring to the detective programme set around small English villages. Bella shook her head and set about making tea and cutting huge slices from a homemade gingerbread with the icing still soft and spilling over the sides.

'Don't you think it's unusual? I mean, all those deaths in three months?'

'They're old, Mars. Isn't that an occupational hazard of being old... *death*?'

'They weren't all even that old. Alister McDuff was only sixty-three – same age as Callum.'

'Said the woman who told me Callum was old.'

'Well, it's no age at all really,' said Marcie, trying to justify her findings. 'Elsie was sixty-five.'

'Oooh, never pictured Alister as a *toyboy*. Elsie, what a *dawg*.' Bella laughed to herself, dropping onto the kitchen chair.

'It's NOT funny!' said Marcie, getting annoyed at her friend and her casual dismissal of her findings.

'Mars, seriously – what do you expect me to say? It's a hard life out here, plus you know Jamie. If there was the slightest suspicion of foul play, he'd be on it like a car bonnet. You're coming up here and going all Miss Marple... Or Jessica What-serface... the *Murder, She Wrote* woman...'

'Bells!'

'C'mon, Marcie!' said Bella, putting down her mug. 'It's not only people who are dying here. The whole place is on its last legs. It's a hard life here with people not having the same access to healthcare and all that wellness palaver that you lot have in the south. So, they die; some after a good innings like Lisanne, and some after a lifetime spent out in the shocking weather like the fishermen and farming folk. The winters are hard here, don't forget. It wouldn't surprise me if Callum sold up and left.'

Marcie stared at her friend. 'And where do you think he would go if he were to sell up?'

'Costa del Sol. That's where I'd go. Endless sunshine. Sangria by the pint. All those hot Spanish bullfighters.'

Marcie shook her head, gathered up her notepad, all her paper clippings and folded them into one big pile and said, 'I'm off.'

'Just when it was getting interesting...' Bella sighed with a wistful look. 'So, when *is* your leaving do?'

Marcie shook her head and went out to the stable yard. She

missed what her friend shouted after her and strode over to her car. She heard a car reversing out of the entrance to the stable yard. She caught a glimpse of broad black tyres but not the vehicle itself as the low gorse bushes around the entrance kept it hidden. She ran back to her car, put her hand in her pocket, then the other but couldn't find her car keys. She looked inside then cursed. She ran back to the kitchen where Bella was washing up the cups at the sink.

'Apology accepted,' Bella said without looking around as Marcie grabbed the keys from the table before running back out to the car without a word.

She took off in a loud screech of tyres and headed out to the main road. She looked both ways, but the vehicle was nowhere to be seen.

Marcie drove as fast as she could to take her as near to the high ridge as possible then she leapt out of the car and scrambled up onto the viewing area of the all-round vista of Strathkin. Nothing. Not a car on the road. The air was still. A cloudless blue sky. The single-track roads she could see were empty.

Swanfield stood strong and silent on the other side of the loch. Beside it, Sweet Briar next door looked deserted.

No smoke rose from the loch side cottages. A bird squawked its noisy arrival over the picture-perfect Highland scene.

Maybe Marcie was mistaken. Maybe the driver had been a tourist taking a wrong turn or someone dropping off a child for a trek, not the same man she'd seen talking to Brodie. Why was she so on edge?

She went back down to her car and headed back to the big house. She had a box of fresh eggs in the car which Douglas had pressed into her hand when she left Lochside Croft. She poached and ate them with the last heel of bread at the kitchen table, and planned to find out everything she could about her newly inherited property and everyone who had lived – and died – on *her* estate before she went back to her old life in London. She'd start tomorrow with a good look around Sweet Briar, to find out where her uncle was or had been. She'd assumed he was avoiding her, but now she feared a much worse reason she hadn't seen him for a while.

## TWENTY-TWO

Fastidious. That was the word Lisanne used to describe her only son.

For a country cottage, Sweet Briar was spotless. Callum was always concerned with cleanliness to the point of OCD, and every room looked like it could be a showroom or prepped for a glowing report in a magazine. It certainly still retained a cottagey feel with the front 'parlour' sporting a large chintz sofa facing the imposing fireplace, and two love seats on either side. Marcie peered around the broad white painted door then entered the room; only the sound of a ticking mantel clock broke the eerie silence. The old oak floorboards creaked beneath her feet. Her hand ran along the back of one of the sofas as she walked to the window and turned back.

Marcie didn't know what she was looking for or what she might find. Was she better to start elsewhere? She could recall that her uncle had an ancient bureau desk which she imagined was upstairs, but the thought of entering his bedroom, everyone's private space, made her stomach churn with nerves. What was she doing here? How could she invade his privacy like this?

Marcie took in a deep breath as if bracing herself, and turned to go upstairs, only to find Callum in front of her.

'I can help you if you tell me what you're looking for?'

She gasped as the sight of her uncle gave her a start.

'Callum! I was so worried,' she exclaimed, but instead of rushing towards him, she felt as if her feet were rooted to the spot. It was as if an invisible wall had been built between them in the preceding days and it would take more than a few steps to knock it down.

'I didn't hear you at the door?'

Marcie's heart thundered. 'I didn't knock. The door was open.' She took in the man in front of her and how different he looked to the first meeting when she arrived at Swanfield just weeks before.

His skin looked almost paper thin, grey, lined. He looked tired and so unlike her vibrant uncle when they sat having their picnic not long ago, sunglasses atop his head, his smile easy and natural, his warmth palpable.

'I'm sure I locked it,' he stated, and it sounded oddly like a veiled warning.

'Where have you been? I've been so worried... you missed—'

'I know what I missed.' He stood with his hands in his pockets, distant, aloof, seemingly unconcerned.

Marcie felt her shock turn to anger. What had happened to Callum since they last met? He looked so different, and this tone was something new to her. She was confused and somewhat blindsided.

'Ruaridh was really badly injured.'

'I know.'

'The MRT, they lost—'

'I don't need a running commentary,' he interrupted.

Marcie was taken aback at his words. She stepped towards him, only for him to turn and head into the kitchen at the back of the house.

She quickened her step to catch up as he reached for the kettle, switching it on and drawing down the tea caddy and two mugs from their shelf; such a normal act, but with his back to her he seemed so distant.

'Was everything okay at the mart? I mean, it's normally a one or two-day trip.'

Marcie waited for an answer. None came, and she watched as he completed the ritual of warming the teapot, swirling round the water then dispensing with it and dropping in three spoons of loose-leaf tea. She heard him say in her head – *one each and one for the pot* – before he replaced the lid carefully and placed the pot in the centre of the table beside two coasters with mugs on top. A tea strainer rested on its stand, and he slowly filled a milk jug and placed it between them. Callum sat down, inviting her to sit opposite with a simple nod of the head.

'My friend Alister passed away. I was at his funeral,' Callum said quietly, his face almost crumpling at these words. He looked far away for a moment as if recalling moments in the past. She watched closely as he looked into the middle distance, and she saw his eyes well up. She reached out but he moved his hands away.

'I'm sorry, I heard about his death. But where...?'

'You young people. You're all so spiritual, allegedly, trying to find yourselves. I'm allowed to do that, too. I went up to Broomfield. A lot has happened, and I needed to think away from all this.'

Her uncle didn't allude to what *all this* meant. She thought he was referring to Sweet Briar but maybe not. Marcie waited, knowing the power of silence is a motivator for those who want to express fear, anger, displeasure or even love. She moved her warm hands from the mug of hot tea to reach across the table, but he shot his hands down to rest on his knees as if anticipating her conciliatory gesture.

'We need to talk, Cal.'

His eyes were down. 'There's plenty of time for talking.'

She tried a different tack. 'Where's Broomfield? I can't remember.'

'Other side of the glen,' he responded with a nod to the left. 'Old Murdo McCormick's place until a few years ago. He's in the Eventide Home in Inverness.'

'Lucky escape,' she muttered, and Callum looked at her oddly.

Marcie noticed his strained expression, as if he were fighting to cover his emotions. 'I've had a lot to take in during recent days.'

'I'm so sorry, Callum. The death of Lisanne must have really affected you.' She looked at him and her head moved to one side as she gazed at his profile. For all her wonderful communications skills, she was struggling for words to say. She knew that grief affected people in so many different ways and was sure she wouldn't really grieve properly herself until she found herself in Simon's arms.

He sighed deeply. 'And the rest.'

Marcie looked away, staring through the window to the hills and greenery beyond, trying not to catch his gaze. She couldn't avoid the subject any longer. 'I take it you've spoken to Richard?'

'I called him to make an appointment, and he suggested I speak to you first, so it was pretty obvious what that was about,' he said sharply.

'I'm sorry, I had no idea. It's not as if I wanted to be stuck with—'

Anger flared in his eyes. 'Stuck with? Stuck with what? My home?'

He was irritated and annoyed at her comment. A throw-away line from her that almost sent him into a rage.

Marcie sat back in her chair and sighed.

She was struggling to express herself and felt she had to

walk on eggshells. *What was Lisanne thinking?* Was this what had driven the wedge between her and Callum? She hoped against hope that it would not cause the kind of resentment that broke up so many families and fragmented previously loving familial relationships.

A vehicle pulled up, and she saw the Hilux pick-up pull into the yard at the back of the house, then Brodie got out, making his way to the back door. She closed her eyes and listened as he came into the kitchen.

'Ah! You're back!' Brodie smiled broadly and leaned against the sink. 'You get everything you needed to buy?'

'Aye, son, aye.'

Brodie caught Marcie's eye and gave her a wink. He leaned back, very comfortable it would seem in his surroundings, and shoved his hands in his pockets.

'No cake today?' he asked, laughing, but he was the only one.

'Outside,' said Callum, sharply, and he noisily pushed his chair away and headed for the back door, Brodie dutifully following him to the yard.

Their conversation was animated but unheard by Marcie as she sat almost rooted to her seat. After a moment, she got up and headed out in time to see Brodie throw himself into the pick-up and drive off hurriedly.

'What's all that about?' she asked Callum, who simply stepped past her back into the house. She quickly followed. 'What's happened? What's happened to us?' she asked hastily and perhaps a little aggressively.

'You've stolen what's rightly mine, Marcie, that's what's happened to us.'

'I stole nothing,' she responded. 'I knew nothing about this!' She was both angry and disbelieving of what had happened to them. *Does Callum really think she knew anything about this?* she thought. Mistrust had crept into what had been a loving and caring relationship, and now she was questioning her grand-mother's motives.

'I had plans, I had a future.'

'You *still* have a future. I don't have any plans and I'm certainly not going to move up to Strathkin.'

He looked at her incredulously. 'What? Sell up?' he asked, his face a horrified expression.

'Well, what am I going to do with a zillion acre estate?' Marcie found herself shouting and watched as her uncle dropped his mug onto the floor. The loud smash made her gasp and cover her mouth with her hands.

She made her way to the back utility where mops and brooms were kept, but he shouted after her, '*LEAVE IT.*' The venom in the words again startled her and she hurriedly rushed out the door and ran back to Swanfield, trying to stifle tears as she slammed the door so hard she could hear it reverberate around the stillness of the house.

Marcie ran upstairs to her bedroom and hurled herself on the bed. Her shock at her uncle's behaviour was so intense that tears didn't come. What had happened to them? Just days ago, they were as normal and affectionate as always. Surely it couldn't only be about the estate. What had happened to sever their unbreakable bond, their wonderful loving relationship?

# TWENTY-THREE

Marcie's suitcase was packed, and it sat in the vestibule. It was an overnight decision she had tossed and turned over throughout the wee small hours, wondering if she was making the right choice. She couldn't get through to Simon and she was feeling increasingly alone and isolated. There were several flights a day to London, so if the late-morning flight was full, she'd find a seat on the later plane, even if it meant spending time in the small airport with a coffee and a magazine.

But her plan was about to change.

It took her a moment of digging in her tote bag before she realised it was the landline that was ringing. She rushed along to get to the back hall, wondering who still used a landline. She wasn't surprised when she found it was Richard on the other end of the line.

'So, a little bird told me you're about to fly the coop?'

Marcie looked back at her carry-on case and tote bag sitting in the hall and wondered if Richard had a hidden camera in the house. She instinctively looked up to each corner of the ceiling.

'What?' she asked incredulously.

'It's okay, I don't have a crystal ball. I called the airport rent a car for a client and they told me they were expecting a white X5 back today. Since they only have one white one it didn't take long to figure out that you were on your way back to London.'

'I know up here is fuelled by gossip, Richard, but that's a new one on me. I *was* going to call you,' she explained.

'Not a problem, Marcella!' he responded in his usual jovial tone.

'I don't have time to drop in. I'm trying to get the late-morning flight,' she said, by way of a hint, but she knew it would make no difference. Richard went at his own speed no matter what the prompt.

'So, we do need to talk,' he said. 'When I say there's not a problem, it's a problem we can solve, I'm sure...'

'Uh?'

'Callum is contesting the will.'

Marcie was taken aback. She leaned against the wall.

'Now, if he's taken advice from anyone, I can assure you it's not me.'

'Can he do that?'

'Oh yes, it's perfectly reasonable of him, particularly in Scots law where it would be – or would *have* been – normal practice for the entire will – the estate in the broadest sense of the word – to be turned over to the eldest son, to carry on the crofting succession. Very, very particular in the Highlands, you'll understand, being from a legal background yourself. I remember when I was a young law student...'

'Richard, I really don't have time for this. I have a plane to catch.'

'But we *do* need to talk, Marcella. I'm advising, if I may be so bold, that you delay going to London and I'll happily tell my other client he's going to have to go for the Skoda Yeti and not hold out for the BMW X5.'

'I'll see you soon, Richard. As soon as I can, I'll call

Margaret for an appointment,' Marcie replied, raising her eyes to the ceiling in tacit agreement.

'*CALLUM!*' Marcie muttered under her breath as she replaced the old-fashioned phone back onto the cradle. *I can't get you to speak to me, but you speak to Richard.*

She looked at her suitcase. She had about twenty minutes to make up her mind if she was to catch the late-morning plane. She rushed out the back door and up the rise to Sweet Briar. This time the back door was locked, and so she banged on it furiously. With no Land Rover or Hilux in the yard, it was obvious there was no one at home. She gave a cry that she was sure afterwards would have been heard across the loch and possibly as far as Strath Aullt if the weather had been clearer.

Dark, heavy clouds were rolling in over the mountains with a harsh wind behind them, and within the hour the rain would be battering against the windows and visibility would be low. *Was this the day to drive to the airport?*

Marcie felt rain begin to spit at her as she ran back to Swanfield. She made her way to the well-stocked drinks trolley in the drawing room. With a shaking hand, she took a bottle of twenty-five-year-old Dalwhinnie and poured the whisky neat into a crystal glass. She downed it in one, the way she had seen people do in the movies when they needed to calm their nerves, but it didn't have the hoped for effect. She felt giddy for a moment as she gulped in air then ran to the kitchen and vomited it back up in the sink, removing any effect it would have had in one fell swoop. Lisanne wasn't a big drinker, and jokingly referred to it as *Amnesia Juice*, although the drinks cabinet was always well stocked for the frequent visitor. On this occasion, Marcie realised she would need a lot more than simply a glass or two of malt to make her forget what had unfolded since she had arrived back at her childhood home just a few short weeks ago.

She sat on her grandmother's old reading chair, and wished the woodburning stove was lit as the rain began to batter against the windows. The temperature dropped. Even though it was April, there was often a frost this far north, and she stirred as a chill swept over her. For all she knew it could be snowing within the hour and, glass of malt aside, it was not the day to be travelling on a bleak and empty road, not in this mood.


Early afternoon she woke in her grandmother's chair, and indeed there had been a flurry of snow. A light dusting was spread across the ground at the back of the house and disappeared on the white hire car in the rear yard. The sky had darkened and although the snow had stopped, the landscape out of the window looked inhospitable; inside, the house felt miserably cold. She was glad she had reset the fire after the night the Balfour boys had stayed. She lit the kindling in the front room and looked across the water to Lochside Croft, watching as a plume of black smoke drifted out from the chimney, was caught in the strong wind and sucked up to join the grey low cloud that covered Strathkin like a blanket. She pulled a tartan rug from the back of a sofa and wrapped it around her shoulders to warm herself until the fire took hold.

Once she was warmer, Marcie picked up her mobile and dialled Callum's number, only to find that his phone, once again, was switched off. Who else could she call? Bella, like her, would be hunkered down at home. No one would dream of heading out for a trek in this grim weather. It was clear from the smoking chimney across the way that the Balfours would also be settled in for a long one on this ugly day, the range likely to be churning out light-as-air home baking, with warming smells that the boys would remember all their days. Heather? She thought about her friend and her probable betrayal. Had Callum heard from Richard, or had Heather blurted out the Swanfield secret? She dialled Heather's number, but although it rang, she didn't pick up.

## TWENTY-FOUR

The next day was crisp and clear after the pitiful weather the day before and, after a quick breakfast, Marcie plucked up the courage to head next door. But there was still no vehicle in the yard, and a brisk knock on the back door brought no joy.

She headed back to Swanfield and to the safe which was installed in the bottom of the wardrobe in Lisanne's bedroom. She wanted to check whether the original dated will was still inside, as Richard had said it would be. Quietly, almost reverentially, in her grandmother's old room she pulled open the window to let air into the somewhat sealed space, and opened the wardrobe. Clothes let out their musty smell and a moth fluttered out. The already fading scent of her grandmother hung faintly in the still air before being whipped away by the wind coming in through the open window.

Marcie kneeled. The code to the safe wasn't exactly stored in the most private of places. She carefully ripped off the piece of paper that was sellotaped to the side of the box, pressed in the numbers written clearly on it, and the door released with a heavy click.

A couple of old green velvet jewellery boxes sat on top of

some papers, and she opened them both to find her grandmother's wedding ring in one and a set of drop sapphire earrings that had belonged to her mother in another. The rest of the jewellery she'd been left in her grandmother's will had been safely stored at Richard's office in Inverness before her grandmother died, and it would remain there until she was ready to take it all to her own home. She didn't want the most precious of gems left in an empty house, particularly now that Jamie MacKay had been warning about break-ins in the area. She wasn't entirely sure she wanted to take them back to London either, until she had a secure place to store them. So that was yet another thing to add to an increasingly long list of To Dos.

She reached in to fetch some papers which were held together with an ancient dry elastic band that snapped as she pulled them out and shot into the air. The envelopes were old with faded writing on the front. One read:

*Copy Deeds, Swanfield*

*Copy Estate Plans*

She opened the plans and pulled out a large, folded map that was beginning to fray at the edges and separate at the folds, and she gingerly placed it beside her on the floor.

Dotted around a map of the estate, in faded text, it showed the outline of the estate and the little cottages within it. She read the names of the tied cottages and tenanted crofts including Sweet Briar next door and Stratheyre, Lubnaig and Kintyre cottages, and Broomfield at the far end of the estate near the hill road to Strath Aullt and Tigh-na-Lochan on the opposite side. Lochside Croft was also listed but a handwritten note in heavy black ink stated that it had been *sold to Lyndsey Balfour*, Ruaridh's father, in 1979. The price was unreadable, but it was in the hundreds of pounds, which made Marcie smile. *It would be hundreds of thousands now*, she thought. Another couple of cottages were listed as farm property but as they were across the folds, they were unreadable. She folded the large map down into its A4 shape and placed it gently into its old manila envelope, itself starting to come away at the sides.

Marcie examined the other envelopes, sifting through them like a deck of cards until one fell out. She was about to put it back in the pile when she realised it was a new envelope with fresh writing. Puzzled, she opened it and pulled out the newly folded piece of paper.

She set it down, leaning back on her haunches. She scoured the piece of paper, unable to make sense of the words in her frantic state. Surely this couldn't be? Was this why Callum had gone *walkabout*? None of it made sense to her. She ran her finger over the outline of her lips then through her hair. If this was hidden away as a secret, then that it is how it should remain for the time being.

She pulled her mobile from her back pocket, smoothing out the paper on the rug where it met the wooden floor, and quickly took a photograph, then another close-up just to make sure. As she shuffled the paper into the pile, she glanced back into the safe as something caught her eye. Trying to lift it, she felt the lip on the bottom of the safe. It was loose, like a false floor, but no amount of effort would make it budge. Looking around she saw on the dressing table a letter opener with the elaborate letter 'L' making a design at the top. She grabbed it and returned to her sitting position in front of the safe. The sharp end opened the bottom easily. One piece of folded paper sat inside. She opened it carefully, once again sitting back on her haunches to try to decipher what it meant. She took out her phone. She zoomed in on her grandmother's writing, which had been blanked out with white Tippex or the like. Marcie looked up, staring into space for a moment, her brain trying to make sense of these two pieces of paper.

She folded the piece of paper she was holding back along the same lines, lay it on the bed and thought for a moment. Leaning back into the safe, she ran her hand along the sides and base and at the back she found her hand circling a wad of money with a twenty-pound note holding it together, the elastic band long since disintegrated. There was maybe a thousand pounds or slightly more in mostly twenty-pound notes.

Marcie gathered everything together and placed it back where she had found it, carefully lining it up to look untouched, and closed the safe over with a resounding 'click' and a hearty push to make sure it was securely closed. She pressed the paper code back against the side of the safe until it stuck. Then she sat back, unfolding her legs, and shimmied up to lean against the bed, lifting the piece of paper she had laid there. She was baffled and confused at what she had found. But it was something she was not ready to reveal to anyone, not yet.

# TWENTY-FIVE

The only clock in the universe with a lounder tick than the mantel clocks at Swanfield and Sweet Briar was the clock on the fireplace in the office of Richard MacInnes, Solicitor, in Inverness. It marked down the seconds and minutes that Marcie had been sitting in the chair opposite Richard's large and imposing desk. It was drowning in manila folders tied with various coloured bands and reams of paper grouped together with treasury tags. It was indeed stepping back in time – literally. It was as if nothing had moved or been dealt with since her last visit.

She heard his heavy footsteps approaching, and she flinched as the door flew open and he breezed halfway in before stopping and bellowing, 'Margaret!'

He flew past her to his desk, only briefly pausing to place his right hand on her left shoulder to give it a gentle squeeze.

'Marcella. Good drive?'

'Interminable,' she responded with a sigh.

'Grateful for you coming over. Weather's not been great. Got two of my main men off so couldn't really take the whole day out to come to you to do the inventory and so on. So grateful, grateful.' He thanked her and disappeared behind his desk, opening a thinner, less colourful folder than the last time she was here.

Richard was about to speak when she heard the rattle of crockery behind her, and Margaret slowly came into the room with a tray of tea. She sat it down gingerly on the edge of the desk, the only part of it not covered in paperwork, and poured two cups. She handed Marcie a cup of water with a vague hint of tea and offered a plate with two oat biscuits. With a nod to Richard, she backed out of the room, and Richard raised his eyebrows as the heavy door closed.

'So,' he began, 'disputed grant of confirmation. How up to speed are you?'

'Not my bag, I'm afraid,' she stated as she took a sip of tepid water disguised as tea, made a face and replaced the cup, never to be touched again. 'I know this is your bread and butter, Richard. I'm a different facet of the law and English law at that. I'm happy to bow to your greater experience in these matters. Happy to take onboard any of your wise counsel.'

'Bottom line – it's mediation or we'll have to go to court. No jury, of course, civil court. An appointed judge will hear all the evidence and make a ruling based on all available information at the time. Of course, if he decides the will *is* valid with the codicil, the estate is administered as is. Of course, he could do a lot of things but my suggestion? Mediation. But of course, it depends on how long you wish this to drag on. As I said, I'd rather go mediation. If you think Callum will be amenable. We are talking a long time here. This is a big estate, a lot of assets. A considerable time, Marcie, considerable.'

She looked down at her handbag resting against the desk, and could see her phone resting in the side pocket. She sighed as she looked at the pink casing. How easily she could flick to photos.

'I'm happy to try mediation.' Her voice cracked. 'I don't

want to lose him. Richard, he's all I have left.' She swallowed hard.

'I can understand, I can understand.' The solicitor nodded and bit his lip. 'I can call him, see what we can do to move this along. You'll be wanting to get back to work at some point so I'll move as quickly as I can, but I have to say, Marcie, I've come across a lot of disagreements between executors and beneficiaries and in my experience it gets dragged out. I'm dealing with one at the moment – thirteen years. It's not a healthy experience for families. And it might not be straightforward. You know my old boss here had a phrase, *where there's a will, there's a relative*, and he was right. Even when it's more assets than large sums of money, in your case an awful lot of valuable land. Be in no doubt, Marcie, I've seen families torn apart,' explained Richard solemnly.

'Thanks, Richard,' said Marcie with a sigh.

'I'm being realistic, Marcella.' He leaned forward on crossed arms, suddenly looking more concerned than she'd seen him before. 'This is not professional discourtesy to my other client, but money and property causes so much damage to what were previously closeknit families. I've seen this family torn apart by what can only be described as greed on the part of one member – causing division and mistrust over what used to be their playground. I know you both well – I don't want to see that happen to you.'

He sat back as if he'd finished his lecture and Marcie gazed past him to the blue sky outside. 'But let's not dwell on this.' He checked his watch. 'Let me take you to lunch. The Fat Pheasant is just along the way.'

'Actually, anywhere but there,' she said, standing and gathering her belongings. Her hand felt for her phone. Was it the right time to show him what she'd found? Her lawyer's brain told her, *full disclosure, Marcie, full disclosure*. 'Richard?'

'Yes, m'dear?'

She put her phone back in her bag. 'Let's do The Mustard Seed across the water.'

'Excellent choice,' he agreed and, despite the spring weather, reached for his thick, green wool Loden coat.

## TWENTY-SIX

As the road stretched ahead, Marcie could see dips and turns for at least two miles through what looked like a moonscape, with jagged rocks and boulders on either side of the single track. She was glad that the clouds were clearing, and it wasn't as dreich as her previous drive. Her mind darted from one thing to another. *Why hadn't she been honest with Richard? Why wasn't she standing up to Callum and just telling him what was what?* Even in the restaurant when the conversation had turned to holidays and Richard and his wife's love of Mediterranean cruising, Marcie could easily have brought the subject back to why she was *there – her concerns over Callum, his future, their future* – but she chose not to. She'd suggested that Judge Uisdean McLeod could be unprofessional, but wasn't this exactly what she was being?

She became aware of something in her rear-view mirror, a dark car with lights on, some distance away. She caught glimpses of it as the road undulated and the camber changed; the car was there one minute, out of sight the next. She kept going at a meandering speed and soon the vehicle had caught up with her own. A black Range Rover; she recognised it as it nudged closer to her then pulled back. She sped up, as did the other car, then she slowed, as did the other car. Her heart began to beat a little faster. She knew that a few miles ahead, the road joined a main road again and she sped up, ever mindful of the occasional sheep feasting on grass at the side of the road. She heard Callum in her ear, who had taught her to drive on these very same roads years before: *head down – foot down*, he would comment to the learner driver, meaning that if a sheep was tucking into a grassy lunch, it was more interested in that than stepping out in front of a speeding car. She checked her rear-view then each of her side mirrors. The Range Rover was gaining. Marcie put her foot down harder to put more space between them but still it loomed behind her, weaving through the glen. In the far distance an occasional car passed as the main road drew closer, but so did a tricky bend near to the old Crag Brae Bridge, over the fast-flowing water, meaning she would have to slow down considerably to ensure she crossed it safely. There was a sign to tell the driver to slow as the hairpin bend approached, but it was clear the following car was having none of it. Marcie's foot hovered between the brake and accelerator as the bridge approached. A glance at her dashboard showed she was tipping sixty miles per hour. As she began to turn the wheel, the Range Rover clipped the nearside bumper of her $X_5$, sending it into a terrifying spin. To her horror, her vehicle was out of control and would soon be flying towards the water...

She sat bolt upright in bed, perspiration soaking her spine, her breath laboured. She was panting as she reached to drink from her glass of water on the bedside table. Her hand was shaking so much she failed to grasp it, and it tumbled to the floor, emptying its contents over the carpet. She had never been prone to nightmares. But the events that had played out in her subconscious felt so real that she expected to look out the window and see her hire car in the yard, smashed and undriveable.

She couldn't see her watch but a quick glance at her phone told her it was just after 3 a.m. She lay back down with a heavy sigh. It was too early – or too late – to call Simon, and she didn't have the energy to get up and creep downstairs to make a tea or a hot chocolate at such an hour. *May as well lie here, and plan for the worst.* She was never a doomsayer, being a glass-half-full type, but she felt she was not, and could not, be in control of what would unfold in the coming days. She was right.

# TWENTY-SEVEN

Morning came slowly. As Marcie sat in front of the mirror, hair dried, styled and make-up on, she said to herself aloud, 'Today's the day.' She opened a small red jewellery box to put on her bracelet that sat snug on her wrist under her red friendship cord and went to pop in her earrings, only to find they were not in the box. The silver drop earrings that had been a gift from Simon, and that she had worn to see Richard the previous day, lay on the embroidered white cloth on the dressing table. But the round brilliant cut diamond earrings which she'd received from Lisanne for her twenty-first birthday were missing. She went back to the bathroom to the shelf above the sink and ran her hand across it, but only her toothbrush and toothpaste lay on top. She sat heavily on the closed toilet seat and pondered for a second or two where she could have left them. She was very methodical and had a set place for everything, which messy Simon found perplexing, so when something was out of its usual order, she felt uncomfortable.

Marcie slipped in yesterday's earrings and went over to the window, where her eyes were drawn to The Strathkin Inn, smoke already belching out of the chimney. *Surely not.*

She had been away in Inverness almost all day yesterday and was not sure if she'd locked the back door, never mind the front door. *What was it Heather had said when she saw the large and expensive earrings that Marcie had so absentmindedly been twirling in her ears when they last met?* How Heather said the sale of such expensive earrings could solve all her money worries in one fell swoop. Marcie thought, as she headed out, *surely this would be too obvious?* Her fingers instinctively moved to trace a line around her lips. She thought less, *today's the day*, and more, *how is this going to go?* when she climbed into the – thankfully undamaged – car and nervously drove over to the Inn on the other side of the loch.

Guests were checking out when she arrived, and Heather was laughing heartily with two couples as she walked them to their car, rolling two sets of keys around between her fingers as she joked about the previous day's April snow.

Marcie stood aside, hands tucked in the pockets of her cream gilet, and smiled to the couple as they checked their roof bins were secure, nodded and pulled out of the car park to the front of the building.

'Hello, stranger,' said Heather as she strolled over. 'I've been over a couple of times to see you. You complained Callum is never around, *YOU'RE* never around...'

*So, she* has *been to Swanfield*, thought Marcie suspiciously. 'Just stuff to sort out back in Inverness. I keep forgetting it's nearly an all-day trip.'

'All sorted? When are you heading back down the road?' quizzed Heather nonchalantly.

'Why is everyone desperate to see the back of me?' Marcie asked, wondering why her friend wanted her out of the way. 'What's the big rush?' she continued but this time more wary of her tone.

Heather smiled. 'Well, the sooner you go down the road the sooner I can come visit.'

'I thought you were *skint*? I thought you were worried about the bailiffs at your door?' Marcie pressed, watching Heather for any clue and eyeing her distrustfully.

Heather looked away. 'I've had a bit of a windfall.'

Marcie bit her lip to stop herself from blurting out her theory of where her friend's newfound wealth had come from, and was immediately glad she had. She was dubious of the manner of this windfall but was also conscious of her normal behaviour of jumping in with both feet. She moved from foot to foot, watching her friend sceptically.

'To be honest, Mars, it was just awful what happened on the mountain. I don't know if it's the rubber-necking gloomsters and doomsters, but my bookings have shot up and people are stopping for lunches after detouring on their way west so, silver linings, eh?' she said and nudged her friend as she walked back into the Inn. Heather looked back with a smile that Marcie felt was unconvincing.

Marcie followed her friend through past reception and the kitchen and into the back office where she hung up the keys on a rack, leaning around to switch the kettle on in the servery. She picked up a large diary and flicked through it.

'Might be the first year to break even in a while.' Heather put the book back down on the desk, and Marcie cast her eyes over the dishevelled paperwork. Her eyes locked on a small blue velvet jewellery box half hidden on the desk.

'Have you any hot chocolate?' Marcie asked her friend.

'Er, probably in the back store, I'll have a wee gander.' Heather headed to the rear of the kitchen into a large storeroom where boxes of hotel supplies were piled precariously on metal shelving.

Marcie leaned over and picked up the box, opening it quickly while her friend was out of the room.

Two sparkling diamonds gleamed back at her. They were dazzling. And they were hers.

'I'm afraid it's only the diet stuff,' said Heather, coming round the door clutching a bunch of sachets of hot chocolate that would normally sit on a hospitality tray in one of the bedrooms.

'What's that?' she asked Marcie, who was holding the open box.

'You know very well what it is...'

Heather looked closer at the velvet box. 'Where did you get that? Did you bring it over as a donation? For the raffle, the tombola?' She smiled.

Marcie regarded her dubiously.

'These are mine,' she said.

'What are you doing with them here? Are you going to get them valued at Strath Aullt?' Heather asked.

'I'm about to ask you the very same question. Where did *you* get them?'

Heather said in disbelief. 'You don't think...? Mars, they're not mine,' she said, holding her hands up, palms facing her friend. 'Seriously, I've no idea what they're doing there,' she went on, her face flushing at the accusation.

'So, business has picked up? Have you already sold them on?'

'Whoa!' Heather barked back at her friend. 'Back off!'

Marcie clipped the box shut and searched for words that didn't come as the two friends stared each other down, both in fury. The scene was only broken by the sound of the drayman yelling from the backyard with a warning that he was pushing a keg of beer through the door.

Marcie turned on her heel and headed straight for the front door with Heather in hot pursuit.

'Marcie!' Heather yelled as her friend threw herself into the car and pulled away, steering up the incline and onto the back road. She didn't look back.

## TWENTY-EIGHT

Marcie leaned on the car looking down on the village from the high ridge. A shaft of light tried to break through the cloud, and shadows danced across the loch and the steep mountains on the opposite shore.

'You know,' said a voice behind her, 'I used to watch cowboy movies when I was wee, and sometimes I'd come up here and pretend I was really in one. Need to buy a Stetson, mind you.'

Ruaridh slid off a horse he probably borrowed from the trekking centre. His face was healing, she noticed as the clouds began to split high above them.

'I'll need to get Dina to tie a big bit of string to it to go round my chin or I'd lose it in five minutes up here in the wind. Find it in Norway in a week's time probably.' He strolled over to her. 'Howdy, partner!' he joked, doffing an imaginary cowboy hat as he joined her to lean against the car. He surveyed the vista.

'I can't imagine living anywhere else, you know,' he said as his eyes moved across the wilderness that unfolded in front of them. She followed his gaze along the mountain range rising behind the small village. All those years ago, on this very spot, she remembered how they'd pledged never to leave Strathkin, and to bring their family up in this magical part of the country.

She reached for her necklace, gripping the pendant to run it across the chain back and forth.

'Cat got your tongue?' Ruaridh asked and nudged her.

She glanced at him. They had been so close for such a long time, she and Ruaridh. She wanted to say, we need to talk, I need to share something. But instead, she continued to play with her jewellery, confused and bewildered. 'I don't know if I could ever come back,' she said finally. 'It's changed so much.'

'Maybe it's you that's changed,' he said. Marcie glanced at him again, then looked away. 'Nothing ever stays the same. Even in sleepy wee Strathkin.'

'I can't wait to get out of here,' she muttered.

'Here! That's a bit of a wild statement!' he said, shocked.

'I lost a pair of earrings – the earrings from Lisanne – well, I thought they were lost. I found them at Heather's. I think she stole them,' she blurted out, her shoulders rising and falling in anger.

'Now, that's a bit of an accusation. I hope you've got proof because I wouldn't go casting aspersions on someone's character without evidence. You of all people should know that,' he warned.

'How on earth did they get from Swanfield to the Inn? I was only away a day.'

'There will be an explanation. She'll have picked them up by mistake or something,' he said, trying to make sense of the situation.

'Did they swim across?' Marcie suggested with a shrug.

'I dunno. Did you ask her?'

'I didn't wait for an answer. Last time I was wearing them she said how diamonds that size would get her out of her money problems, then suddenly, she's laughing and joking like she hasn't a care in the world, saying her money issues have been solved.'

'Well, in her defence, Mars, the place has been a bit busier since the, well…'

'So she said.'

Ruaridh looked at her sadly. 'And you don't believe her? One of your oldest friends. Why?'

'I don't know what I believe anymore,' Marcie said with a harrumph and pushed herself away from the car.

She marched forward only to be pulled back by Ruaridh, realising with a fright that she was, in fact, standing at the very edge of the ridge.

'Feck's sake, Mars! Careful!'

She had shocked herself back to reality and snapped out of her mood. 'Thanks!' she gasped, realising how close she had come to certain death.

'I'm not going through all of that again. Not now that…'

'Now that?' she urged.

'Och, she told me what she'd said to you that night. That night, a lifetime ago!' His face relaxed into a smile, the broadest grin she had seen on his face in a long time.

Marcie's mood lifted and she wrapped her arms around him, feeling him wince slightly, realising his deep bruising must still be giving him pain. 'I'm so happy for you.'

'A wee lassie. AT LAST,' he almost yelled into the air. 'I'm not taking anything for granted, though, after what we all went through. I've told her we're telling nobody until I've got that scan in my hands from Raigmore.' He gestured, referring to the hospital in their nearest city.

'I've not said to the girls,' qualified Marcie, 'but as soon as she starts digging out those voluminous smocks the game's up. I mean, your boys were all HUGE!'

'Take after their dad,' said Ruaridh, proud as punch. It was true; he was tall, broad and strong and somewhere in his DNA beat the heart of a Viking. 'Listen, Mars, can I give you some advice?' he offered, and went on, not waiting for a response. 'Everyone here is going through a period of adjustment – you included – so just cut people a wee bit of slack, eh? Sometimes you have a touch of a bull in a china shop vibe. I'm saying that as a friend,' he qualified.

He was right – she did have a *jump feet first* approach. But there were strange goings on in her little village, and somehow, she seemed to be at the epicentre of them. Marcie wasn't yet sure what she was going to do, but she had to do something. She knew she would have to ask difficult questions. The thought of jumping on a plane back to London couldn't be further from her mind.

# TWENTY-NINE

Bella eyed her friend, incredulous. She stopped piling tagliatelle into pasta bowls while pondering what she'd just heard. Putting down the pot and strainer, she picked up the block of parmesan and grater, slicing off several shards on top of the pasta. She handed Marcie a filled bowl. She then picked up her glass of Sangiovese and took a long drink.

'I don't know how or why, but surely it can't be true.'

'She stole them – plain and simple,' stated Marcie, drinking a glug of wine. She was staying over at the house attached to the trekking centre and fully entering into the spirit of *Amnesia Juice*: she would forget the last few days if she could.

'Now, did you not tell me Jamie said there had been break-ins in the area?' asked Bella.

'Well, yes, but they're hardly going to just take a pair of earrings and leave everything else and then leave them in another house, are they? I'm sure even Jamie would agree they'd be rather incompetent burglars.'

'Ah, true.' Bella wrapped some pasta round and round her fork aided with her spoon, before scooping it up to be devoured. 'But why?'

'She's skint.'

'We're all *skint*, Mars.' She pointed her fork towards her kitchen. 'This spanking new kitchen that I have? Came from the school before they shut it down. It was destined for the skip. The only new thing is the worktop. And this? This is the most I've eaten since Tuesday.' Once again, she pointed the fork, this time into the half-filled bowl.

Marcie noticed the last slice of gingerbread still lying on the counter. To ensure the horses and ponies were being cared for, her friend was doing without. 'Listen, if you need help...'

'I'm not asking for handouts, Mars, but seriously, what if she *did* steal them, what are you going to do? Report her? She can't afford a fine. None of us can, to be honest.' She tucked into her pasta. Marcie knew her friend's supper was made from the supermarket 'basics' range and it struck her once again how fragile people's lives here had become when money was harder to come by.

'*Jessica Fletcher!*' Bella blurted out. 'That's the Cabot Cove woman I couldn't remember! You're more her than Miss Marple. Speaking of which, how's the cosy murder mystery?' she asked, changing the subject.

'I just find the whole thing suspicious, and I don't consider it *my* estate yet – we're a long way from that as far as I'm concerned.'

'That's the lawyer in you. All that forensic stuff you needed to learn about. They just died of old age, though, unless you have an *investigative theory*. Yeah, I admit it – I watch *Murder, She Wrote*.' Bella dropped her fork onto her empty plate, collected the dishes up and placed them in the sink.

'Fancy a blast from the past?' She stretched into the fridge, taking out two small glasses. 'You remember coming back from school when it was Lisanne's time for tea and she gave us the most amazing pudding?'

'Butterscotch Angel Delight!' replied Marcie, and they both laughed.

'Well, miracle of miracles, you can still get it in Roddy's shop.' Bella put a glass with a teaspoon sticking out on the table in front of Marcie.

She laughed as Bella spooned a large scoop into her mouth and closed her eyes in fake ecstasy.

'I think the sell-by is probably 2004, but I'm trying to make your last days feel like the old days.'

'Why is everyone trying to get rid of me so soon?' asked Marcie, downing the rest of the wine in her glass and pouring another.

'I think if we keep going on it'll be like reverse psychology, and you'll end up staying.' Bella reached for the corkscrew, smiling at her friend across the table.

'Be careful what you wish for,' replied Marcie, holding out her now-empty glass.

# THIRTY

'It looks different in here,' said the police officer as he looked around the drawing room at Swanfield, taking in the expansive view from the huge windows – the loch, the cottages on the opposite shore and the mountains that rose steep and sharp beyond.

Marcie poured coffee from the French press into the bone china cup on the tray, handing it to Jamie as he sat down opposite her, adjusting all his various items as he did: airwave radio, defender torch, handcuffs, taser gun and baton, none of which had ever seen any action in Strathkin.

'I'm best doing without,' he said when she offered him the milk jug. 'We've started switching the electricity off at the police station, so the fridge is always full of our sour milk.' He took a slurp of the thick black coffee. 'I'm quite liking it,' he said, pleased with himself. 'You know, I've only ever been in the kitchen.' He looked around the room, placing his saucer and cup down on the side table. 'So...' he urged her.

'So,' Marcie began. 'Everyone in the village probably knows by now that I've inherited "the big house".'

'Aye, lucky you.' He looked up in awe at the high ornate ceiling cornices and intricate mouldings.

Marcie went on, 'And obviously that includes the estate and all.'

'Aye.'

'And all the tied crofts and tenanted farms.'

'Aye.'

'I'm just curious to learn about some of the people who live on the estate. I mean, I don't really remember them, you know. I left when I went to university and never really returned,' she explained.

'You're coming back now, though, aren't you?' he quizzed, looking at her as if he was about to question her at the police station. He had slipped into police officer mode as he leaned forward.

'Well, that remains to be discussed,' she said firmly.

Jamie sighed. 'I've not seen much of Callum in the last wee while, come to think of it. How's he doing after his mum passed?'

'My uncle is why I wanted to ask you a few questions,' Marcie replied.

Jamie chuckled. 'A wee bit of role reversal there, Mars. It's usually me doing the questions.'

'The funeral the other day, of...' she began, unable to remember the deceased man's real name.

'Aye, the Duffer. Sad, really. Same age as my dad.'

'What did he die of?'

'Think he drank himself to an early grave if I can remember. Up at Kintyre Cottage, was it? I get them a wee bit mixed up because I think there was one at that other cottage not that long ago.'

'Lubnaig?' she pressed.

He pulled his notebook from his top pocket and started flicking through the pages. 'Aye, that's the one. What's this got to do with anything? There was nothing suspicious about those deaths.' His tone suggested defensiveness at the quality of his investigation being questioned.

'I'm just asking questions. I mean, they were Lisanne's tenants, were they not? And she and Callum must have known them personally. Just wondering if I should write to their relatives to tell them I've inherited Swanfield and offer any support.' She was trying to keep Jamie on side but couldn't tell if she was doing a good job of it.

He continued to look at his notebook. 'Nope. Don't think there were any relatives to be contacted. Except the old guy, McAskill... think he had a cousin in Australia but not sure we traced him.'

'Stratheyre Cottage?' she questioned as, once again, he checked his book with a sigh.

'Cailean McAskill, Stratheyre Cottage. Think that was an epileptic fit, poor old guy. Bit of a mess.'

'I don't think the victims were that old, Jamie, that's what I'm saying. Were they not all early sixties? I didn't know about them but look at how fit Callum is at that age.'

'Aye, indeed, he is a fit bloke for his age,' he agreed with a nod.

'But it's no age at all...' she found herself repeating. She stood up and paced to the window, looking out at the view across the loch and the mountains beyond. Maybe the harsh reality of living and working in such a remote and sometimes unforgiving place had taken its toll. She ran her finger over the outline of her lips. Maybe all of this was just coincidence – it had been a particularly cold winter. But no. She wasn't convinced. She made her way back to where the police officer was still sitting, nursing his cup.

'So, what are you saying, Mars?'

She sighed with frustration. Did she have to spell it out? 'I just think it's suspicious.'

'Suspicious? They all died from natural causes, according to the postmortems.'

'Was toxicology done?'

Jamie held his hands up. 'Hey, Marcie, we're getting into dangerous territory here. The pathologist at Raigmore Mortuary recorded "non-suspicious death". You know as well as I do it's called an "unexplained death" until the results of the PM. They all had underlying health conditions. Believe me. You're straying into territory that's maybe a wee bit out of your depth, with all due respect.' He stood up. 'No offence, Mars, you might be taking over the big house, but you'll not have the same sway over the villagers as your grandmother. Things have moved on, you know. You can't come up here and act like the Lady Laird, like Lisanne, sitting here like the villagers owed her their living.' He brushed imaginary crumbs and dust off his trousers to smarten himself up and stood to his full six foot two.

'Are we done?' he asked, and Marcie realised how much she'd insulted his policing prowess. She nodded in response.

'I'll see myself out.'

Instead of walking to the front door, Jamie headed out the rear hall into the yard. Moments later, he pulled away sharply in the police car. As Marcie watched on from the window, he didn't look back or give her his usual friendly wave as the Battenburg liveried vehicle slipped onto the road.

'Well, that went well,' she said aloud to herself, realising she had just alienated yet another good friend.

# THIRTY-ONE

'Mars, you're unreal,' Simon said over the phone. 'I honestly don't know where you're getting this from.'

'It just doesn't make sense,' she repeated.

'You staying up there on your own in that vast empty house doesn't make sense. It's not good for you, with Callum giving you the evil eye, as you say.'

'He's not giving me the evil eye, per se,' she replied, 'and the girls are here. Well, Dina and Bella.'

'But he's going to contest the will? That just doesn't sound like him, Mars. Look, I can't get away right now, unless you tell me *I'm* really a secret millionaire and can walk away after closing at midnight,' he joked.

'Well, you would be if I sold everything, but to be honest, I think we've inherited a money pit.' She could hear the glasses chinking in the background and the murmur of people out enjoying themselves, and she suddenly had a longing for Simon and for their perfect little life that had changed with one phone call.

'Listen, why don't you head back pronto, and we can sit and talk about it with one of your famous lists? A pros and cons sheet of paper and a large glass of red. If you decide not to go back...'

'What?' she exclaimed.

'IF, if you decide not to go back, we could just take off, have time to ourselves for a while and do all that travelling we keep talking about. Maybe a bit of space between you and Cal might be the ideal answer to your problems, hmm?'

'Hmm,' she said back to him and took a moment to ponder his suggestion. She didn't like it. While she was desperate to get back to Simon and some sort of normality, she was also determined to see everything in Strathkin come to a conclusion – whatever that conclusion may be.

Once they'd finished their call, Marcie went upstairs to her room and stood at the window. All was peaceful, no strange cars tonight, no bizarre goings on at Sweet Briar. She nursed her hot chocolate with a splash of brandy in it to help her sleep after her nightmare of a few days ago. The wind had died down and she thought about her last meeting with Heather. She hadn't mentioned it to Jamie, as she didn't think it was something worthy of a police investigation: for one, the earrings had been found and she really had no solid evidence that it was her friend who had stolen them; for another, she had now alienated the only police officer for miles by suggesting he had made an error, or *errors*, in his investigation into the deaths of the tenants on the estate. Maybe she was wrong about everything. Bella was probably right. It was a hard outdoor life this far north and no matter your stamina, your body would give up at some point, even though Marcie still thought it was *no age at all*.

Still cradling her hot drink in one hand, she pulled the heavy curtains closed around the large oriel windows and switched on the ornate bedside lamp beside her bed, before heading out to the bathroom for her evening rituals. Who knew what tomorrow would bring?

# THIRTY-TWO

Despite Ruaridh's attempt to calm the children down as he stuffed their backpacks full of provisions, the house resembled a carnival of chaos. Dina and Marcie agreed that the best form of defence was to ignore the chaos, otherwise they would be drawn in with a frustrated 'let me do it!'

'So, what do you think?' asked Dina, sipping tea and simultaneously breaking off a bit of sliced fruit cake to pop in her mouth. 'Fancy the party?'

'As long as it's not a leaving party,' moaned Marcie.

Ruaridh struggled to be heard above the shrieks of young children, anxious to be out of the house and on a speedboat with their father. 'It's mostly a fundraiser for the MRT and Heather suggested we just combine them together – with your leaving do.'

'I'm going back to London; I'm not sailing around the world like you guys look like you're doing.' Marcie nodded as more and more bags appeared.

The young boys insisted on putting on their life jackets, even though at least two of them were still in pyjamas, while repacking colouring books in their own backpacks as soon as their father's back was turned. Marcie, witness to it all, made to get up to help, but a shake of the head from Dina was enough to make her sit back down.

'Give me a minute guys, c'mon!' pleaded Ruaridh with arms raised in the air as he shook his head. 'Personally, and Dina *doesn't* agree with me...' he began, with a glance to his wife.

'Yes?' urged Marcie.

'I know Heather wanted to do a thing at the Inn for you, but I think 'cause you two are, well, *on the outs*, I think she's proposing a compromise by having the ceilidh in the hall and then it's all wrapped up in one go so to speak.'

'I've never asked her to organise anything. Anyway...' Marcie glanced at Dina for support, unsure if she was aware of the full circumstances of the falling out.

'Ruaridh told me about the earrings. I mean, I know we're all a little bit hard up, but it really shocked me,' confessed Dina.

'Ditto,' sighed Marcie, running her finger around the rim of the cup.

'What would she have done with them? I mean, they're so distinctive, she'd never have gotten away with wearing them, and if she took them to the pawn shop in Inverness, surely someone would have recognised them, or something. She'd have to tell them of their provenance, their history, no?'

'Maybe she had a fence for them already?' suggested Ruaridh.

'How come I get called Miss Marple and you're the one who knows all about *fences*?' asked Marcie, laughing.

'Late-night TV when the team are in bed. *Manchester Coppers* and *Night Beat*. Plus, Bella told me you're more Cabot Cove than St Mary Mead.' He took a drink of Dina's tea as she looked at him quizzically. 'Alibi Channel,' he said and pointed to himself and his healing face. 'Obviously, when I was in recovery,' he justified with a shrug as Dina raised her eyes to the ceiling.

With another flurry of blond hair, and a little more coaxing, the boys left with their father, and Dina and Marcie were alone.

'You know, with all the noise, sometimes I can't hear myself think, and I take myself off to the room at the back – your room – and I close the door and I just sit. I deliberately wanted it at the back of the house, and I can tell you it's bliss,' said Dina, closing her eyes. 'Then after five minutes, I come out and they're all sitting quietly drawing and it's like now – quiet – and I'm not sure I like it,' she finished, with an almost wistful look around the toy-strewn room.

Marcie looked around and thought of their school days and their hopes and wishes and dreams and what had happened to them all in what was just a small part of their lifetime. Her fingers played along the red corded friendship bracelet, and when she looked down, she noticed that Dina had pulled hers out from under her cream-coloured fleece. She, too, was absent-mindedly playing with it.

Marcie left Dina to enjoy her rare solitude and began to walk back to the big house on the other side of the loch, starting along the shoreline and then walking up to the single-track road that ran alongside it when the rocks became too difficult to clamber over.

Her eyes caught something on the other side of the loch, on the jetty, and she realised it was Callum, standing alone, surveying the scene. She quickened her pace as much as she could, thinking about how much she'd stand out on the other side of the water with her red Berghaus fleece, albeit from a long distance. *Would he wait for her?* she thought, as she kept glancing over to where his tall frame lingered on the platform.

It was almost half an hour later by the time she made it to

her uncle. He sat at the edge of the jetty and, although he had clearly seen her, he made no effort to get up as she climbed up beside him. Marcie hoped her breathing would quickly get back to normal after her rush along the shoreline.

'Beautiful day,' she offered as she made her way along to him, leaning down to touch his shoulder. He pulled away with a flinch as she touched him.

'Oh, I'm sorry,' she apologised, realising she had maybe, quite literally, touched a nerve. He seemed very sensitive to her touch, or maybe he was still in his bad mood. She sat down near to him, not up close next to him as she would have done previously, and turned to start speaking but she was shocked into silence by his appearance. He looked drawn, pained even, ill like people who had recently been so very sick, almost wan.

'My goodness, Callum – are you okay?' she asked.

He didn't respond for a moment, continuing to look forward as if in a trance, taking laboured breaths.

'You look...' She searched for a word. 'Ghastly,' was what she settled on.

'You could say I'm under a fair bit of stress,' he said, but his voice sounded weak as if he was struggling to gather the words and say them out loud.

'I'm so sorry, Cal, but this wasn't of my doing. I wasn't responsible for the will. I didn't know, I was as much in the dark as you. If only you'd spoken to me about it instead of...' She wanted to say, *speaking to Richard*, but stopped short.

'Has to be done,' he said in almost a whisper.

Marcie shimmied across the jetty on her bottom and placed her hand on his arm. She was startled when he flinched away from her again with a gasp.

'Are you okay?' she repeated. 'You didn't take a tumble from one of the ponies?'

He didn't respond. Instead, he closed his eyes and pointed

his face towards the weak sun now pushing its way out from the clouds, his hand reaching down to his hip to rub it slightly.

She studied him closely for a moment and realised suddenly that he looked so much older than he did just days ago. He was becoming greyer, if that was possible, than the last time she saw him. The open and charming, fun man who had greeted her so warmly appeared to have aged considerably. He looked tired to the point of exhaustion, his fresh outdoor complexion taking on an almost dull tinge.

'Have you seen a doctor?'

'Why would I see a doctor?' he asked, clearly aggrieved at his situation.

'Callum,' she said firmly. She stood up and leaned down to take his arm to haul him up at least partway. 'C'mon. You're not well. I'm calling Doctor Mooney.'

'I don't need a doctor,' he whinged, wincing as he pulled his arm, and she thought he looked almost distressed. A look of concern spread across her face, and she turned and ran back to the house.

Though he worked in the GP surgery in Strath Aullt, the next biggest town, Doctor Mooney was not averse to a house call to his near neighbours in the small hamlets nearby. Marcie was lucky enough that when she called he was at the surgery and was out the door and in his car before she had headed back to collect Callum, who was slowly walking with some difficulty back to his house, appearing feverish.

'I think you should come to Swanfield,' she pleaded.

'I'll go to my *own* house,' he said, settling the matter firmly.

Marcie helped him across the not inconsiderable distance back to Sweet Briar and in through the front gate. What had been the dining room had long been converted to an office with a day bed, and it was as far as they could make it, with him throwing himself down heavily before dragging his feet up onto the wide seat.

She pulled a heavy tartan blanket off the chair at his desk and placed it over him. Then she waited for what seemed like an age, sitting in a heavy plaid reading chair opposite him, a worried look slowly spreading across her face. He appeared sore to the touch and even a slight brush against his skin made him flinch and grimace in pain.

When he arrived, Doctor Mooney was caring and soothing, and she left the two men alone, not wanting to intrude on this private moment. As she closed the door, she heard Callum explain how he'd been managing his pain with stronger drugs and realised that the hip she'd seen Callum frequently stretch out and rub was clearly giving him more discomfort than he was letting on. She hovered in the sparse kitchen, and made a large pot of tea, setting out what were called the Denby 'good' mugs, on the table, knowing that the medic would no doubt stay for a short break before starting his journey back over the hill.

'He's got a wee touch of a fever still; has he maybe been doing too much? Overexerting himself?' said Stuart Mooney as he sat down while Marcie fussed about looking for the remnants of a piece of cake or even something vaguely resembling a biscuit.

'I've no idea. I don't think so.' She shrugged and watched as he helped himself to tea with an inordinate amount of milk in it, the kind she called 'baby tea' in her office.

'He's a bit worn down. Wouldn't be surprised if it is a wee bout of flu on top of everything else. But he's got a touch of tenderness too, a bit of nausea and diarrhoea,' said the doctor, 'and of course the hip playing up. I'll keep an eye on him, but I'd like to do some more tests, get him over to the surgery. But he's not up for it just now. Still as stubborn as his mother.' He took a gulp of tea while his eyes darted around for an elusive biscuit to dunk in his tea latte. 'Lucky for him, he has that young lad helping out. A godsend, if you ask me.'

'He's very fit for his age,' Marcie interjected.

'Oh, early sixties, mid-sixties even – it's no age at all,' he said.

'I knew it!' she said, thumping her closed fist on the table, making him jump as he looked at her. 'Sorry,' she apologised. 'While you're here, doctor, can I ask you...'

'Anything,' he encouraged.

'There's been a lot of, how can I put it? "Unexplained deaths" on the estate recently.'

'*Unexplained*?' he repeated, puzzled.

'Well, I was just speaking to Callum the other day after Alister's funeral.'

'Ah, the Duffer. Tragic. Alcoholic neuritis.'

'Oh?' Marcie raised her eyebrows.

'Such a sad case. Was never the same after Elsie. Poor Alister.'

'It's just I never put him down as a drinker,' she said, trying to sound convincing.

'You knew Alister?'

'No. but... His wife used to clean here, you know. Well, next door, at the big house. What about the death of Angus Fraser?'

'Sad. He was found by... now, what's his name?' mused the doctor. 'Callum's man? You know, the one I was talking about, the one that helps him out. Cracking bloke.'

'Brodie, Brodie Nairn,' Marcie muttered. She wondered how long it would take for his name to come up.

'As I said, he's been a godsend to Callum, you know. Does all the heavy lifting, so to speak. We're all getting into that club we don't want to belong to. "The old timer's club." Sadly, none of us is getting any younger. Hard life up here, Marcella, and not just in the winter.'

Marcie stared out the window at the Hilux. *So, he has the Land Rover today*, she thought. *And where is this young man who has charmed everyone in the village?*

'You know, it always puzzled me because, poor Angus, I

must have missed his epilepsy; it wasn't in his notes. Nothing even from the locum when I went on holiday. He's sadly missed at the Strath Flower Show. Produced fruit and veg from the polytunnel. Superb specimens. Never be the same without him,' he said wistfully, and followed Marcie's gaze to the yard.

'Keen to get on, are you? Well, then, I'll be off. If I leave a prescription, you can give it to Roddy down at the general store. The pharmacy van does a drop-off there or to be honest, paracetamol will do the trick to get his temperature down. Until I can persuade him to come over to get some more bloodwork done, anyway. Maybe when he's up and about? You'll have to bring him, mind. Not fit to drive, in my opinion.' He stood up, collected the mug and took it over to place it in the sink.

'He's got his work cut out here.' He looked past the yard to the land beyond. 'Rather him than me.' He gathered up his black leather bag and country tweed jacket from behind the chair and headed to the door. 'Will I see you at the ceilidh later? Someone said it's not just the MRT Fundraiser, but you're heading back down the road?'

'Possibly,' she replied, trying to muster a smile. Instead, she bade him farewell and went back to where she had left her uncle lying on the day bed. He certainly looked less distressed. The pained expression on his face had lifted but he still had a grey tinge to his skin. Marcie rushed up the stairs and checked his room, taking a hand-sewn quilt from the cupboard and putting it across his bed before heading back down to turn on the heating. She pondered about building a fire in his bedroom but thought a quick burst of heat from the old oil-fired radiators would make the place warm enough.

When her uncle had mustered up enough strength, she helped him up to his room, untied his heavy walking boots, and put him to bed fully dressed in T-shirt and fleece. No words were exchanged. Once tucked in, she quickly ran back downstairs, and with barely a thing in the fridge, she returned to

Swanfield where she prepared a thick ham sandwich and a flask of sweet tea, which she took over to Sweet Briar in a basket. She sat it on the floor at the side of his bed and, when her uncle fell sound asleep, she carefully and deliberately locked both the front door and back door before she went back home to Swanfield.

## THIRTY-THREE

Cooking and domestic chores were never top of Marcie's skills, but she excelled at making scrambled eggs and baking. She piled the well-seasoned, light and fluffy eggs onto homemade bread (both gifts from her last visit to the Balfours), then put a plastic cloche over the plate and busied herself with juice and tea. She warmed the teapot and then spooned in leaves to the silver Carlton, leaving it to infuse before straining it into one of the many flasks that were normally kept in the larder. She placed everything in a large basket to transport it next door, to be left on a bed tray when she got to Sweet Briar.

She had gone over just after seven and when she heard the snoring coming from upstairs, it satisfied her that Callum was alive and well and having the rest the doctor ordered.

She rushed out to the back garden and, with a pair of scissors, knelt and hurriedly cut some small late-blooming daffodils to brighten the breakfast tray. When she stood up, she gasped as she saw her elusive nemesis standing immediately behind her, so close she could feel his breath on her neck.

'I never thought you looked like the nursing type,' he said, and she was sure it came out almost like a violent hiss.

'What have you done to him?' Marcie replied, immediately apportioning blame.

'I'm here to look after him,' was Brodie's response.

'You're getting nowhere near him.' She turned around to face Brodie squarely, sharp shears in her hand.

'I think I'll make that decision,' he said, his ice-blue eyes burying into her. 'Maybe it is time you went back to London and left us to live our lives here. Strathkin is no longer your home.'

*Say nothing*, she thought. *Do not give the game away.* Marcie wanted him to threaten her, so she had something concrete to go back to Jamie MacKay with. *Everyone loved him,* she mused, *his thoughtfulness, his helpfulness, his looks, his charm.* She had no idea why she had this burning desire to expose him as a fraud. She thought it must be women's intuition or just her naturally suspicious nature, but she was certain something was just not right.

'You left this behind,' he said as he pushed something into her free hand. He closed her fingers around the item, squeezing it with his large soft hands, surrounding hers so tightly she felt her nails digging into the smooth flesh of her palm.

He turned and headed for Sweet Briar, and she waited until she heard the door slam shut before she unfurled her fingers and saw the old, broad deep-red elastic band that used to circle the items in the safe at Swanfield. It had unceremoniously snapped off when she took out the items and pinged away out of her sight. So, he had been in the house in her absence. *Her* house. He had been in her grandmother's bedroom, *and* he knew she knew the secret.

Marcie's mind was racing. *What if it was Brodie Nairn who had, in fact, stolen the earrings and it wasn't Heather after all? If he could wander freely around the big house, what else could he find, or plant or steal?*

'Feck!' she said aloud. At a time when she needed all her

best friends around her, she was beginning to sound like the girl who cried wolf. Certainly, Jamie MacKay from the local constabulary was starting to think she'd lost the plot, and her relationship with one of her best friends was on very thin ice. Marcie was as stubborn as her uncle and grandmother, and even now, when it was looking like she was very clearly in the wrong about Heather, she wasn't looking forward to making a fulsome apology. She hurried into the big house, looking under the sink for a vase and settling on an older marked milk bottle from the local dairy, long since closed. As she set the flowers into the basket, her hands were shaking uncontrollably.

Marcie carried the wicker basket next door, slipping through the back door to Sweet Briar, and took it upstairs to Callum's bedroom.

Brodie had pulled up a chair and the two men were laughing heartily when she entered, struggling somewhat with the heavy basket. She was surprised when the younger man leapt to his feet in a gesture of help.

'Oh, let me get that from you, Marcie, this is too kind,' said Brodie with a wide-open smile.

She looked at him incredulously as he placed the large basket at the side of Callum, who was now sitting up, head resting on several recently plumped pillows.

'You're looking so much better,' she said with a smile, to break the ice.

'I'm being well looked after,' he stated with a glance to Brodie, now returning to the seat that Marcie had set aside for herself the night before.

She noticed there was no attempt by Brodie to get another chair from another room for her. The basket she had left the night before was untouched. She spotted some foil and a crust on the bedside table next to a bottle of Lucozade, a bottle of

Highland Spring and an apple core. Brodie had clearly been providing sustenance for her uncle.

'Maybe we should have a chat if you're feeling up to it?' she suggested to Callum, but before he could reply, a response was quickly in the air.

'I think we'll leave it for today, hmm? Didn't the doctor say rest?' said Brodie, looking to Marcie then to Callum.

Callum certainly looked less grey, she noticed, a little lighter in mood since yesterday. She picked up the now-empty basket.

'I'd be happy to bring that over for you,' offered Brodie.

'I can manage,' she snapped, turning towards the stairs.

As she made her way back to Swanfield, Marcie was seething. She wanted to scream and yell and shout. *What was happening to her life that she felt it was slowly crumbling around her?*

## THIRTY-FOUR

'And how exactly are you going to do that?' asked Bella, sweeping her currycomb over one of her broad-backed fell ponies in the yard of the trekking centre.

'I don't know,' said Marcie, shrugging her shoulders, dunking homemade butter shortbread, provided by her friend, in her tea, and searching in her head for the words. 'I'm sorry – I made a mistake.'

'Gotta eat it. The old humble pie,' said Bella as she ducked around the pony and came to Marcie's side, brushing the pony's long and carefully tended mane. 'I mean, she's throwing you a party. She's not going to be doing that if she's also stealing from you. It makes no sense to me but I'm more of a Maggie O'Farrell than Miss Marple.'

'You know I'm no good at apologising.'

'Well, you've never apologised to me,' clarified Bella, pulling horsehair from the comb, and Marcie's eyes followed it as it drifted into the air to become part of a future nest in a nearby fir tree. 'I think the problem is, if I may be so bold, you've been away too long in the big city and your lawyerly type brain is working overtime. Some guy comes to help Callum and you're suddenly thinking he's usurping you; you're the cat that got the cream.'

'*Usurped*?' Marcie said, aghast.

'Yeah, you taught me that word. Plus, what do we need money for up here really? Look around you,' said Bella, throwing her arm out to gesture at the view that surrounded them.

Today was a clear April day; the hills behind them were majestic and glowing and the sky was a vivid blue. Below, the water danced in sparkling light, glistening and rippling as the yard stretched out then dissolved into the grass and shingle beach.

'Scenery doesn't pay the rent,' said Marcie, with a vision of her Southampton Row flat, four floors up from a row of shops with the ever-increasing sound of traffic on the busy road below.

'Well, *I'd* have stolen them myself if I thought I'd have gotten away with it,' said Bella, then reeled back with hands face up. 'I didn't, though,' she explained, palms outstretched.

Marcie bit her lip and sighed. 'Have you ever read *Alice in Wonderland*?'

'We read it in school together.'

'"Everything is real and not real." That's what I feel, here, now. I want to wind the clock back. I want none of this to have happened. I want a remote to press rewind.'

'Gotta deal with the cards you're dealt, Marce,' said Bella, sitting down on the side of the white harled stone trough beside her friend.

'If I'd told those German doctors to stay *that* night at the Inn, they would still be here,' said Marcie, her head down, voicing a regret she'd been harbouring since the accident.

'You don't know that.'

'You're right, I don't. But I do think Callum has had a break-down after all the stuff he used to do on the hill. I think the accident has brought back all that trauma. He's just retreated into himself. I think it's *him* that's lost the plot, not me.'

'Marce, is this what this mood is all about? Do you want me to call Simon?'

'No, I'm just ruminating.'

'Ruminating?' queried her friend. '*Ruminating*,' she said again and rolled the word over in her mouth.

'Contemplating my situation,' explained Marcie, 'and considering whether I should go and see Heather.'

'Ah!' said her friend. 'Well, I'll be considering whether to open a bottle of wine for when you come back later with a black eye. Note to self: "Must get some ice in the freezer".' She laughed and then nudged her friend.

'Come on, let's get the ponies tacked up and I'll take you for a wander up the hills,' suggested Bella, and Marcie poured what was left in her cup onto the ground, deciding a canter through the hills was probably just what she needed, rather than a confrontation with one of her oldest friends.

# THIRTY-FIVE

Marcie pulled two trays of sausage rolls out of the Aga and kicked the door closed with her foot. She put them on the well-used kitchen table beside her phone which was on loudspeaker.

'Are you sure they don't need me to bring anything?' she asked.

'To your own party?' quizzed Dina, who was also knee-deep in freshly baked savouries across the water at Lochside Croft.

'Well, I'm not doing it for me. I'm cooking some stuff for the MRT.' She pulled open the oven door and removed two fruit cakes made with Lisanne's own homemade mincemeat, jars and jars of which Marcie had found in the larder, some up to three years old. They had been well macerated in brandy, and the kitchen had a distinctive festive smell drifting out the door on this crisp spring day. Piles of home-baked goods now stood on every spare work surface, and cakes and mini pies were in large plastic tubs ready to be transported to the village hall on the other side of the loch. She had started the night before with the thought that if she was concentrating on something other than her own personal circumstances, then maybe the knot in her head would unravel and things would become much clearer.

The large cardboard box that Ruaridh had brought his boys' snacks over in was full of Bakewell slices and shortbread. Ruaridh had delivered all the provisions from her list on his latest visit to Inverness, as the local shop didn't have an adequate supply when the whole village was baking up a storm.

When Marcie heard the back door open, her heart jumped. To her relief, it was Ruaridh coming with a spare box of icing sugar. 'Your husband is here,' Marcie told Dina on the phone, 'so I'll catch you later!'

'You look like you've seen a ghost!' commented Ruaridh when she'd hung up, placing a large shopping bag on the table next to a ready-to-ice tray of Empire biscuits, a tub of cherries beside them to adorn the sweet treats.

'I just got a fright. I thought it might have been Brodie.'

'Haven't see the Brodster in a couple of days. He still playing Nurse Ratchet to Callum?'

'You talk in riddles sometimes,' she commented as she took a bowl of water to the sink to empty a little out. She sprinkled a large amount of icing sugar into the bowl.

'Dina does that the other way round.'

'Each to their own.'

'Says it's safer.' He nodded as he watched her mix the water into the sugar until it became a thick paste. She then took her spoon and made thick lines up and down the biscuits, instead of the customary thick blob of icing in the middle.

He stood over her, hands in pockets. 'Ooh! Controversial! Glad this isn't Ye Olde Strathkin Baking Fayre. I think you'd be disqualified for that. Not a *real* German biscuit now, is it?'

'It's my interpretation,' Marcie explained, tongue out in concentration as she continued along the row of biscuits. Ruaridh followed her across the table, placing a cut half cherry in the middle of each round.

She came to an end and looked at her masterpieces. 'Could be in *The Bake Off*,' she said aloud, admiring each perfect little biscuit with its cherry jewel. She leaned down to straighten up the ones Ruaridh had managed to nudge slightly when he was being the sous chef. They were disturbed by someone clearing their throat.

'Oh, Callum. Good to see you up. I'm just helping Mary Berry here,' explained Ruaridh as he leaned over to readjust an errant cherry.

'Could at least have said Nigella,' sighed Marcie, under her breath.

'Whoever you're pretending to be,' said Callum, which caused Marcie to take a sharp intake of breath. She didn't know if Callum was being funny, snippy or insulting. It was so unlike him, this gentle loving man, to be filled with such scorn. She was puzzled.

'Here, Cal, you're a brave man,' Ruaridh joked, clearly trying to lighten the mood, as he walked over and leaned with his back to the sink, hands in the pockets of his utility trousers.

He glanced at Marcie who hadn't responded. 'So, who's on yer dance card then, Cal?'

Callum was stony faced.

'I hear it's Peat & Diesel coming over from the Strath. They're a bit of all right, eh? Not charging either for their services, I hear, so all ticket money will go to Lachie's men. That's a bit of all right, too, eh?'

'I can see Marcie is trying to break up your marriage,' Callum said.

'Oh, here, wait a minute!' said Ruaridh after the words sank in. 'That's a bit salty, Cal!'

'She doesn't want anybody to be happy.'

'That is NOT true,' said Marcie with a shake of her head.

'I was just over here dropping stuff off. I dunno what you think you saw, Cal, but you're barking up the wrong tree here, mate.'

'I know what I saw. I know what I see every time you pair are left alone.'

'Oh, for Pete's sake.'

Marcie sighed and walked over to the sink to wash her hands. Ruaridh moved away quickly. It seemed when he realised she was coming towards him, he didn't want it misinterpreted.

'For the record,' she said, 'I'm very happy in my relationship, which has absolutely nothing to do with you.' She regretted the sharpness, realising that this was a situation that could very quickly deteriorate into a slanging match which all three would come to regret.

Callum threw an envelope onto the table, and it came to rest on top of some of the newly iced biscuits.

'Aww, Cal, come on! Uncalled for, uncalled for...' said Ruaridh as he moved to pick up the letter before it became a sticky mess.

Marcie felt as if Callum wanted to say something, but instead he turned and left the kitchen, closing the door quietly behind him.

'Jeezo! What the...?' said Ruaridh, blowing his breath out to make his cheeks puff up. 'Look, I know you're happy with Simon, top bloke. I mean, what Callum said. Nothing's going to break up me and D, if you think...'

'I'm not trying to do anything like that! Callum is havering. He's not well. The doctor wants him for tests,' explained Marcie. 'It's this flipping house! Seriously! We're all going mad here!'

'Well, spiteful or not, that was out of order. I'm not happy about that, not happy one bit,' said Ruaridh. 'In fact...' He made towards the back door; she could tell that this was not the moment for strong words.

She grabbed his forearm. 'Leave it, Ruaridh! Leave it. Please. He's just saying these things to get a rise. He's not been well. Let's get tomorrow over,' she said, referring to the ceilidh the following evening.

'If any of this gets to Dina,' he said through gritted teeth. 'If anything happens to her and this...' He stopped short of saying any more. It took a lot to rile mild-mannered Ruaridh Balfour, but anything that affected his wife and children would turn him into a raging bull.

'Nothing is going to happen, Ruaridh. He's not well. This with everything... I just want to go back to where we all were.'

It took Ruaridh more than a few minutes to calm down. With no more said between them he started to lift the boxes of already packed baked goods out and into his old Land Rover, parked in the rear yard. It took a few trips and when he came back a final time, Marcie was examining the iced biscuits to see what could be saved.

'Thanks for your help.' She smiled. 'I'll bring these tomorrow.'

With a nod he was out of the door.

Marcie took the biscuits that had been ruined and piled them onto a metal tray, walked to the back of the house, and launched them furiously into the bin.

# THIRTY-SIX

Marcie looked around the smallest off-licence section in the world at the general store. She picked up a giant bottle of what looked like sparkling wine. The bottle was one she didn't recognise as being in her own repertoire of 'special' drinks, but she bought it, nonetheless.

'You definitely don't have Prosecco or Champagne?' she asked Roddy McLeod for the umpteenth time, and for the umpteenth time he sighed, shook his head and said, 'We don't have much call for it here.'

If people wanted a *big proper shop*, as she liked to call it, they would make a monthly pilgrimage to Inverness to the large superstore for groceries and provisions, stock up their garage with alcohol and their freezer with the best that Marks & Spencer had to offer. She kicked herself that anything of the 'decent' variety she had purchased in her few trips had already been demolished.

She picked up two bottles of Campo Viejo Rioja which Roddy described as 'fancy wine' and when she went to pay, she looked behind the counter for gin.

'I'll have that bottle of Bombay Sapphire, please,' she said as she fumbled in her bag for her purse.

'Oh, that one's just for show. Fills the shelf. Not much call for gin round here. Give me a minute, I think I have a bottle of something in the back.'

He disappeared into the rear store with a careful glance at the mirror on the back wall that showed the goings on at the counter, just in case she was stupid enough to steal his display bottle. Marcie noticed a space where the usual bottle of Old Inverness stood proudly and expected to see it later at the ceilidh. Roddy came back with a bottle of Plymouth Gin that had clearly just been dusted; she asked if he had tonic.

'Och, I won't get that till I get to the big city next week,' he explained before swiping her card for a thirty-two-pound bottle of gin and a Rioja that cost her a startling eleven pounds a bottle.

It didn't take her long to get ready. The girls had agreed to meet at The Strathkin Inn for a quick drink before they walked the few hundred yards to the village hall. She searched the larder for tonic water and eventually found an open, but flat, bottle of Schweppes on the drinks trolley. She filled her glass with tonic water and ice in the kitchen.

She heard a noise outside and stepped back into the kitchen and away from the window as Callum and Brodie drove past in the Hilux. Callum looked pale but better than when they last had their encounter. They were both laughing, clearly easy in each other's company.

She wasn't looking forward to tonight in so many ways: there was the Heather issue; the Callum issue; the police officer issue; and the fact that most people, it would seem, were looking forward to their chance to say goodbye to her.

On the short drive to the Inn, she took it very slow, mainly to give herself thinking time. Once in the front car park, she practised her deep-breathing exercises, before leaving the car and walking in the front entrance for the first time since Lisanne's funeral.

Bella was the first person she saw as she entered, standing holding several drinks at once and dispensing them to people hovering about the large vestibule. It was extremely busy as people gathered before the doors opened to the hall and the festivities begun. She saw some of the MRT gathered at the foot of the stairs and nodded an acknowledgement to them. She muscled her way into the bar area and caught a glimpse of Heather juggling orders and money, ably assisted by Ally.

As Marcie reached the counter, Heather whispered something to Ally who turned and caught Marcie's eye. 'Can I help you?'

'I'll have a large G&T, please, and can I put money in for a round for Lachie and his team?'

'Sure – that's... twenty-eight quid,' said Ally, simultaneously holding up a drinks list, putting the tonic in her glass and punching the numbers into the card reader.

'That's cheap! You sure?' asked Marcie, her mind mentally working out the size of the team and her usual London prices.

'Most of them are on juice or tap water,' clarified Ally.

Marcie nodded an '*I see*' and looked around to see anyone else she could buy a drink for and engage them in conversation, but most people she knew were hanging about at the entrance. It was getting thicker and thicker with people. Marcie realised that her dress seemed a bit out of place for this Highland gathering, as most were more practically dressed for the ceilidh.

Then out of the corner of her eye she spotted the unmistakable blond mop of hair and the smooth manner of Brodie Nairn. He was talking to Ruthie Gillespie, soothing her by stroking her arm. She moved further into the area, struggling to see him as people jostled back and forth to the bar. Ruthie tearfully walked away, and Marcie noticed that Brodie was now with the men she had originally seen in Callum's yard.

Marcie stayed where she was, not wanting to lose her vantage point. She caught sight of Callum; a quartet of secrets, she thought, as she gazed on the scene. But she couldn't keep a close eye, as she was pushed from side to side by the crowd and eventually found herself out in the hallway again, where Bella was in full throttle with Dina, who had arrived with the four boys. Douglas, excited to see her, wrapped his arms around her waist and looked up to her with adoring eyes.

'Hello, darling.' She smiled and bent to kiss his forehead before he took off with his three siblings, running out the door as they saw their father arrive outside.

'Aww, the Marcie Fan Club, all one of it,' joked Bella as she looked out to where the boys had surrounded the tall, broad figures of Ruaridh Balfour and Lachie Bateman, who had gone out to join him.

'He is adorable.' Marcie swooned, looking at Douglas.

Dina sighed as she gazed out to the five most important people in her life, with one little flop-haired six-year-old taking centre stage.

'Did you speak to Heather?' asked Bella, draining her glass.

'No, she's avoiding me, I think.'

'Told you, you should have come before tonight to apologise,' warned Bella with a shake of the head.

Dina looked puzzled but took a sip of her champagne flute filled with Appletiser.

'It's been such a while since we had a good old ceilidh. I mean, the boys are beside themselves. Dax has his eye on Isla in his class, and I think tonight's the night when she falls under the Balfour spell.' Dina sighed.

Bella made a noise, stuck imaginary fingers down her throat and the three of them laughed. As they did so, one of the men who had been in the quartet in the lounge bar came out, nodded to them and made his way to his black Range Rover which was sitting outside.

'Any idea who that is?' Marcie asked.

'No idea,' said Dina with a shrug.

'I've seen the car around but not a clue,' said Bella. 'Top up?' she asked and took Marcie's empty glass as Dina signalled a 'no' with a shake of the head.

Dina and Marcie watched people come and go until friends and family started drifting off to the village hall. Meanwhile, Ally, the bar manager, came out with two large trays piled with the final boxes to be taken to the venue. Two men stopped her and offered to take the food, which she gladly handed over before making her way back to the bar.

'Ally, is Heather heading down to the hall?'

'Sure is, we're just going to tidy up a bit here then we'll walk down. Gus is going to mind the shop, but I don't think he'll be overstretched.' She smiled and went back into the lounge bar.

Marcie looked in and saw that the room was now nearly empty, realising that Callum, Brodie and the spare man must have left through the back door to head to the hall. Bella came out with two drinks and joined her friends as they made their way slowly to the front entrance.

'Coulda got me a pint,' complained Ruaridh, now left alone with his boys, the rest of the party having headed to the event just down the road.

'I think you dropped enough drinks down there earlier!' laughed Dina, referring to his very substantial and already delivered carry out as she walked up to him to be surrounded by her troop.

Both Bella and Marcie took their drinks with them as they made the short walk down the road. Ruaridh signalled to the boys to run ahead and grab a good table near to where he'd set down his box of drinks. All four boys happily ran off as if in a race. Ruaridh held back a little until they'd all caught up, and he stepped between Bella and Marcie, signalling her to slow down to his pace, which she gladly did.

'Have you spoken to Cal?' he asked once he realised that he was out of earshot of his wife and their friend.

'No, he's kind of retreated into himself even more,' explained Marcie. She felt her stomach flip as she realised she would, once again, come face to face with him and Brodie.

'Don't know what's got into him,' said Ruaridh. 'He looks awful.'

'Hmm,' she agreed. 'Did you see him in the bar?'

'Through the window, aye. To be honest, Marce, I'm still not over what he said to me, so I better watch myself on the beer a bit tonight.'

'Did you see who he was with?' she asked.

'Aye, Brodie...' he responded.

'And the other two?'

He frowned. 'Other two?'

'The two big guys in the tweed.'

'Oh, I've seen them around. Big fancy cars.'

'Who are they?'

'No idea.' He shrugged, completely disinterested, as they reached the hall.

Once again Marcie took a deep intake of breath before entering the village hall that had been the venue for so many of her childhood victories and defeats.

'Once more into the breach, dear friends, once more into the breach,' said Ruaridh and strode ahead to find his seat for the night.

# THIRTY-SEVEN

Once inside, Marcie found the hall was much busier than she'd imagined. She struggled to see her friends as they set out the glasses and drinks on their table at the far end of the large space, next to the stage, and it was only the frantic waving of the highly excited children that drew her to their spot. The table was piled with glasses and napkins, soft drinks for the children and a small plate of sandwiches. The rest of the food had been carefully stored in the kitchen servery for setting up during the interval from dancing and revelry in a few hours' time.

Marcie sat on the seat next to Bella, who was opening a large bottle of fizzy juice with no label.

'You're going to have to bite the bullet. Heather has just come in.' Bella poured a plastic cup full of the clear liquid.

Ruaridh slapped down a basin of ice into the middle of the table as the children started fishing out ice cubes into various paper and plastic cups. Douglas lifted the cup next to Marcie, only to have Bella take it straight back.

'*Auntie Juice!*' she declared and put ice into the container, then winked at Marcie. 'Pre-mix.' She handed the cup back to

Marcie, who tasted it. It was indeed a heady mix of a lot of gin, with not a lot of anything else.

'Tonic is so expensive!' explained Bella with a 'cheers' to her friend who shook her head with a wide smile. The gin was taking effect when Marcie saw Heather heading into the kitchen with some boxes of crisps. She swiftly followed in behind her.

Heather turned to leave the kitchen and found her way blocked. 'Hi, Heather. I wanted to say thanks for doing this.'

'It's for the MRT, really.'

Marcie took her gently by the wrist and swept her through the kitchen and straight out the back door.

'Look, I might have been too hasty.' Marcie looked for the right words, not quite finding what she wanted to say.

'*Too hasty?*' repeated Heather as she was bumped by someone heading for what could effectively be called the biggest ice bucket in the world. The two women stood for a moment in a standoff: one angry, with an accusation hanging over them, and the other trying to find a way to apologise.

'I still don't know how my grandmother's earrings ended up on your desk,' began Marcie.

'You think if *I'd* stolen them, *I'd* leave them lying about? Seriously? Give me some credit!'

'Well, maybe you're not a thief, but—' said Marcie before her brain warned her to choose her words carefully.

'*Thief?*' Heather flinched. 'You know what you are? You're just a rich, entitled...' It was only an intervention of the most unlikely kind that stopped the conversation from deteriorating further.

'Ladies!' Brodie Nairn beamed as he came out the back door to lean on the ice hopper, only to be pushed out of the way by a particularly large member of the Strathkin MRT, who leaned in and filled his own large basin with ice. He smiled with a nod before heading back inside, a quarter bottle of brandy poking out of his back pocket.

'I'm hoping you'll both make sure I take you for a reel.' Brodie smiled with a look to both Marcie and Heather. 'I have always enjoyed myself on the dance floor.'

Marcie regarded him with her usual suspicious gaze. 'Everything was fine until you turned up on the scene,' she spat.

'Some might say the same about you, Marcella Mosse. Although, I'm not entirely sure everything has been all right here for a long time.' He smiled though his eyes remained ice cold.

'What kind of dance do you like? Strip the Willow? Highland Schottische? Kalinka?' Marcie asked, the former being part of a normal ceilidh, the latter being a traditional Russian folk dance. There wasn't a flicker of recognition from Brodie.

He smiled benignly, looking from Marcie to Heather. 'I shall make sure to seek you out.'

He slipped back inside as the music began to pick up. Marcie realised that they'd missed any opening speeches, and the sound of heavy feet on wooden floors made her think it was time to join the party.

'I'm sorry, Heather. It's a special night tonight. Thank you.' Apologising had never come easily to Marcie, or to anyone in her stubborn family.

Heather bit her lip and looked away. 'I would never steal anything from you.' Heather was almost too quiet to be heard as Ruaridh burst out the door, clearly already a few bottles in of the Black Isle Brewery's finest offerings.

'Eeny, meeny, miny, mo...' He pointed to them, his finger coming to rest on Heather, grabbing her hand so vigorously she almost flew into the back door. When Marcie followed them into the hall, she could see her friend being twirled around in a reel so fast that her feet were quite literally off the ground.

She was making her way around the edge of the dancers when she felt a tap on the shoulder. It was Jamie. He bent down to whisper in her ear but the loudness and tempo of the band and screams of delight from the dancers meant she struggled to hear him. Even putting her hand to her ear to encourage him to come closer and speak louder made no difference. He gesticulated for a dance later, and she gave an exaggerated nod in agreement.

Marcie looked across the hall to the table opposite as dancers swirled past her. Callum was sitting with a couple of older members of the MRT, deep in conversation. Behind him sat the two large men of Marcie's nightmares, observing proceedings, nodding and tapping feet in time to the music. And in front sat Brodie, legs out and crossed in front of him, hand on the table, fingers drumming in time to the music and eyes firmly fixed on Marcie.

Couples danced past, but his eyes never left her. Far from feeling intimidated, Marcie decided, *if you want a staring match, game on.*

The first slow waltz of the evening brought a lot of people back to their respective tables for a bit of rest and sustenance. Ruaridh was heading back with his latest dance partner. Marcie noticed that Dina had been avoiding the gaze of Roddy from the corner shop for much of the night. She and Ruaridh both slid effortlessly back on to the dance floor, this time together with broad smiles and not insignificant perspiration from their exertions.

'Gawd, you need to be fit for this lark,' sighed Bella as she sat next to Marcie and reached out for a paper cup, downing the contents in one.

'Yuck! Water!' she said, making a face then burst out laughing as the two friends enjoyed a joke. Bella picked up the next plastic cup which, even with plenty of fresh ice, was a strong 'home pour'. It was then Brodie appeared before Marcie. He held out his hand and all eyes settled on her. She glanced around quickly to smiling faces and encouraging glances from the women on the other side of the room. Bella returned her gaze wide-eyed with a shrug of the shoulders. Marcie didn't know what to do either.

Brodie led her to the centre of the dance floor, and she tried to keep a distance between them, but he pulled her close. She could feel the rings on her fingers being squashed into her hand, but she said nothing as he slowly led her around the room in a silent waltz. She looked away and caught the eye of Ruaridh, who was still dancing with his wife. By his expression she could tell he could see her discomfort in Brodie's grip.

'SWAP PARTNERS!' the band leader suddenly shouted as the waltz changed into a very fast Gay Gordons, and Marcie was suddenly snatched away into the arms of Ruaridh.

'What's going on?' he asked urgently, his eyes darting between Brodie, now dancing rather energetically with Ruthie Gillespie, and his unhappy wife, who was in the arms of Roddy McLeod. Callum, meanwhile, was now seated in the chair vacated by Brodie at the edge of the dance floor.

As they swung past their table, and Ruaridh twirled Marcie around, he shouted over to Bella, 'Get Callum up!'

'What?' queried Bella, above the noise. Ruaridh jerked his head towards the seated Callum. Understanding her mission, Bella was out of the blocks and across the floor like a greyhound, despite still being in recovery from her energetic start of the night, dancing with Ruaridh.

Callum at first rejected Bella's advances, then she bent to his ear, and he relented. Marcie wondered how he would get on after his recent health issue, but as the couple drifted past, he seemed to be in a lighter mood and was certainly entering into the spirit of the evening.

'SWAP PARTNERS!' shouted the band leader again. 'Grab someone quick who's still sitting! Get them up for an Orkney Strip the Willow.'

Marcie hurried to the back of the hall where some of the younger members of the MRT were filing out of the kitchen with plates held high. She grabbed one of them and half of the sausage roll he was holding, encouraging him to put his plate down. She wanted to be as far away from the start of the lineup, where she saw Brodie and Callum and one of the Range Rover crew, who had now taken off his tweed jacket, to reveal a blue shirt absolutely soaking in perspiration on this warm late April evening.

The lineup for Strip the Willow was long, almost everyone in the hall on the dance floor. The first couples bounced their way into the centre, arms linked, before they began to work their way down the line with feet thumping and kilts swirling, men on one side and women on the other. The music was loud and boisterous as the second couple moved down, reeling first to one side then the other. As they neared her in the line, Marcie noticed that Brodie and Bella were a pair. Marcie was clapping hands and trying to join in, but her heart was thumping. Just a few steps behind was Callum. Marcie looked round but there was no escape. She wished she'd had considerably more to drink as the reeling came closer. Suddenly, it was her turn, and Brodie took her hand and swung her around. She was convinced she saw him reach into his pocket as they turned, but he was turning with Bella and away to the next woman in the line too quick for her to see. The young MRT member next took her hand and threw her round with equal energy. Only two dancers away was Callum. He took Marcie's hand, and she felt herself shouting, '*Be careful!*' without knowing exactly what she was warning him about.

Smiles were wide and people were shouting and laughing and suddenly it was the big man in the damp shirt in front of Marcie, clapping and cheering and grabbing her firmly to swing her round. She could smell his whisky breath and his expensive cigars as he clearly enjoyed his Scottish night out.

And then Marcie was locked in a crossed arms circle with the other big man, with Brodie on one side, the other menacing man to her other side – she felt trapped. *Was she imagining it?* The big man spun her around and around, and she saw Brodie once again reach into his pocket, the one where he normally kept the rag she'd frequently seen him play with. She saw a flash of silver as she was reeled around – the rest of the dancers clearly enjoying the fact that these new people were fitting in easily to relaxed Highland life. And now, she could feel the grip from the man holding her tighten; the smile disappeared from his face as he began to slow her down ever so gradually. People flashed past her quickly, but she saw them as if in slow motion.

Marcie thumped her foot on the ground, to bring herself to an immediate stop. The man staggered slightly, and she fell to the opposite side of Brodie, falling onto the feet of the MRT leader who had stopped dancing with Ruthie Gillespie. Lachie bent to pick her up at the same time as Ruthie, just as Brodie leaned forward, but she was now far enough away for him to not be a threat.

Lachie helped Marcie to a nearby seat, reached over and put a plastic tumbler of wine in front of her. Then he rushed back to join the line as the next couple came dancing, swishing back and forth from partner to partner with hoots of delight. The three men, the two big ones and the slighter Brodie, were left at the end of the Strip the Willow line alone, as their partners had gone during the short distraction. Though they looked one to the other, very few words were exchanged, and then they drifted back to their table at the far end of the room. Brodie, separating from them, hand still in pocket, left through the front entrance, only to return moments later, smiling, whooping and clapping with both hands. He ignored Marcie, seated only a few feet away.

Marcie watched him refresh their drinks and rejoin the dancing before she slipped outside. She didn't know what she was looking for. Something wrapped in a rag, maybe? *What exactly had Brodie been holding?* There were only a few cars parked outside, most people choosing to leave their vehicles at home. At the cars nearest the front door, she pulled on their doors, but all were locked. Marcie looked around again. Whatever it was he was trying to get rid of, it was well gone, who knows where, and so she cursed herself before heading back inside, where a Dashing White Sergeant was in full swing. She went back to the table her posse had claimed at the rear of the hall near the stage.

Heather was standing, as if about to give a speech to the table, but the combination of Bella's home-poured gin and tonics and the Balfours' secret recipe for Strathkin Scottish Cream was making it a difficult task. Ruaridh was shaking his head.

'Oh, it's too late for speeches,' Heather said and launched herself heavily onto the chair.

Marcie sat down just as her friend leaned over, placing her head on her shoulder. Dina gave a beatific smile at the sight of the reconciled friends.

Bella sat down next to Ruaridh with a thud, perspiring heavily, straight from the dance floor; her make-up was starting to slide from her face. She gesticulated to the people at the table next to her to open the fire door to let in some air, which they duly did.

'Thank goodness these no longer come around so often. I mean, seriously, you need to go into training. See all those soldiers down at Spean Bridge training to be special forces? Give them two hours here once a week, I tell you, forget yomping on the hills – they'd be as fit as fleas,' Bella said, ending with a hiccup and a loud sigh.

People were starting to drift off, and Marcie noticed that the party opposite her uncle and the three other men had also gone. She had missed their departure and wondered where they had gone to – Sweet Briar or back to the Inn? The music had quietened somewhat, and a slow waltz was announced. Through the thinned-out crowd, Marcie saw Jamie coming towards her.

He smiled to her and put down his can of Diet Coke on the table. 'I'll collect my dance now.'

Marcie held out her hand so that he could lead her to the dance floor through the remaining couples preparing to dance what was left of the night away. She was hoping to tick another friend back on to her list as he led her steadily round the room, gently, as one of the few sober people left in the hall.

'I'm sorry about the last time we met, Jamie, I was out of order,' apologised Marcie for the second time that night.

'Not at all,' replied Jamie. 'Tensions always run high after a death in the family. Believe me, I've had worse thrown at me.'

'I wasn't challenging your investigative skills, honestly.'

'Don't worry. If you don't mind, I sent a note of our conversation down to Inverness just in case. They came back to me this afternoon.'

Marcie stopped and drew back. 'And?' she queried, as if she had suddenly sobered up.

'They're happy with what took place. Non-suspicious deaths. Underlying health conditions, as I said.'

Marcie's shoulders sank in his arms.

'It is what it is, Marce.'

They continued their waltz around the room quietly while Marcie took in the news that her new life as an amateur detective was fatally flawed.

# THIRTY-EIGHT

'Of course, *he's* still in his bed!' said Dina, clearly annoyed she had been left with the boys for the morning. She'd thrown them outside in the fresh clear day, while dealing with the three piles of laundry on the floor.

Marcie poured herself another dark coffee from the cafetière and realised, on reflection, she had been wise to stop drinking when she did, particularly considering the strange events that had taken place during the dancing.

There were a couple of knocks at the door and Heather came in, followed by the troop of children who had clearly noticed the large cardboard box full of food in her hands. They were looking at their mother with pleading eyes and back to Heather's haul. She placed it on the coffee table, and they all sat down quietly on the sofas and chairs that surrounded it, still, silently, lined up like cattle at feeding time.

'Extras,' was all she said before she flopped onto a chair next to her friends around the kitchen table. Though it was a bright day, everyone knew she wasn't wearing sunglasses to shield her eyes from the glare outside.

'Oh, can I still say, you look remarkably better than him upstairs,' said Dina.

'Lock-in,' explained Heather. 'Not been to bed yet.'

The party had clearly continued at the Inn long after Marcie left. 'Ouch,' she said.

'Gawd, those friends of Brodie can drink!'

'Friends of Brodie?' queried Marcie.

'I think they enjoyed the ceilidh so much they wanted to go straight into another one. I've never known the Inn to run out of alcohol. Well, good malt, maybe, after a particularly long wake, but ooft. Not a drop of vodka in Strathkin. The good stuff – the cheap stuff I secretly serve later in the day,' she said through cupped hands so that only those at the table could hear. 'Everything. I've got Ally doing a stock take, but to be honest, I think she'll probably be in her kip.'

Her friend finished with a long, loud yawn. Marcie was about to apologise, again, while everyone was still in a subdued mood. But before she could, their quiet discussion was interrupted by the sound of a high-pitched noise outside. It was easily distinguishable as a siren.

They all looked at each other with concern as this unusual sound broke the normal sounds of the village.

Marcie moved swiftly to the door; Dina shook a hand to the children to allow them to dig into the sandwiches and savouries that had been delivered by Heather only moments before, to take their minds off what may or may not be happening outside.

The three women stood at the threshold, still hearing the *woop-woop* of the siren, but the vehicle itself was out of their line of sight. Heather walked out on to the grass with her hand over her eyes to shield the blinding morning sun despite her heavy dark glasses, looking at the road that ran along the back of Lochside Croft.

'I can see it over there, it's at the end of the village,' she said, and Marcie went out to join her in time to see an ambulance disappear up a farm track.

As if wakened by an alarm, suddenly Ruaridh was at their side, blinking furiously. His body seemed to have gone into emergency mode, and he was immediately alert through a fog of stout and whisky.

'Where's it gone?' he asked urgently, as he searched the vista.

Heather pointed. 'Is that Ruthie's house?' she pondered as they all watched the ambulance turn left and slowly navigate the single-track road and come to a stop outside a small white cottage.

'Oh, poor Ruthie,' said Dina, 'just after Geordie, probably all those exertions last night. She was really enjoying the reeling.'

Marcie felt the colour drain from her face. 'I've got to get over there!' she half shouted, stepping into the garden, then stopping dead. She didn't have her car; she had walked over to the Balfour house.

'What have you got? A jet pack?' asked Ruaridh, hands firmly pushed into the pockets of his pyjama shorts.

'I don't think any of us is fit to drive, Marce,' said Heather.

'Well, I could,' said Dina, still bedecked in her dressing gown.

'What are you going to do when you get there?' asked Ruaridh. 'Sadly, she's probably had a fall. You being there is just going to get in the way of the paramedics or whoever is there. Might not be Ruthie; she might have visitors or maybe someone who was looking after her.'

'If she feels she needs to go then let's go – we can take some food over if the animals haven't scoffed everything you brought,' said Dina.

'There's food?' asked Ruaridh, suddenly seeming more awake.

Dina raised her eyes to the sky and went inside.

Marcie didn't really know how to explain to them what she was feeling. Was there a lot more going on at the ceilidh, or was that just her vivid imagination?

Dina put on some yoga pants and a pink sweatshirt and pulled her blonde hair up with a clip. She still managed to look as if she had a glow around her.

As Dina pulled out on to the road, the nose of the Land Rover was almost clipped by the police car that drove past them so fast Marcie thought at one point it had left the road.

'I was sure you were going to say follow that car,' Dina joked, but little did she know that's exactly what Marcie was thinking.

They took it a lot slower than Jamie in his marked police car, so that by the time they arrived, Ruthie Gillespie was being wheeled in a stretcher into the back of the ambulance, ready to take her to the cottage hospital at Strath Aullt. Dina ran over to speak to her, though she was barely conscious, while Marcie observed the scene before making her way to the police officer. Jamie looked up and held his palm to her.

'She had a fall at home,' he said, prepared for one of Marcie's conspiracy theories.

'She was fine when she left last night,' she countered.

'Everyone was fine when they left the hall, but everyone's maybe a wee bit more fragile this morning, no?'

Jamie took out his notebook and made his way over to the paramedic who stood at the door. She heard them have a brief discussion about locking the house up, not knowing how long the householder would be away.

'Don't suppose you want to take in a cat?' he asked as he wandered back to her.

'Oh no, Shadow comes and goes through the flap. I don't

think there's any need,' said Dina. 'She only goes home to sleep, but I can ask the boys to wander over and keep a lookout if you like?'

Jamie nodded. 'If you don't mind. I'll do a wee walk through, make sure everything's in order, take the keys back to the office.'

'Could I come with—' started Marcie.

'Nope,' was Jamie's firm response as he walked away. She stood with Dina as the police officer went towards the door to check that nothing was out of place. The ambulance pulled away and they watched it leave.

'Poor soul,' said Dina. 'She's in such agony, can't even bear the blanket to touch her. She's so confused. And she's losing her hair a bit. Must be all that strain after Geordie. She was looking so well last night, too.' Dina's concerned look of sympathy stretched as far as the ambulance that was now heading back down the single-track road.

'Gimme a minute,' said Marcie, touching Dina's arm. She marched across the grass and into the quiet calm of Ruthie's house. The small hall had pictures on the wall of farming scenes, which were slightly off centre, and it took all of Marcie's willpower not to start straightening them up.

She heard the static on the police radio and found Jamie in the living room, standing by the hearth; the woodburning stove had kindling scattered around it. Some sympathy and condolence cards were still on the mantelpiece from her husband's recent tragic death on the mountains. Marcie watched as Jamie began examining a small pool of blood on the rug and the stone hearth where it looked like Ruthie must have hit her head as she fell. She knew Jamie's tell – he was biting the inside of his cheek.

'I know you're there, Marple,' he said, not looking up, though she hadn't made a sound other than quiet breathing. 'You're not very good at taking orders.'

'I just wanted to...'

'*You* could be contaminating a potential crime scene,' he said, annoyed.

'I thought it was just a fall?' Marcie asked pointedly, and he looked up with a sigh.

'What are your thoughts on this one then? She's in her sixties, so your age bracket for your so-called Strathkin serial killer?'

For a moment, Marcie didn't know whether he was being serious or sarcastic. He leaned down to look at the blood on the floor.

'Was she on warfarin?' he asked in such a way that made it clear he wasn't really expecting an answer from someone who was technically a visitor to the area, and certainly not expecting the answer he received.

'I think someone tried to kill her...'

Jamie stood up, looking at her resignedly.

'When we were dancing last night, I think Brodie pulled something out of his pocket intended for me and Ruthie got in the way.'

'You really do watch too much telly, Mars.'

'I'm being serious! I thought it was a knife, a penknife or something but maybe it was something different, I don't know.'

'So, Brodie went to a ceilidh, pulled a knife on Ruthie Gillespie but it was really meant for you. Call me old-fashioned, but I didn't see a stab wound.'

'I don't know.' She shrugged. 'There's just something not right going on and I'm going to get to the bottom of it.'

'Whoa, whoa, whoa!' said the police officer. 'Until you complete two years of training and start carrying a badge that relieves people of their liberty, you'll be doing no amateur detective work on my patch. I've already heard your fanciful theories and all I can say is, you've developed a vivid imagination since you left the Highlands.'

'I just think—' she began.

He held his hand up in a firm gesture that indicated 'STOP!' and he pulled his radio to his mouth.

'Control, this is 3773. Can I get a forensics team over to the old post office house at Strathkin? I'll meet them here. Over.'

He didn't meet her eyes, but said, 'Leave it to the professionals.'

With a gesture of his hand, and a finger pointing to the door, Marcie took her instruction and left the house to join Dina outside. She felt a strong sense of compassion and sympathy for Ruthie after all she had been through, but could she unsuspectingly be the one who brought down Brodie Nairn? Marcie looked up to the sky with a feeling of at least a little victory.

# THIRTY-NINE

Dina dropped off Marcie at Swanfield. She felt both a twinge of excitement that her concerns were maybe now being taken seriously and a pressing fear of dread that something more than 'Woman Falls at Home' would feature in the monthly, home-printed *Strathkin Echo* that was snatched up with fervour each month at Roddy McLeod's general store.

What if Marcie *was* Brodie Nairn's target? She thought she'd figured out his motive but was loath to say it out loud. It would mean poor Ruthie had, in fact, got in the way and been hurt in her place. Or had she imagined what she'd seen, all while full of *magic ceilidh juice*? Did she trust Jamie enough to tell him who she believed was behind it all, and why? What if he was part of this whole elaborate plan, whatever the truth turned out to be? Marcie was running out of people to trust, and her inner circle was getting smaller by the day.

Maybe she would be better off, as Simon had suggested, heading back to London and dealing with everything from afar. Being several hundred miles away may – he suggested – put a new perspective on things, let her see things from a different angle.

Part of her wanted to up-sticks and take off, to get into the car and keep driving, but her heart was torn. This was her home, and she would fight for it, even if that fight meant estrangement from her only family. There was still tension between her and Heather, but that could be easily fixed. Bella was just the same old Bella, and Dina, well, she had turned out to be the godsend to Ruaridh that everyone said she would be, and Marcie was beginning to value her friendship and trust Dina above all others.

Callum was as stubborn as Marcie herself. She knew whatever happened next, it wasn't going to be an easy fight. There were secrets hidden in the safe that she just couldn't get to the bottom of, which were playing on her mind more and more.

Marcie made herself a strong coffee and took it outside. She sat on a bench at the back of the house, halfway up the garden, under an arbour with wild clematis growing over it. She looked back at Swanfield and then to Sweet Briar sitting in its shadow. *Did the upstairs curtain move?* A light breeze blew through the house, so perhaps the light was playing tricks on her. No one could be at home; neither the Land Rover nor the Hilux were in the yard. She should enjoy this moment of calm and peace without fear of an encounter with her nemesis, Brodie Nairn.

# FORTY

Marcie couldn't let anything lie. Her university tutor told her she was tenacious, which was an ideal trait for a lawyer. Her schoolteachers told her she was stubborn. Her friends consistently told her to 'leave it'. She listened to none of them, which was why she found herself in the car park of Strathkin Village Hall, counting steps from the main door to where Brodie could have walked to before he came back in the previous evening. It couldn't have been more than a minute or two. In her head she drew a circumference.

'The cars were parked over there,' she said quietly to herself, pointing to the corner. But he'd have had to pass the front windows to put anything inside, and she knew that didn't happen. She paced to where the ice hopper was but couldn't see in as the sides were too high. Even so, she discounted it as a place to discard a knife or whatever it was she'd seen flashed in front of her.

She walked in straight lines then turned and walked back in a rudimentary grid system. She cursed herself for not bringing a piece of paper and pen so that she could draw out her search area. Seeing something glistening at her feet, she leaned down, only to find it was a shard of glass from a pint tumbler, the markings clearly still visible.

'Yo!' she heard a voice shout. 'Dropped one of those expensive earrings? I'll help you look if it's finders keepers.'

Beyond the low wall at the car park at the front of the hall, Ruaridh, hand in hand with his youngest, was walking along the shoreline. Douglas, with his dinosaur wellingtons on, was picking up pebbles and small shells and sorting them in his hand before discarding those that didn't make the grade and pocketing those that did. His pockets were so full that every time he bent down, several fell out, and when he turned, he picked them up again and triaged them so that some returned to his pocket and others were tossed into the water.

Ruaridh stepped over the wall and walked up to Marcie, looking down to where her eyes settled on the piece of broken glass.

'Hope it wasn't full when it was dropped. That's a waste of a good Guinness otherwise.' He stepped back, his hands going into pockets. 'Seriously, though, did you lose one of those earrings? 'Cause I'd definitely get down on my knees and help you look.'

'I don't actually know what I'm looking for,' Marcie said, eyes closely scouring the gravel car park as she walked her imaginary grid. Ruaridh followed her, looking down, glancing up occasionally to check son number four was still within sight, which he was. He started humming as he walked alongside her to the tune of U2's 'Still Haven't Found What I'm Looking For'. It was only when his humming got slightly louder, and more out of tune, that Marcie stopped and gave him a look of despair. Ruaridh was not known for his singing voice.

'Sorry,' he muttered.

'Something happened at the dance last night,' she said.

'Oh aye,' he replied and nudged her. 'Was it Brodie? I saw him looking at you.' He smiled, winked and looked over the loch to Swanfield. 'Have you left him having a wee long lie-in?' He laughed, then by the look on his face realised it maybe wasn't a joke that Marcie appreciated, especially given that she had a fiancé. 'Clearly not. Trot on, Ruaridh,' he stated firmly to himself and continued to follow Marcie's gaze along the car park.

Marcie took a deep breath. 'I think he tried to attack me or something.'

Ruaridh stopped and looked at her in disbelief. 'The Brodster? No way!'

'There was just such an uneasy feeling about it. One minute we were dancing and the next...'

'Daaaad!' shouted the boy across the low wall from the pebble and sand beach.

Ruaridh was off like a train at his son's voice and leapt over the wall with ease, rushing to his side as he bent down to match Douglas's line of sight and peer at what he was casually pointing at.

'Marcie!' Ruaridh yelled, and she hurried across, taking the wall less elegantly than Ruaridh, given that she was considerably shorter. She joined them in looking down at an object that was rarely found on a remote Highland beach, and which Marcie suddenly knew was exactly what she had seen Brodie holding the previous night.

# FORTY-ONE

Jamie looked down while the police officer next to him took photographs on a camera.

'Didn't think you still used them. Not just use your own phone?' asked Ruaridh to his friend.

'You're not another one that thinks he's an amateur detective?' asked the police officer, before gesturing for Ruaridh and his son to take a further step back away from the imaginary police cordon.

'Are you putting, like, that barrier tape and all that around it?' Ruaridh continued while Jamie simply looked exasperated.

'Now, you're sure about this?' Jamie asked Marcie.

'Definitely. Almost one hundred per cent.'

'*Almost* one hundred per cent? That could be a bit more positive.' He sighed as he bent down, wearing blue nytril gloves, and picked up a syringe, dropping it into a bag that had the words '*EVIDENCE: DO NOT TAMPER*' clearly written in large capital letters across it.

'What's the latest with Ruthie?' asked Marcie.

'Not sure. Waiting on the blood results coming back. But

let's see what this had inside it. Probably left by some druggie from down south, mind you. One of these wild camping folks.'

'Well, my wee man here scours these beaches every day and, believe me, it's the first time he's come across this type of debris washed up.'

Jamie closed and sealed the bag, signed it and handed it to his colleague. Then he slid off the gloves, took another plastic bag out of his pocket and dropped them in before sealing that bag, too, and shoving it back into his pocket. The three friends stood for a moment. Even Douglas was quiet as he looked up at the three people standing above him, firmly holding his father's hand, his eyes wide with the excitement of seeing a uniformed police officer up close.

'I'll need a statement, Marcella,' Jamie stated. Things had moved up a gear now that her old school friend had started using her Sunday name.

The group walked back to the police car and then drove to the police station that would be open specially for the occasion of taking her statement. They were trailed by a pair of binoculars. The operator cursed under their breath. The cord of the binoculars momentarily caught in the red friendship bracelet worn around their operator's wrist, and it took several attempts to separate them, before they put them securely back in their case, and were on their way.

# FORTY-TWO

Jamie had become increasingly frustrated with Marcie and her wild accusations over the previous days, but surely now he would realise that what she had been saying about Brodie was right all along.

He wanted her to make a statement right away at the police station, but to be more relaxed and, more importantly, to get a decent cup of coffee, Jamie decided they should instead go around the loch to Swanfield. Marcie was pleased when Ruaridh took up her offer of moral support, and Douglas was delighted to come along for the ride, especially as he had been offered the back seat of the police car.

'So...' Jamie sighed as he opened his little black notebook and steadied his pen, 'take me through the events of yesterday evening.'

Marcie began to recall the evening's events up until her dance with Brodie. Ruaridh was listening to her intently as they sat around the kitchen table, while Douglas raced around the big house in a repeat of the night he and the boys stayed with Dina at the sleepover, arms outstretched, making plane noises.

'I didn't see what it was he was holding, but I knew it was something sharp.'

'How did you know that?' pressed Jamie.

'Erm, I'm not sure. I just think I knew. Saw it shining in the lights. Knew it was something long and thin.'

'You *just think you knew*,' repeated Jamie with a nod and a scribble in the notebook. 'Drink had been taken, I assume?'

'Well, yes, but...' Marcie admitted. 'I mean, you were there...'

'What had you been drinking?'

'I'm not too sure. We had some G&Ts then I think some wine then some homemade concoction when we arrived at the village hall but...'

As someone who had indulged before in a *homemade concoction*, Jamie was immediately suspicious. 'So, how much in volume, would you say?'

Marcie swallowed. 'Volume?'

'Yes. Volume.'

'They weren't pissed, seriously, not like they were the last time they were all out together,' qualified Ruaridh. Realising he'd probably done more harm than good, he made an apologetic face at Marcie while mouthing the word 'sorry'. 'Er, I'll shut up. I'm away to find the wee one.' He left the table shouting for his youngest son before he could do any more damage.

Marcie sighed deeply, shoulders resting high then falling.

'Don't lose the rag with me, Mars, but if I can be honest with you, you do have a vivid imagination. Brodie is well liked around here, and these are pretty wild allegations. I just need you to be sure of what you're accusing him.'

Suddenly Marcie began to doubt herself. *What if she was wrong? What if she had imagined most of it – had she really been binge-watching too many crime dramas lately?*

'Maybe he's diabetic,' stated Jamie with a shrug, 'and was on his way to the loo and then came across you?'

Marcie gave him a look. *Has he got to you, too?* She dismissed the thought. She pulled herself up from the reading chair and went to the window at the sink. No cars in the back yard of Sweet Briar. *Where was everyone?*

'Maybe I did imagine it,' she said quietly, almost to herself.

Jamie stood up and strolled over towards her.

'Look, if this is too much, let's just forget about it...'

'I believe you, Mars,' said the police officer, his hand resting on her shoulder. 'I just want to make sure you're okay about this before I file this report and start this inquiry. As I say, he's well liked – it's going to upset the equilibrium in the village when I start asking questions. You know what our wee village is like?'

Marcie knew all too well what the incestuous nature of small village life was like.

She also knew if she was to throw accusations around, she had to be firm in her belief that she was right. Was she prepared for the ramifications to follow if she was wrong? She slid her phone out of her back pocket and swiped through her photos, resting on the one she had taken recently and now realised she should have shown to Richard at their last meeting. And now she had to ask herself – if she was wrong, was she prepared for what was to come? And if she was right, how would it change life in Strathkin for those involved?

## FORTY-THREE

The four friends sat at the window table of The Strathkin Inn while Marcie updated them on the latest happenings. She had decided to keep some details to herself for the time being – but seeing the looks of incredulity on her three friends' faces made her feel she had done the right thing in being as open as she could with them for now.

'I can't believe this about Brodie, though. Why would he want to harm anyone? He's been a godsend to us, really,' said Dina in protective mode.

'Agree. Plus, I don't mind watching him lift my bales of hay, to be honest. Are you sure?' queried Bella.

'I remember him comforting everyone at the hall that awful time. It's so very hard to believe that he's trying to do something to you. I mean, why?' Dina shrugged.

Marcie wasn't being fully open and honest with them, but she was intent on studying all their faces. No one gave anything away. Dina shivered and looked around at her friends.

'Nothing like this ever happens in Strathkin. I don't like it. It's making me uneasy.'

'It's okay for you,' said Bella, firmly. 'You've got a big bruiser looking after you. What if Marce is right and we're next?'

'Next for what?' asked Heather, suddenly unnerved.

'I don't want to start anything here. I'm just thinking we should look out for each other. Why don't you come and stay with us at Lochside for a few days?' suggested Dina to Marcie.

'You've already got a houseful!' said Bella. 'You can come up and stay at the barn. There are always people around. Swanny can be so quiet.' She used their childhood name for the big house. 'All those ticking clocks. It's like a flipping museum.'

'Got plenty of spare rooms here,' suggested Heather, indicating the empty hotel, with a worried look creeping across her face.

'I'll try to speak with Callum,' stated Marcie.

'Haven't seen him for a few days,' Bella replied.

'He'll just be busy,' replied Marcie, though they probably knew she was lying.

Heather pulled herself off the large tartan chair. Marcie studied her as she walked into the centre of the large bay window which looked out over the loch and across to the house.

'Maybe you should go away,' Heather suggested, gazing out the window. Her friends stared at her, then at Marcie, and at each other.

Bella mouthed, '*What?*' to Dina.

'It all started when you arrived. Maybe it'll stop if you go away.'

'What exactly?' asked Bella. 'What exactly will stop?'

'Well, everyone seems to be looking over their shoulder. Brodie came here in good faith, and he's being blamed for everything.'

'Oh, hello!' said Bella. 'At the risk of repeating myself – what exactly will stop? Marcie's kinda right. Sometimes he can be a bit...'

'Creepy?' suggested Dina.

Bella frowned. 'Well, I wouldn't have used the word *creepy* but, maybe, *different.*'

'I didn't force him to come here!' Heather snapped, turning to face them. 'None of this is my fault.'

'None of what?' asked Bella slowly.

'All the stuff with Callum and the big house and all this...' She was gesticulating wildly, and the three friends looked at each other.

'No one is blaming you,' said Marcie. 'You're not responsible for anything. I just think we all need to be careful.'

'I love him,' blurted out Heather, and the three friends were wide-eyed. There was an awkward silence as they all struggled to find the words to follow such a confession.

'Who, Callum? Well, we all do really,' said Bella, glancing at Marcie, then Dina, startled.

'Heather?' Marcie said, tentatively.

Heather was breathing as if consumed by anger, consumed by something inside that had been eating away at her and something that had remained unsaid for such a long time.

'I think you treat him terribly,' Heather suddenly said. 'After everything he's done for you. All he wants is his rightful inheritance and you've come up here and stolen it away from him.'

'WHOA!' stated Marcie, standing up to face off with her friend. 'Where has all this come from?'

Heather seemed on the verge of tears. She bit her lip, while Marcie was lost for words. 'I think we all just need to calm down. I know that me coming back has stirred up mixed emotions in, well, me as well as you three but let's not get ahead of ourselves.' Marcie firmly gripped the arms of the sofa. 'Callum and I have a lot to discuss and we've all not been ourselves lately.'

'Callum's not been well. I think the stress, it's getting to him,' Heather went on. 'You'll be responsible if something happens to him.'

Bella didn't so much walk but march herself over to the bar, slide in behind it and grab a balloon glass which she pushed up against the optic containing brandy. She put in two large measures and turned on her heels to come back and shoved the glass into Heather's hands.

'You need to get a grip. Drink that. Now!' she warned, and Heather slowly raised the glass to her lips, took a sip then slammed it down on the windowsill, its contents spilling over onto the painted wood.

She turned and walked silently but firmly to the door and they watched it slam behind her. They heard a *thump, thump, thump* on the stairs, indicating that she had taken herself off to one of the bedrooms, followed by a slam as a door was evidently shut in fury.

'Oh my,' was all Dina could muster in wide-eyed surprise.

'Flipping heck!' was Bella's response. 'Didn't see that coming.'

A deep sigh blown out through puffed cheeks was Marcie's answer to what had just unfolded.

*Did not see that coming*, thought Bella as she moved across to the bar, gathering up three glasses this time and an open bottle of wine. She poured three glasses, half full, handed one to Marcie who downed it in one, and another to Dina who politely refused with an upturned palm, so Bella handed it straight over to Marcie.

Marcie took a sip. 'I'll go and see her in a minute.'

'I think maybe you need to give her longer than a minute,' stated Bella, taking a large gulp of wine.

'I mean, as you said, everyone loves Callum...' started Dina.

'I'm not exactly sure that's what she was meaning,' replied Bella. They both studied Marcie's face for her reaction and guidance on where to go next.

'I don't know what Heather means,' Marcie said honestly. 'But I do know it's him, I'm telling you. All of this started when Brodie Nairn showed up unannounced.'

'Maybe it's not all Brodie's fault. Maybe Callum has been under a lot of stress lately what with Lisanne passing away,' offered Dina, trying to be the voice of reason.

'Your problem,' responded Bella, turning to her friend, 'is you see the good in everybody. Even the bad guys.'

'He's never done anything to me,' Dina returned, justifying her statement.

'He's never done anything to me either but turns out he's trying to jab our friend here with a needle. What do you think was in it?' asked Bella, turning to Marcie.

'No idea. Could have been just air. Jamie has sent it away to Inverness.'

The three women sat for a moment in silence. They were disturbed when a local appeared at the doorway carrying a copy of the *Press and Journal*, taking his usual seat in the corner with a glance over their way. Bella poured wine into a spare glass and took it over to him. They exchanged a few words ending with 'on the house', and she made her way back to her friends. After a few more minutes of strained silence, Marcie decided she couldn't wait any longer.

Upstairs, she knocked quietly on the bedroom door, fully expecting to be denied entry, but the door opened smoothly and even the creak of the floorboards beneath her feet didn't disturb her friend who was lying on top of the huge bed, facing the wall.

Marcie was surprised at how beautifully the room was decorated and imagined Dina must have had a hand in its stylish colour and design. She was just as astonished at the view across the loch from the high window, directly above the room she had just left. The vista was stunning on this bright day with high cloud, with Swanfield standing majestic on the other side of the water. The sight drew her in as she walked to the window which had modern thistle designed curtains with heavy thick lining. She ran her fingers over the material as she gazed out to the mountain on the other side of Strathkin Loch, mesmerised by its beauty. Marcie turned as she heard a disturbance behind her and saw Heather pulling herself up on her elbows to rest against the pillows piled high against the tall headboard.

'I'm not apologising,' started Heather with a look that moved between regret and fury.

Marcie sat on the very edge of the bed opposite her friend.

'There's no need to apologise...'

'As I said, I wasn't going to.'

'It's a lot for everyone to take in.'

'You always said you'd never move back,' said Heather, and she wasn't wrong. Marcie had always said her life lay elsewhere, away from the confines of a Highland village, no matter how idyllic. 'And you can't help who you fall in love with.'

Tears began to well up in her friend's eyes.

'I thought you were joking at Lisanne's funeral when you said you could be my auntie.' Marcie smiled, trying to bring some lightness into the conversation.

Heather remained impassive. 'Like that's on the cards.' She shifted herself on the bed, leaning down to pull up the thick wool ANTA throw that had been so carefully placed along the bottom of the bed. She pulled it close and hugged it around her.

'I've loved him since we were young, you know. He was like the father I never had. He was always sober so that was a start, compared to what I was brought up with. And when I came back after it all went south with Scott, you know, "the marriage that never was", he was so good to me, better than my own dad. I think he was probably missing you by that time; you were away. I think it just grew from there. He was so kind, so gentle, just so different from all the men I'd ever known. He always hugs you like he means it and smells so fresh, not like the other guys around here that smell of silage and engine oil.'

Heather reached into the back pocket of her jeans and pulled out the remnants of a ragged paper tissue, sniffing. Marcie went into the en-suite but couldn't find a box of tissues; instead, she pulled the spare toilet roll from on top of the cistern and unravelled several sheets. This time she sat down next to Heather on the bed, propped up on a pillow, and handed her the thick paper.

'We went to one of the MRT ceilidhs a year or so ago. People were desperate to get some fun back into their lives, remember? They just wanted to get out and go a bit mad. Well, I certainly did. I tried it on with Callum after a slow dance and he was horrified. I don't know who was more embarrassed, but I told him next day it had been the drink talking, that I was just a bit tipsy. Well, more than tipsy, to be honest. He was utterly *mortified*; I mean, you know what this place is like for gossip. He said he thought of me the way he thought of you, as family. And I was absolutely panicked, so I went into hiding then I took off. I couldn't get far enough away. That's why I ended up on the other side of the world and finally met *you know who*. I'm sorry, Mars. If I hadn't been stupid, then I wouldn't have had to leave and I wouldn't have met Brodie. I'm trying as hard as I can to wind the clock back. This is all my fault.'

'No, no, it isn't,' said Marcie, taking in everything Heather had shared, and leaning over to give the cuddle of friendship she had needed for a long time. 'Don't blame yourself. We're not in control of who we fall in love with. And who even knows what was going through Lisanne's mind when she changed her will? None of that – *any of it* – is your fault.'

Her friend looked at her, and Marcie knew the revelations weren't over. 'I think Lisanne saw them.'

'Who?'

Heather was silent for a moment. 'Callum and Brodie. I didn't know Callum was gay. I don't think anyone did.' She wiped her eyes. 'But I did know Brodie was. I saw him with a guy on our last night in Thailand. Never in a million years, though, did I think he'd follow me here to the back of beyond.'

'What did you tell Brodie you were in Thailand for? The scenery? The temples? Did you tell him why you'd *escaped* to the other side of the world?'

'Not immediately, no. But after a couple of weeks, yeah, I told him I had an "indiscretion" with... I think I called him the uncle of a friend, a wealthy farmer, just to beef up the story, of course.'

Marcie sat back on the bed. 'A wealthy farmer, who was single and just happened to be gay, like him?'

Heather turned away. Marcie's eyes didn't leave her friend.

'And,' Marcie began, 'did you?'

'Have an indiscretion with Callum? I tried until I was turned down in no uncertain terms. And don't give me that look, Mars. I didn't know. I was young and stupid. Still am, truth be told.'

Marcie had long thought Callum was gay, but it was never discussed. As far as she was concerned, whoever he was attracted to was his own business.

It was never discussed. It was never spoken of. It just was.

Marcie stood up and walked to the window, gazing out over the glistening loch.

Heather gave a long sigh. 'It's not a setup, Mars. There are only so many ways to say I'm sorry. If only this, if only that.' She shrugged with a resigned sigh.

Marcie went back to her friend, reached out and comforted her like a child before she sat back, her mind racing. Everything was becoming clearer just as everything was unravelling.

She gave Heather a quick goodbye, hauled herself off the bed and went down the stairs. On the way past, she glanced into the front lounge, the only patron being the gentleman with the day-old paper. In front of him stood an empty glass of wine which she noticed had been supplemented with a large afternoon *help yourself* dram. She looked outside and saw that the back yard was empty; Bella had clearly strolled back to the trekking centre which lay after the village hall, while Dina would have walked the few minutes back to Lochside Croft.

Marcie jumped in her car, screeched out of the car park and drove to Swanfield and Sweet Briar. She pulled the car around to the back of her house and almost broke her shoulder as she tried to get in what she believed was an open door. She gave a scream of frustration and leaned down to a plant pot containing an old hydrangea and pulled out a single key. Opening the door, the kitchen was empty and quiet, and the house stood, as Bella had remarked, like a museum.

She ran back out and along to Sweet Briar, which also was locked up, but this time, when she reached into a similar old terracotta plant pot, she found no key.

'Jeez!' Marcie muttered under her breath and ran back to her car to dig out her mobile phone from her handbag. Jamie's phone was not responding. He was probably on his way back from a call somewhere in the area, she decided, knowing the surrounding mountain terrain made mobile signals notoriously poor.

Marcie went back into the kitchen and sat down at the table to think, but found it was impossible. She ran upstairs to her bedroom, her heart beating a little faster. She stopped dead in her tracks as she saw both her suitcase and her carry-on case upturned and emptied around the room. Clothes and shoes were scattered on the floor, and drawers were opened and rifled through. She ran through to Lisanne's room to find the same scene before her. She looked in the wardrobe where the safe was; it remained deep inside but with the door open and the contents gone.

Marcie pulled her phone out of her back pocket and called the previously dialled number. No signal, so she sent a text, as previously instructed.

Marcie looked out the window across to the cottage on the other side, and then quickly took a photograph of the scene and returned to her room to do the same.

She was glad she had remembered the best way to hide something – in plain sight. In her room, on the dressing table, under the white embroidered linen cloth with her brush and straighteners on it, sat the folded piece of paper, unseen and untouched.

## FORTY-FOUR

'Tranquilo, tranquilo,' said Ruaridh with his hand outstretched to calm Marcie down after she arrived with a screech of tyres at the side of the house. 'We've got a Spanish lesson going on here before an exam, so this had better be good.' He stood up from the bench seat in front of the cottage, placing the open textbook he had on his knee next to Dax, who was looking at her suspiciously.

'Have you seen anyone go into the house from here?' she asked breathlessly.

Ruaridh glanced over to Swanfield. 'Na. Been busy today. Homework before they can get out on the water,' he replied with a nod to his eldest son, whose nose was firmly back in the Spanish language tutorial book he had open in front of him.

Ruaridh directed her into the cottage where Dina was peeling vegetables at the sink.

'Oh, Mars! So sorry I had to leave. Ruaridh's on study time and I'm on dinners this week. Is everything okay?' She smiled unknowingly.

Marcie sat down at the kitchen table while Ruaridh swept

away books, an Iberian map, crayons, a broken abacus and large basket of bread middles. 'I think Brodie's trying to kill Callum!'

Ruaridh and Dina exchanged glances.

'Let me just get this straight – I thought you said that he was after you? I'm a wee bit confused,' said Ruaridh, with a perplexed look. Dina, meanwhile, wiped her hands on a towel and came over to her.

'Marcie, are you sure? These are kind of wild allegations.' She pulled out a seat next to her friend and sat down heavily. The front door opened, and Douglas came into the kitchen until Ruaridh held his hand up gesticulating a firm 'stop', and the boy immediately backed up and went out again, obeying his father's silent order.

'Maybe we just need to wait until Jamie comes back and see what he has to say. I told Dina about the syringe, but who's to say that hadn't been lying there for days, weeks even. Like Jamie said, there's always a chance it belonged to a wild camper.'

'To be fair, darling, we don't get a lot of wild campers here, and not ones who use syringes, unless it was a diabetic wild camper?' suggested Dina, before pulling a face at her own wild explanation.

Marcie looked at Dina and then to her husband.

'I'll be frank, Mars,' began Ruaridh, 'everything seemed fine until you turned up.'

Marcie looked at Ruaridh, horrified.

'Listen, don't get me wrong,' he went on, 'things in general in Strathkin are not brilliant but everything was going along swimmingly until, well, Lisanne passed away and you came back.'

Marcie was stunned. She stood up hurriedly but was stopped in her tracks when Ruaridh grabbed her arm, firmly encouraging her to sit down again.

'Now, let's just calmly and slowly work it all out,' he said. 'What happened with Heather after Dina left?'

'Heather told me that Brodie and Callum might be an item.'

'That's no surprise, we all know about Callum,' said Dina quietly.

'It's a well-kept secret in the village, him being gay. Callum is Callum and he's so loved by everybody. But I didn't know about Heather's feelings until Dina told me all about it,' said Ruaridh, finally releasing Marcie from his grip.

Marcie sighed and lay back in her chair, eyes facing the ceiling, looking at all the little and not so little cracks, the cobwebs, the badly painted corners, the bent nails in the beams. Nothing was as it seemed in Strathkin. It was time to share what she'd discovered in the safe.

'I need to tell you guys a story,' she began.

# FORTY-FIVE

'Daydreaming?' asked Brodie, standing a few metres behind Callum on the edge of the high ridge, overlooking the village, but far enough back not to be seen by prying eyes.

'Aye, just a wee bit,' said Callum, surveying the land and loch that stretched below him, placing his hands in his pockets and sighing deeply as he took in the vista. He ran his hand over the painful hip that was starting to give him sleepless nights.

'We'll soon be away from all of this. Are you taking a last look?'

Callum didn't answer but silently contemplated his future. A future away from Strathkin, from gossip and quiet, whispered words. But for how long?

The bracken crunched quietly under Brodie's boots as he crept up behind Callum, very, very, slowly as the older man looked down and then up to the scene before him. As he neared, he made his way to stand firmly and directly behind him and raised his hands up. He slowly let them fall to rest on Callum's shoulders, and the surprise of another person's touch so close made him gasp.

'I'm sorry, did I frighten you there?' asked the young man as he squeezed Callum's shoulders.

'I was just lost for a minute,' he responded. Lost. Lost for a moment... or lost for a time, a long time, a lifetime?

'It won't be long now. It'll be all over,' reassured Brodie, whispering close to Callum's ear.

Callum felt a shiver run through him. He stepped to the side, away from the sheer drop to the gorse and broom and scree below.

'I wonder if you would be found here if you fell?' asked Brodie as he leaned over the ledge, edging his way towards the drop with the sidestep of the truly fearful when they looked imminent death square on.

'I don't think it would take long. They have all sorts of infra-red stuff nowadays on helicopters and on rescue teams.'

'Hmm, but you think, for sure, they would bring that here if they thought a nobody had fallen over?'

'A nobody?' asked Callum, perplexed.

'Well, you know, not a famous or well-known person. A person who was just *anybody*.'

Callum frowned. 'Everybody is important. Everybody is a someone special to another person. Even you,' he said with a weak smile. He thought it a strange thing for Brodie to say, then decided it was probably a translation issue and not anything of great importance.

Callum walked back to the Hilux while Brodie remained on the high ridge looking down, wondering if a body would ever be found there if you told the police that you saw them driving off in the other direction and away from Strathkin, a diversion if you will. He smiled. And then he went to join his lover in the vehicle that would take them back to Sweet Briar for the last time.

# FORTY-SIX

The two men had only just started unloading bags of feed and boxes from the pick-up when they were disturbed by Ruaridh's booming voice behind them.

'Aye, aye, lads!' Ruaridh shouted, stepping towards them, hands in the pockets of well-worn cargo pants.

'Ruaridh.' Callum nodded as he hauled a sack over his shoulder with the strength of a man several years younger.

'Been down to the bustling metropolis of Strath Aullt, I see,' Ruaridh said with a nod to the provisions and stock in the rear of the pick-up. 'Dancing girls and casinos, and feed for the beasts when you're there,' he joked, and as soon as he had said it, he seemed to realise he was rambling in his nervousness.

Callum gave him a look of curiosity.

'I'll give you a hand,' Ruaridh offered, to try to make amends, and lifted a large bag of feed pellets from the truck, dumping it at the side of the barn. Brodie started to take them in and place them neatly on large shelves slightly off the floor and away from the rodents that frequented the large shed.

'What can I do for you, son?' asked Callum as they passed each other, conveying the stock.

'Er, I was looking for Marce, actually. Dina's got a list of questions about a possible trip to London.'

Brodie came out of the barn and gave Ruaridh a look. 'Well, maybe if you go back to your own house – that's where her car is,' he stated sharply, and he looked at Ruaridh suspiciously for a moment before hauling a large sack over his shoulder.

'Came in the back way.' Ruaridh nodded by way of an explanation, with a finger pointed to the Drovers' Road that ran behind both houses.

Ruaridh went back to the Hilux and pulled out a case of bottled water and left it outside the back door. He went to take out the second case and realised that some of the bottles appeared to be leaking, as the floor of the truck was wet. He pulled the two dozen bottles towards him and looked closely but they all seemed new and sealed, although the plastic packing around them was wet and had pools of water. On closer inspection, some bottles were only half-full.

'They stay in the van,' warned Brodie to Ruaridh sharply, suddenly at his side, so close it made Ruaridh jump.

'We usually just drink the water from a burn when we're out on the hill,' said Ruaridh, 'but you've got some duffers here; they're leaking all over the van. You want me to toss them into the recycling?' He felt the young man's hand on his arm.

'As I said, they stay in the van.'

'No problem, pal.' Ruaridh smiled, realising that the voice he'd just heard wasn't Brodie's usual friendly voice, but something that had a slight air of menace to it.

Marcie's words rang in his head. *I think Brodie is trying to kill Callum.* Suddenly her theory had a bit more weight after hearing Brodie's vicious tone.

Brodie pulled himself up into the cab and started up the vehicle. Ruaridh leaned into the back of the flatbed and grabbed a half-empty bottle of water and quickly put it behind his back as the vehicle pulled away. He placed it on the passenger seat through the open window of the Land Rover, and then went back to the barn where Callum had just finished organising the sacks into the right order.

'He's a great help around here,' said Ruaridh casually, hands in pockets.

'He is that,' said the older man, taking off thick gauntlet-type suede gloves.

'Everything okay, boss? You seem a wee bit distracted. All okay again with you and Marce?'

'Everything's fine, son,' stated Callum with a nod to Ruaridh to move out of the way so that he could swing the heavy door shut. They both walked silently out into the yard. Normally both men would shoot the breeze, talk of village life and laugh at some issue or other that had befallen a villager, but not today. Today felt different. Ruaridh felt he was intruding on these two men and whatever was going on.

'Och, well, I better get back to the zoo. Think there's some sort of cakeage going on so if I'm not fast, I'll be last in the queue for the crumbs.'

'You will that,' stated Callum.

'I'll pop over tomorrow with leftovers. Grab a brew?' he suggested.

Callum smiled weakly and turned to head back into Sweet Briar.

'Yeah, like that's gonna happen,' muttered Ruaridh under his breath, going to his Land Rover. He leaned into the glove compartment, pulled out an old plastic carrier bag from a super-market long gone, and carefully placed the leaky bottle inside.

'Right, let's see what's going on here,' he said, and turning the vehicle around, he pulled out of the yard, into the driveway of Swanfield and onto the road that would take him around the loch and back to Lochside Croft.

## FORTY-SEVEN

'So, why would you keep leaky bottles in the back of your pick-up?' asked Dina. 'Why not just pour out the water and dump the plastic in the recycle bin?'

They were all standing at the sink in anticipation as Ruaridh tentatively pulled the half-empty bottle of Highland Spring out of the bag and held it up to the light.

'Dunno,' he said, perplexed.

'I'm really not sure what we're...' began Marcie.

Ruaridh sighed. 'You started this,' he exclaimed. 'You think Brodie whatever his name is, is out to get Callum, so maybe there's a clue here.'

'In an empty bottle of water?' asked Dina.

'Half empty,' said both Marcie and Ruaridh at once. Ruaridh squeezed the bottle, and a steady stream of water squirted out of the bottom of the plastic.

'Oooh!' exclaimed both Dina and Marcie at the same time; Ruaridh squeezed the bottle again and the same thing happened. He lay the bottle on its side, then went to a box in the corner full of children's toys and started rifling through them. He came back to the sink with a magnifying glass. He looked through it while holding the bottle upright and giving it, this time, a very slight squeeze in case all the liquid inside escaped.

'Found it. A hole. Looks like it's been pierced. That's why they're leaking all over the shop. One of the cases has been...'

'Tampered with,' said Marcie in a loud, lawyerly tone.

'Think so,' agreed Ruaridh, examining the bottle again.

'Could they have been pierced with a syringe?' asked Dina, and they both looked at her, before briefly looking at each other. 'Sorry, I watch too many Channel Five movies,' she explained.

'We need to get Jamie on to this,' said Ruaridh decisively, and reached up to a shelf by the sink for a pair of scissors. He snipped two pieces of kitchen roll, crossing them over the bottom of the bottle and sat it back in the bag, upside down on the windowsill.

'I wonder if there's enough there to analyse. There's not a lot left,' thought Marcie aloud. 'Maybe we need to get another one at least.' A drop had splashed out onto the worktop and Ruaridh leaned out to place the tip of his finger in the water and raise it to his mouth to taste it. He felt Dina's hand sharply on his forearm and as he turned to her, she shook her head vigorously in a firm NO.

The three of them looked at each other, realising they were beginning to play a game that may not have a positive outcome.


It was that crepuscular time of the day when nature draws down a veil before night-time creeps in. Gloaming. Marcie had never been on a stakeout, a raid, call it what you will, and her heart almost beat out of her chest when she heard the crack of gravel underfoot. She relaxed when she realised it was Ruaridh skulking up the drive, having walked around from the other side of the loch to ensure his Land Rover remained firmly out of view from prying eyes across the water.

Marcie opened the front door slowly, and he slipped in. He was dressed completely in camouflage gear, and she almost made a joke about not seeing him, but fear got the better of her. She pointed up the stairs. Ruaridh looked at her quizzically for a moment before realising what she meant, and he quickly took the stairs two at a time, she following behind him with a less agile gait.

She pointed first to Lisanne's room and then into her room, and Ruaridh looked around at the devastation wrought by someone who had clearly meant to frighten her by breaking and entering. He came out of her room and shrugged his shoulders, then pointed next door to Sweet Briar. Silently, they went downstairs and out the back door into the back yard.

In black yoga pants, boots and a black fleece and beanie hat, Marcie crept along behind Ruaridh as they crossed the path into the property next door. Ruaridh pointed at the Hilux parked up near the barn. He would have to walk past the kitchen window to reach it to grab more bottles.

'Do you want me to go?' whispered Marcie. 'I'm a bit nimbler.'

Before he had time to answer, they heard another vehicle. Marcie gasped when Ruaridh's gloved hand quickly covered her mouth.

'Ssh,' he said, quietly, as a black Range Rover passed them just a few centimetres away. Marcie felt her heart was going to explode as she pressed back further into the wall to try and make herself invisible.

The vehicle pulled up to a stop in the yard just in front of the Hilux. Marcie recognised Brodie's two acquaintances as they climbed out of the sleek black car with an air of joviality and went into Sweet Briar through the back door.

Marcie peeled away Ruaridh's hand from her mouth. He raised his finger to his lips and once again gave her a 'ssh' sign as he crept slowly along to the kitchen window. Hidden by a wild clematis in full bloom, they managed to gaze into the kitchen window unseen.

The two men were receiving large tumblers of whisky from Brodie as Callum poured from a new bottle of Tamnavulin. Ruaridh nodded to himself as if to say, 'nice choice'. They heard hearty laughter and the word *Nostrovia* as glasses were raised and liquid drunk. One of the men reached into his jacket, and they both saw a holster and a gun under his tweed.

Ruaridh watched with wide-open eyes. This was not what he expected, and he felt his heart beat a little faster. He and Marcie continued to watch for a few moments more as a paper was signed, followed by another cheers, this time *Slàinte Mhath*, and the chink of glasses echoed around the kitchen.

Marcie watched Ruaridh tiptoe around the Range Rover to the back of the Hilux and look in the back of the flatbed. He swore silently when he found it empty; he went to the front of the cab to check the footwells. He tried the door, and it opened effortlessly, and sure enough, they found a small puddle of water. He reached in and took out a bottle that was almost full, gave it a slight squeeze until water come out of the bottom, and lifted it out.

Marcie froze, as, suddenly, the back door opened, and all four men tumbled out laughing.

'It has been pleasure, Callum, pleasure. You will enjoy money. It is what makes world go round.' The more corpulent visitor laughed.

Callum outstretched his hand, and the man pulled him towards him in a great hug. Callum looked shocked at this gesture but accepted it. The man then kissed Callum vigorously on his cheeks, three times. Marcie watched the scene with unfolding horror as she saw how close they were to uncovering Ruaridh, who was now lying under the vehicle. The men slapped and hugged Brodie, and she thought for a moment she was going to give the game away by throwing up unceremoniously into the yard with fear.

Callum went to the back door, so close to her, as Brodie bid his farewells to the two men who had climbed into the Range Rover and turned the car round sharply, headlights sweeping around the yard. Marcie breathed in, closed her eyes and pushed herself against the wall in an effort to blend in to the shrubbery. Brodie then turned and made his way to the Hilux. Marcie gave what could only be described as a silent gasp, her hand covering her mouth, as she watched him climb into the front seat, switching on the engine.

Ruaridh was a tall, well-built man and it was clear it had taken him all his effort to squeeze under the pick-up to hide from the gun-toting duo. Marcie held her breath, knowing that when the engine switched on, the slightest reverse could drag him out and possibly under the front wheels.

'Leave it till the morning,' shouted Callum.

Brodie waited for a moment before turning off the engine. He slid out from the driver's seat and then, laughing, returned to the back door, throwing the keys to Callum who caught them deftly with one outstretched hand. The back door was closed with a hearty thud and suddenly all that could be heard was the owl that nested in a tree in the garden and the laboured breathing of a man under a car in the yard.

Ruaridh lay under the vehicle for some moments, until the light in the kitchen went out. His breathing was shallow as he forced himself out from under the pick-up and up onto the grass. Together, they pushed through the bushes and down into the yard of Swanfield and made their way to the porch door.

'Gawd almighty!' Ruaridh said. Marcie could hear his heart beating through his thick padded jacket. 'There's clearly a reason I live in Strathkin and never joined the SAS.'

Going silently into the unlit house, Marcie grabbed a bottle of malt from the pantry, her hands shaking while she took the cork out of the bottle. Ruaridh looked for glasses, before deciding to drink directly from the bottle of Dalwhinnie Winter's Gold in two large gulps.

He let out a long sigh, eyes closed, as he propped himself up against the wall. They stood for a few minutes in silence then they took a seat.

'I'm too old for this shit.' He shook his head, hand tight around the neck of the bottle.

'You're thirty-two,' Marcie reminded him.

'I tell you what, I've aged in the last twenty minutes,' he qualified. 'What in the actual is going on?'

'Did you see that gun?'

'Looked like a Glock 9mm.'

'These things don't happen up here, Mars. That kind of weapon isn't what I'd call entry level. That's hardcore. Whatever is going on, Callum has done some sort of deal with these people. Signing papers and stuff with those guys, the friends of Brodie. I could take Brodie, or whatever he's called, out but I couldn't take down two bruisers with their guns – that's serious stuff. They shouldn't be carrying that kind of metal up here, there's laws against that, there's children around, MY children,' he said angrily, finger stabbing at his chest.

'Don't do anything stupid,' Marcie warned as she heard the worry in his voice.

'Whatever this is, it's bigger than Jamie can deal with,' he stated.

'Should I dial 999?' Marcie asked, mobile now in hand.

'Feck, I dunno. And say what? I want to report two guys drinking whisky and laughing in someone's kitchen while in the possession of semi-automatic weapons?' Ruaridh said sharply. When she didn't answer, he said, 'Sorry.'

Marcie encouraged Ruaridh to go home to his family, but he was reluctant to leave.

'What if they come back? You need to come to Lochside.'

'No,' insisted Marcie, 'I need to stay here. We need to decide what to do with this bottle and what we need to say to Jamie. I can come round to you first thing?'

'No, I'll come back. Let me have thinking time. *You* need thinking time.' Ruaridh reluctantly left, after making her promise to lock all the doors and call if she needed anything.

As soon as she was alone, Marcie shoved her beanie hat on and headed for the back door. She had to know what was on the papers her uncle had signed. She found Sweet Briar still in darkness, and to her relief the door was unlocked. Marcie slipped inside the spotless empty kitchen. The papers were still lying on the table. She stood for a moment at the door, waiting until her breathing slowed and she felt a bit calmer, before she picked up one of the pieces of paper and studied it.

She felt the presence of someone else in the room. She had heard of people dying of fright and she thought – *so this is how it happens*. To her relief, she inhaled the fresh citrus scent of her uncle rather than the aroma of animal that lingered around Brodie.

'Found what you were looking for?' asked Callum. Marcie didn't turn around. 'You know the house should have been left to me. I've been left with almost nothing.'

Marcie put the papers down on the table, the only light from the table lamp in the hall illuminating the scene. 'You've sold everything? That's what this is all about. You're selling the estate to those guys?'

'I was only selling what was rightly mine,' Callum stated. 'I'm contesting the will, you know that, and I know Scots law will dictate that I...'

'No, it won't,' stated Marcie, still not turning round.

Callum walked around to face her. 'Don't come here with your big city lawyer ideas, Marcella. I know the law as well as you. Your vindictive grandmother thought I was only good for farm work. But I had my nose in books, too.'

'And your *husband*? Did he put you up to this?' asked Marcie, watching the shock grow on Callum's face. 'I found the marriage certificate in the safe. It wasn't the best place to hide it. You only went to Aberdeen. I'm surprised no one saw you. This part of Scotland is like a big village. You know that.'

Callum put his hands in his pockets. Now that her uncle was close to her, opposite her, she saw again how frail he looked, like the time she saw him deliver his eulogy at the church. He was still ill, and she was beginning to unravel the reason why.

'Your husband tried to kill me,' she stated. 'I think he's doing the same with you.'

'I don't think so. I'll go when it's God's will. I'm not here to fall out with you, Mars,' said Callum, calmly, in his usual manner. 'We all know we have limited time here on Earth. Why don't we just all get on?' he added in almost a sigh.

'I think you need to sit down,' Marcie suggested, and started towards him, but he held up his hands.

'Make another appointment to see Richard, there's a good lass.'

He was swaying now, his eyes glassy. She grabbed him by the forearms to sit him down on the chair next to the empty table, but he shrugged her off. He winced, hand on his hip.

'Did you drink that whisky on an empty stomach?' Marcie asked, looking at him closely, the bottle and glasses now on the handmade kitchen cabinet.

'I knew you were out there. Ruaridh had a lucky escape.'

'I'm going to call Doctor Mooney.'

Marcie reached into her back pocket, but her uncle stopped her.

'Ca' canny, lass. We're all a wee bit uptight at the minute. Why don't we all have a good sleep, and you come over here for tea tomorrow and we'll talk it over?'

'No, I want to know everything, *everything*, now.'

'You always were an impetuous wee besom. You're in my house now, so...'

'*My rules*' they both said together, but not in their usual jovial tone – this time it sounded almost threatening.

Looking at his weak smile, Marcie's mind was racing. 'Okay, I'll leave you to rest. But we'll talk first thing.'

She went to walk away, then turned back and gave him a long, tight hug, his familiar scent embedded in his clothes. This time, he held her tighter than usual, and she could feel how thin he was becoming. She looked at him carefully as she drew away. There was a sadness in his eyes, and it was almost like he was struggling to see her. A melancholy expression of hope and love and fear had crept across his normally ruddy but now almost grey face. He raised his hand and pressed it against her cheek, and his soft skin on hers made her well up.

Arriving back at Swanfield moments later, Marcie was teary and emotional. She felt decidedly uneasy. It was after midnight and Doctor Mooney's phone went to answer service. She texted Jamie, then scrunched herself up on the sofa, pulled over a blanket, and lay there in a half sleep until the early hours.

# FORTY-EIGHT

The pinging of her phone awoke her – a text from Jamie.

> I'M ON MY WAY TO SWANFIELD. STAY TILL I
> GET THERE

She wasn't sure if this was a police order, being all in caps, or if the sometimes hapless Jamie simply couldn't work his phone. She rubbed her eyes awake in time to see Ruaridh walking down the drive. He pointed to Lochside Croft across the water and waved to his sons who were already out on the shore.

'Thanks for coming back. Jamie texted; he wants us to wait here until he arrives.'

'No, Marce, he wants *you* to wait here. I just popped back around to check you're okay. I need to get back to Dina and the boys. I'll call you later so that I can speak to him on the phone and give him this.' He held up the bag with the small bottle of Highland Spring and whatever else the water contained.

'I spoke to Callum last night. He looked so awful. I'm really worried. I just wish I knew...' she began.

'He just left.'

'What?' Marcie was astounded.

'He just passed me on the drive. Gave me a wave,' explained Ruaridh.

'Wha...' But before she could finish her sentence, a revving engine startled them both. Brodie swept past them at speed in the Hilux. He was going so fast Marce couldn't catch even a glimpse of him, and Ruaridh had to jump from the drive for fear of being taken out.

The pick-up took the corner on almost two wheels. Ruaridh sighed, and shouted to Marcie, 'Get your car keys.'

They both raced back to Swanfield, throwing open the front doors. Marcie picked up the keys from the hall table as Ruaridh rushed to the hire car at the rear of the house. She ran through the back door and threw the keys to him, shouting, '*wait a minute*', as she scrambled across to Sweet Briar. The kitchen table was bare but for an envelope with her name on it. Grabbing it, she rushed back to where Ruaridh was revving the hire car like an F1 driver.

They screeched, engine roaring, down the drive, and took the corner on to the single-track road in front of the house like Brodie had done just moments before. They hadn't seen either the Land Rover or the Hilux on the road into the village, so they turned right at the end of the first single-track road. It was only as they raced up the incline that they saw the pick-up in the far distance.

*Head down, foot down*, Marcie repeated in her head as they raced past sheep grazing at the side of the road, knowing that if they hit one, the car would take off and leave the road like a rocket.

Marcie tried to open the envelope while the vehicle bumped and bounced along the pothole-filled road at pace. She was still tearing at it when on the other side of the loch she saw the police 4x4 speeding in the opposite direction. Marcie hoped it was because it was heading to their side of the loch to catch them up.

'STOP!' she screamed at the top of her voice as they reached the crest of the hill. They had climbed it at speed and were now looking down on the glen. Ruaridh put his foot down so hard they both braced a hand against the dashboard.

Marcie was staring straight forward, paper held in shaking hands, and Ruaridh snatched the letter from her grasp, then looked at her, shocked. His foot hit the pedal and the car pulled away with a screech of tyres on the dry road. But no matter their speed, nothing would prepare them for the scene that lay ahead.

The sight of the upturned Land Rover made them both gasp. Smoke was rising from a burned-out engine. Even from this distance, Marcie knew the crash was most probably fatal. Ruaridh sped up as fast as he could, then dropped his speed considerably as they neared the scene of the crash. In the background Marcie heard the blues and twos of the police 4x4 getting closer. As they stopped, Marcie saw in the far distance the Hilux coming to the end of the road. Rather than turn back the way it had come, it took the high Drovers' Road, no more than a dirt track, which dropped back into the village.

Marcie sat motionless, shock beginning to make her shake, as Ruaridh climbed out and made his way to the vehicle in the ditch some hundred or so metres ahead of them. *Please don't be Callum... somehow... please.*

Ruaridh clambered down the steep banking to the ditch, leaned into the vehicle and stood back shaking his head. Marcie could hear the police car getting closer and closer, until it screeched to a hard stop behind her, and Jamie jumped out. She opened the door as he got nearer, a horrified expression on his face as he realised what he was dealing with.

'Are you okay?' Jamie asked quickly, grabbing her hand.

'Yes, yes.'

He let her hand go and rushed over to the scene. She could

hear Jamie talk quickly into his airwave radio, instructing whoever was in the control room about the resources he needed. But as hard as the realisation was to contemplate, even Marcie knew that an ambulance with lifesaving equipment on board was most probably not required.

She looked down at the letter in her hands. At first, she'd been alarmed. But she'd soon realised the suicide note was not in her uncle's beautiful handwriting.

If Callum was in that Land Rover, this was not an accident of his own doing. Deep down she was certain that when the police road traffic collision investigation team got here, they would conclude that the vehicle was run off the road, forced into the ditch. Anger began to take over her, and she screamed so loudly inside the hire car that even the two men some distance away looked up. She knew what she had to do.

Marcie manoeuvred across to the driver's seat and started the engine. She drove down to where shortly before the Hilux had turned onto the Drovers' Road. Ruaridh was struggling to climb back up to the road through gorse and bracken, shouting for her to stop. But the red mist had descended. He waved and shouted at her, and she conceded, reversing deftly to where he'd climbed up on his hands and knees.

'I thought you were going to leave me here!' he shouted, almost angry with her, and as she turned to see his face, what he had seen was written all over it.

'I'm going after him,' she yelled.

'No, you're not!' Ruaridh said firmly as he ran around the front of the car. '*We're* going after him.'

He climbed into the passenger seat, and Marcie put her foot down.

# FORTY-NINE

It only took moments before they could see the Hilux in the distance. It had dropped down off the old Drovers' Road, back on to the single-track road, and looked like it was headed back to the village. *He's on my turf,* thought Marcie. She'd grown up on these roads, she knew every turn and corner. She slowed right down as they came to the edge of the village.

'I thought he'd maybe head off,' suggested Ruaridh, holding on to the door strap as they bumped down onto the single-track road, some distance behind him. 'Maybe he's forgotten something.'

'Or someone.'

They glanced at each other, both knowing who that someone would be.

They slowed right down, creeping into the village, and Ruaridh reached into his back pocket, indicating to Marcie to slow down even more, as he dialled a number. She could hear the phone ringing and being picked up.

'Dina, get the boys off the shore and take them inside the house, stay inside until I get there,' ordered Ruaridh. She could hear her friend's voice querying her husband. 'Darling, just please do this for me, eh?' Dina became more compliant as she heard her husband's concerned tone.

The majestic outline of Swanfield was across the water, Sweet Briar sitting in its shadow like a mournful widow. Her thoughts turned to her uncle, and a deep emotion swept over her, and she gulped hard to stop it emerging in a wail of sorrow, concentrating instead on what she was doing. The car moved slowly along the deserted main street of Strathkin. She pulled quietly into the rear car park of The Strathkin Inn. They both got out, doors left open, and entered the silent building.

Inside, the place was empty of patrons, guests and customers. They made their way slowly through to the lounge bar, creeping like they were invading some sort of sacred tomb.

Nothing. Nobody.

'Wait here,' Marcie ordered, in barely more than a whisper, and went upstairs to the bedrooms. She hurriedly looked in all the rooms but found no one. Quickly, she made her way back downstairs and met Ruaridh. He'd obeyed orders and was standing stock still in the hallway.

'Not a soul.'

They returned to the car and drove slowly past the village hall, heading to the trekking centre next door.

They left the car on the road and got out. They couldn't see the Hilux, but they could smell the heat of an engine that was clearly close by. Marcie swallowed so hard she feared their presence would be instantly revealed. They both slowly walked into the square yard just as their nemesis came out of the stable block.

'I commend you on your driving,' said Brodie. 'You took those corners like a racing driver.' He smiled wryly. She could hear his accent now, stronger than before. *So, it was, in fact, all an act*, she thought to herself.

'You've killed my uncle... your husband,' said Marcie, her voice cracking, revealing her shock and vulnerability.

'Maybe his time had come. Death comes to us all,' he said. He brought his arms from behind his back to reveal one hand holding a handgun similar to the one they had seen with the men at Sweet Briar.

'What do you want?' asked Ruaridh, coming up from behind her now that Brodie had displayed his weaponry.

'Well, it seems what I want is what I can't have, thanks to you, well, not right away...'

'You won't get away with it,' snarled Marcie. 'You won't get away with anything.'

An ambulance siren sounded then disappeared as it headed around the loch, past Swanfield, and straight to the scene of the road accident. Marcie's eyes were fixed on Brodie as he smiled, almost maniacally, and then cocked his head, hand to his ear as the siren waned. He shrugged knowingly as it disappeared in the breeze.

Crunching gravel had their heads turning. Heather and Bella walked up from the shore, smiling at some joke they had been discussing. They both looked stunned at the scene that was unfolding in front of them.

'Brodie?' asked Heather. 'What's going on?'

She walked up to him, and Marcie thought, *yes, here's your accomplice,* but before she had time to voice her suspicions, he had grabbed her, pulling her close.

'I'm going to leave now. Are we all okay with that?' Brodie said as Marcie gasped in horror. *Was her friend innocent in all this, after all?*

'Don't you dare hurt her!' shouted Bella in a warning to Brodie. 'This wasn't the plan.'

'*Plan?*' asked a clearly distressed Heather as Brodie pulled her tighter around the neck, his grip fierce, one hand still on the semi-automatic handgun.

Marcie reeled. She looked to Ruaridh then to Bella. What

did Bella mean? Surely, she couldn't have been in on this? Surely not – in cahoots with Brodie all along?

Brodie pulled Heather tighter into his grip.

Marcie opened her mouth to speak but no words came out. She stared at Bella who had turned slightly so that she didn't meet her eye, couldn't meet her eye. For once Marcie was blindsided – she was struggling to comprehend what was going on. Fury rose in her, a venom she had never experienced.

'Was killing Callum your plan all along?' Marcie shouted at Brodie viciously, breaking the silence.

'Callum?' gasped Heather, her throat held tightly in Brodie's grip. She tried to release herself, but he was hooked on tight, and she was taking in great gulps of air.

'Let her go!' demanded Bella, but Brodie only shook his head in exasperation.

'Bella, Bella, Bella – don't pretend you care. You're as ruthless as me,' he stated, and he gave her a look of recognition verging on scornful.

'You didn't say you were going to kill anyone,' Bella shouted at him. 'This wasn't what we agreed.'

Marcie was incredulous. How could this be true? 'Are you really in on this with him?'

'I didn't think it would come to *this*,' Bella responded almost meekly, with a veil of panic beginning to creep over her face. 'All I wanted was money to keep the place going – try to get my horses back – get people back here – try to make this place, the place it once was. Strathkin is dying a slow death. I just wanted to take things back to what they were. He said he'd help me.'

Heather was gagging now as Bella tried to justify her actions, while all the time Brodie's grip tightened.

'I just agreed to go along with some of his plans. He's got a deal with some investors, to bring some money in. They were going to rebuild, and I was in for a cut, *that's all*,' Bella pleaded.

'Bella, dear,' snarled Brodie. 'I think you should shut up now. They don't need to hear this.'

'Yes, they do, if you've killed Callum, and the rest!' shouted Bella, becoming more distressed. '*Please*, let Heather go.'

'The rest?' caught on Marcie. 'You mean people like Alister Duff and Angus Fraser?'

Ruaridh had moved away from Marcie's side and very, very slowly started to edge his way around the yard.

'Well, you didn't think those old people died of natural causes, did you? I helped them out in their houses; I'm kind that way. Collected money for them at the ATM when they asked. Sometimes when they didn't ask. A little for myself, for my troubles. What were they contributing to society anyway? I just helped them along a bit. They didn't suffer. They had a nice drink, and they fell asleep. I sent them to meet their husband or wife in their heaven, so, no harm done.'

'*No harm done?*' repeated Marcie. 'You've murdered all those people?' She shook her head. 'Is that what you were doing with Callum, too? Poisoning him like you did the rest? Is that what was in the water?'

'*Meh*,' said Brodie with a shake of his head and a shrug, 'everyone must drink water. It's easily done. Very kindly deliver those villagers some water, after you've turned off their private supply, and they were oh so grateful. They even offered me tea and cake. As if I would drink the tea!' He laughed, then, at the sound of movement, he turned quickly, deftly raising the gun he was holding with an expert, steady hand.

The sound of a shot reverberated around the yard as Brodie fired near to Ruaridh's feet as a warning. Ruaridh jumped, raising his palms up in defeat.

'I see what you're doing. Back off,' ordered Brodie.

Marcie looked at Heather, who seemed to be minutes from losing consciousness. 'Heather!'

'Release her!' shouted Bella. 'Or I'll tell them everything, Poytr—'

But before she had time to speak another word, a second shot rang out. Marcie watched as her friend crumpled to the ground.

Ruaridh ran to Bella at the same time Brodie released a now unconscious Heather, slipping from his grasp like a rag doll.

Marcie ran to Heather and caught her just in time before her skull hit the solid ground, cradling her head and protecting it with her hand.

'Heather! Heather!' Marcie shouted, slapping her friend's face, to bring her back to life. Heather's eyes rolled and crossed then opened, her chest heaving for breath.

Ruaridh was huddled over Bella, stemming the blood coming from her shoulder with his fleece, while he peeled off his camouflage jacket and scrunched it up as a pillow for her head.

As Marcie reached for her mobile phone, she looked up to see an empty space where Brodie – or the man now named as Poytr – had been standing, just seconds before.

'Where is he?' she shouted, realising that in the commotion Brodie had made his escape.

And he was so adept at being elusive, they didn't even hear the car depart.

# FIFTY

## SEVERAL WEEKS LATER

The drive to Achmelvich in the far west of Scotland took almost three hours, not because the road was busy with traffic, but because Marcie was driving slower than usual, taking more care.

She was mindful of every pothole, every bump, every rough piece of ground so that the car didn't jolt or shudder or wake her passenger. The man dozing in the passenger seat occasionally opened his eyes then drifted off into slumber.

She was going to stop for a comfort break when they reached the halfway point but decided to keep going unless asked. They would normally have stopped at Glen Docherty Viewpoint when on the A832, but it was busy with bikers and caravanners, so she drove on through Achnasheen, Lochluichart, and Gorstan, and then passed Inchbae Lodge as it sat amongst the trees to her left. Ullapool, too, was busy today, so on she drove past Drumrunie, Ardvreck Castle and Little Assynt, until she reached the car park at the far end at this most beautiful spot with its clear white beach.

It wasn't as busy as they thought it would be, and Marcie was glad her plan had come to fruition.

Ruaridh and Dina had driven up the day before, taking provisions to the lodge that overlooked this spectacular piece of coastline. The boys had gone with their father to the beach and played in the soft sand while their mother refreshed the lodge and filled the cupboard and fridge. Ruaridh had stacked wood in the firepit in the morning while his wife started making up fresh beds for their new guests later that day.

Some considered it a miracle he'd survived the crash. It had taken seven weeks in hospital, one major operation, pins and plates from experienced surgeons, and days and days of physio before Callum MacKenzie looked anything like his old self. It was touch and go for weeks on end, and he had a long stay in the High Dependency Unit in Glasgow's Queen Elizabeth University Hospital before he was effectively pieced back together and then allowed home.

Stubborn as ever, Callum did not want to stay in Swanfield but instead was nursed back to health at Sweet Briar. Marcie organised a carer from the local volunteer pool and had a firm from Inverness rip out his old bathroom and put in a zero-step shower. During his recovery, neither of them brought up the subject of inheritance, confirmation, or lost loves. Marcie knew there would be a time for that when he was feeling much better.

That time was now.

She helped him out of the car and onto one of the old Adirondack chairs that sat at the front of the lodge with views of the bay. He adjusted his sunglasses and simply nodded. 'Aye, this'll do,' he said quietly.

In the lodge, Marcie unpacked what little they had taken and after settling him with a blanket, she walked along to the fish and chip van, queuing with the rest of the visitors who had come to 'chase the sun' on this, the longest day of the year, the twentieth of June.

When Marcie came back with two boxes of freshly cooked haddock and chips, he had set the metal picnic table up between the two chairs with paper napkins, extra salt and vinegar and a pot of tea. A bottle of single malt was also on the table for the magical moments later when the sun dipped for the briefest of times.

She handed him a box which she had opened for him and took her own seat. They savoured the first few bites of the salty and soft fish.

'I never thought we'd be able to do this again,' said Marcie finally, blowing on a long and perfectly cut hot chip.

'Me neither, lass, me neither. It's no Orkney, mind,' he said with a cheeky grin and winked at her.

Marcie smiled and leaned over as far as she could to kiss him on the cheek – a red and ruddy cheek now far removed from the grey pallor of his skin not that long ago.

'I didn't want to make any plans too soon. You were *very* unwell,' she added, pointing a chip in his direction.

'I never knew the Balfours still had this wee lodge. It's a perfect spot.' Callum looked behind him to the two-bedroom lodge that was for years packed with bunk beds and sofa beds and had been no more than a pod to sleep in when Ruaridh and his brothers were young.

'They don't use it as much now that big brother Ross is away in New Zealand, but Ruaridh and Dina do still bring the boys up occasionally,' replied Marcie, following Callum's gaze.

'Thank you, Marcie. Thank you for everything,' Callum finally said after he had poured two mugs of tea. He held his up so that they could 'cheers'. He took a sip and sat the mug on the wide arm rest.

Marcie waited.

'You must think there's no fool like an old fool, eh?' Callum began.

Marcie smiled and shook her head. '*You're* not in charge of who you fall in love with. It's the cosmos, it's all of this,' she said, throwing her arm out to the soft glistening sea, the wide, wide sky as far as the eye could see and the small sailboat that was setting anchor near the beach.

'It was my last hurrah, as they say. I was so taken by that young man that I lost all sense of perspective. Someone was suddenly interested in *me*. I lost my way. I was blinded to everything that was going on. When I look back, the worst thing about the whole episode was what happened to you and me.' He gazed out across the water, took in a deep breath.

'Years ago, I did something stupid. I don't think my mother ever forgave me. I met someone, a local farmer, had a brief relationship, but all of a sudden it was out in the open and the family had to leave.'

'Uh huh?' encouraged Marcie.

'I was young, I was stupid, I was indiscreet. Long before you were born. My mother held it against me, you know, bringing disgrace on the family. So, you saying you're not in charge of who you love, it's so true. Your generation have a different attitude. I would go to church and hear whispers and looks of disgust. I fell away from the church. I fell away from everything. I've not lived, Marcie. I've put my life on hold to atone for my sins of the past which nowadays to people of your generation, seems so foolish. I think of those young men on the hill, their lives cut short when all they wanted to do was help people. When the first helicopter passed overhead, I just had to go. I was dreading a call from Lachie to take me back when I realised the scale of it all. I couldn't do it. I knew people would be so caught up I wouldn't be missed until it was all over."

He took a long sip of tea then unexpectedly threw the rest of the liquid out onto the grass, reached over and picked up the bottle of malt. He studied it for a moment.

'Glenfarclas, twenty-five-year-old. That was my mother's favourite wee tipple of an occasional weekend. Your grandmother.'

Marcie nodded, surprised but thankful for his honesty, and

emptied out her mug of tea before holding it out to Callum, who poured a heavy measure.

'I don't know what came over me. Blinded by love, I suppose they'd say. When they told me about the cancer and that I had maybe only a couple of years left, I just decided I wanted that time for me. I didn't think I was being selfish. I'm not like you young ones that jump on the plane at the drop of a hat. I've had responsibilities and obligations and duties, and I couldn't just up sticks. Suddenly this young man made me feel as if I could do anything. I wanted to run away. Me? At my age? Old fool, right enough. A sham marriage in Aberdeen? What in the name of the wee man was I thinking? I couldn't see through any of it. You were suspicious about him from the start. I should have listened. You've always been a meddler, as your grand-mother would say. Had to figure everything out. Of course I should have listened. Of course I should.'

'Call it women's intuition or whatever. I mean, I liked him, let's be honest, he was a good-looking guy, seemed to be helping you and doing a good job, but there was just something. I can't put my finger on it. Just something in his make-up that I felt wasn't right. I met him in Inverness, you know – we went for lunch – then I thought he was a farm hand, a labourer there to help you out. I was delighted. But once we went back to Strathkin... I don't know what it was, but I couldn't figure him out.'

'Aye,' said Callum with a sigh.

'And now?' Marcie asked. 'Have you made new plans?'

'Do I still want to run away?'

Marcie nodded.

'Yes. Yes, I do. I want to feel the sun on my face. I want to walk in the sand, lass. I want to swim in a *warm* sea for once. I love this, I do, and I can't imagine being here with anyone else but you, Marcella, but I want a warmth that I can't get here.'

She nodded again. 'Let's make it happen.'

'I don't need to run away this time. I don't need to be away forever. I don't need to find myself – I did enough soul-searching in that hospital, I can tell you. I've made my peace with him,' he said and raised his eyes and the mug of whisky to the cool, blue, cloudless sky.

They clinked their mugs again and settled into the chair as the evening crept in. Marcie pulled the blanket off the back of the chair and, although the wind had a warmth to it, she held it up to Callum who nodded and she tossed it over for him to catch. She watched as he tucked the soft wool around him and sipped at the amber liquid that was heating her from the inside.

'No sign?' asked Callum, speaking of the man who had stolen his heart and almost stolen his life.

'No sign,' stated Marcie.

They sat in silence as the solstice set in.

'Promise me this, lass,' said Callum, adjusting his sunglasses even at this late hour, 'you'll still make a wish at midnight, the first day of summer?'

Marcie nodded. She wanted to ask him more, about the secrets of Swanfield, but she thought better of exhausting him on this first day out and away from the prying eyes of villagers.

'And...' he went on.

'Yeah?'

'You'll join me next year at the solstice, wherever I am?'

She turned to him and smiled, squinting in the sun.

'Absolutely.'

## FIFTY-ONE

Marcie set the kitchen table with an old German stone tankard full of knives and forks.

The night before, in the barn next door, she'd rummaged in the almost empty freezer, found the very last piece of her grandmother's fruit cake, wrapped tightly in plastic cling film. Inside a Tupperware box, she'd discovered the folded recipe, too, covered in plastic wrap.

She had planned to set up the table in the dining room, but the kitchen table had been the scene of so many dramatic events that it seemed silly to choose somewhere else to have her friends for tea. Thick doorstep sandwiches were sitting piled high under wet linen tea towels, and freshly baked scones were cooling on two wire racks on the worktop. The kitchen smelled homely and inviting and, despite the sadness of the occasion, the first big gathering without Lisanne, the house was absorbing the sorrow and tempting people in to become entranced by its warmth.

The man who came down the stairs and through the hall lifted her hair as she bent over a tray, kissed the back of her neck, took a jug of water from the the table and headed out the back door. A mellow smile drifted over her face.

Marcie lifted the tray and took it outside to a stone table in the middle of the garden with circular stone seats, two people already sitting and in deep conversation.

'Ah!' said Richard MacInnes enthusiastically, his usual ebullient self. He lifted the large tumbler of malt from the tray and waited for Simon to hand him the small crystal jug, the whisky taking the merest hint of water to open its peaty, warm flavours.

Jamie, out of uniform, took the Diet Coke with less enthusiasm.

Richard sniffed at the glass. 'Callum's favourite,' he said as he identified the classic malt with ease.

'Seemed appropriate.' Marcie smiled as Simon's arm encirled her waist.

It was a perfect summer's day and the bird call was only inter-rrupted by the sound of a vehicle coming up the drive and round to the back of the house. With cars already parked, Ruaridh swept his Land Rover into the back yard of Sweet Briar before disgorging his pack out into the sunshine. As they strolled down, he met with Heather coming out of the back door of Swanfield, still enveloped in a Lancaster sling from her broken wrist which took the weight of her unconscious fall, looking paler than normal, her hair noticeably shorter. She acknowledged Ruaridh's arrival, and he rushed over to help her up the few steps to the garden.

'You've had a chance to gather your thoughts?' asked Richard as he led Marcie slightly away from the onslaught of children tearing up the path and to the rose garden, lovingly tended by Lisanne for over half a century, buds straining to burst open as the warm summer sunshine tempted them into a blossom. Jamie joined them, and Ruaridh hurried to catch up.

'I mean, I knew as soon as I saw the suicide note, I knew it wasn't from Callum. It just didn't sound like him and it wasn't his writing, so I was sure something was afoot.'

'I know it was a struggle for him to keep his diagnosis from you but in the end, it was a relief to him to know that you were receiving this place and he needn't bother with all the hassle of a new will, appointing executors and all that nonsense.'

Richard reached into his inside jacket and pulled out a two-page document which folded in two, and he handed it to Marcie who studied it. It was the contract she'd seen her uncle sign that night outside Sweet Briar.

'The name,' he said, before handing the paper to Marcie. '"Calum Mckenzie". It was simply spelled wrong. If you're going to draw up a document with your own, let me say "crooked lawyer" – not a term I use loosely – make sure you get the name right in the first place, as it's open to *technical* challenge and, let me tell you, this would have got nowhere,' he explained. He took a large gulp of malt. 'I think I'd be a bit more careful if I thought I was going to be buying a multimillion pound estate, even if I had plans to get rid of the owner after money did, or didn't, change hands.'

'So the contract is worth nothing?' asked Marcie.

'Worse than nothing,' said Richard. 'He's still a canny man, Callum. Hats off to him, wherever he may be!' He raised his glass high.

Marcie smiled. *He's feeling the sun on his face and his feet in a warm sea,* she mused, *the kind of place he'd dream of while reading travel brochures, and none of them need to know where.*

'But, Brodie, he was still responsible for, I mean, he killed all those people. Innocent people?' asked Heather, taking a seat, before being interrupted by Jamie.

'Well, on the surface it seemed just like a series of unusual or unfortunate events,' he said, 'but once more toxicology was done, yes, it transpired they were poisoned. The bottled water did contain elements of thallium which, I'll be honest, we'd never really come across before. It was taken in low doses but it meant there was a gradual build up, so they became ill over a longer period and that made it look like natural causes. I'm sure Stuart Mooney would agree, a lot of the symptons could be classed as something else: nerve pain, hair loss, dizziness, confusion, old age etc. Bizarrely, it was also found in one of the climbers. We've no idea so far *how* it got there. But just in one of them, so our working theory is that one of them was ill and fell and took the other two down with him. Could they have got the water from Brodie? We'll never know.'

They were in horror at this revelation from Jamie, and Ruaridh shook his head, his mind no doubt flashing back to the terror he felt on the hill.

Marcie thought, *It had to be the water; it'll be Cal, he's given some unwittingly to someone in his open, kindly way.*

'And of course the syringe,' Jamie went on. 'That held quite a large dose, so I think that would maybe have been his downfall. Getting away with it for so long and then just becoming impatient, reckless. It's actually how most people are caught.'

'What about all those break-ins?' Marcie added. 'Did they have anything to do with it?'

'Break-ins?' queried Jamie.

'Cal told me to be mindful; he said you'd warned him about break-ins in the area?'

'I think it was just his way of protecting you,' said the police officer.

'I can't quite take it in that when he was at the big hospital in Glasgow, they found a fair bit in him, too.' Marcie shook her head and looked to Jamie for more reassurance.

'I'm told it's readily absorbed into the body. It masquerades as so many other things, the team said in the High Dependency Unit. So it was a combination of that and his bone cancer, I imagine, that led to him being quite ill recently, too. I've already spoken with Doctor Mooney. All those trips to Inverness for treatment, all those disappearing acts.'

Marcie closed her eyes as Jamie explained further.

'Plus, there were also traces of paint from the Hilux on the back of the Land Rover, so it's certainly the road policing's position that he was run off the road that day,' he concluded with reference to his investigative colleagues, but with a sympathetic nod towards Marcie.

'Where would he have got hold of it?' asked Ruaridh, hands shoved in pockets in his usual stance.

Jamie shrugged.

'Why do you think he did it?' asked Dina, leaning against her husband, his arm casually around her shoulder.

'Money,' stated Jamie. 'It's always the motivator, isn't it? He was in immense debt in Moscow, and the way to get out of it was to set up a deal with those heavies. He was, in effect, the middleman and it was just circumstances and luck that brought him here at the time it did. And all the tenants on the estate – he gave them a little bit of his Brodie charm and they handed over their bank cards. A little bit of money here, a little there, not enough to raise suspicion; but he decided to get rid of those poor people when he turned his eyes to the bigger prize – getting a hold of Swanfield through Callum. He had no need for them after that. Shameful really.'

'It was me, you know,' Heather began. 'Full disclosure and all that, since we're being so open, it was me who called him Brodie. It was a bit of a laugh to start with. My mother is from Nairn, as you know, and we used to go visit the castle at Brodie, so we laughed about it one night and it became a standing joke. I never thought it would lead to this.'

She sounded somewhat melancholy, still suffering the effects of having her last breath strangled out of her and still blaming herself for the killer showing up in Strathkin, using her as an effortless excuse.

Marcie put her arm around her, hugging her, and lifted her wrist next to hers, their red friendship bracelets still attached. They looked at each other with a knowing smile, and Marcie knew that at some point she would have to apologise again to her friend for thinking she was the third wheel in the Brodie and Callum saga, when, in fact, it was Bella.

'How long do you think she'll get? A custodial prison sentence, you think?' asked Ruaridh to Jamie, bringing up the subject they were all trying to avoid.

'Bella? Hard to say. Perverting the Course of Justice is a serious offence. First offence, though? Maybe a few months, maybe a few years, depends on the judge at the end of the day, evidence that's presented by her solicitor and possibly whether she knows where Brodie or, what is it, Poytr Medvedev, is? She might get a suspended sentence. I'm surprised they didn't let her out on bail, but then again, it's a big story. And not just for our wee Strathkin,' he said, standing up. 'But she has, I suppose, mitigating circumstances. Although she would gain from it, too, she was doing it for the benefit of everybody. She wanted everybody in the village to be part of the regeneration, the reinvention of the area, so it wasn't entirely selfish. The judge may look at her case differently because of that.'

'Who knows indeed?' sighed Richard. 'I remember one of my first cases...' he started, and Marcie turned, catching Heather's eye. They knew all too well of Richard's strange ability for cutting his short stories long, and the three friends and Simon stood up and started to walk to the back of the garden, from where the land rose up, over the old Drovers' Road, and then straight up the hill until it fell away on the other side direct to the sea and the Atlantic Ocean beyond.

'You okay?' asked Ruaridh, strolling along, head down as if he was deep in thought.

'I just can't believe that barely three months ago, Lisanne was still here, Callum next door, me in London.'

They were joined by Dina, hand on a growing belly, who wrapped her hands around her husband's waist, and, in turn, he pulled her close.

They stood silent for a moment, taking in the scene, and then all five turned away from the hill and gazed upon the house, a house that had held so many secrets and in time would no doubt release more.

They turned one to the other before strolling back, but Marcie stopped, turned and gazed upwards as a bevy of swans took off from the loch and flew low over the small crowd that was gathering in her garden. She smiled. Douglas ran up to her with a sandwich so large that he had to take it in two hands. He started to balance it in his palm and reached up to her, entwined his little fingers in hers and led her back to the people who meant the most to her in her life.

Marcie looked down to the loch, next day. She hadn't made it as far as the high ridge but halfway up to where the narrow Drovers' Road snaked its way across the hill, still displaying a spectacular view down to the water and the mountains beyond.

No chimney smoke drifted up from any of the little crofts now which sat silently on the edge of the water. The stables looked quiet, and there were no childish squeals from the Balfour boys, who were clearly being kept indoors on what was a tranquil, still day.

She thought back to the Friday evening call that Simon received what seemed like a lifetime ago and what had happened since. Trauma, distress, evasion, deceit. Friendships torn apart. Love lost and won.

A light wind blew up and she tucked her hair behind her ear, hair that hadn't really seen a comb or a brush in days; it was an existence away from her life in London. She looked different, felt different. She felt she had suddenly grown up into the woman she thought she could never be, would never be. She had at once been surrounded by love and by distrust, by jealousy and disbelief. But mostly yearning.

Her life had crumbled and just when she believed it couldn't get any worse, well, it did.

A single tear welled up, under her sunglasses, and while the old Marcie would have quickly wiped it away to save her expensive make-up, the new Marcie let it slowly feel its way down the soft skin of her face and rest at the corner of her lipstick-free mouth and it was only then she raised her hand to brush it off.

She tucked her hair again behind her ear as she heard the roar of an engine as the Land Rover heaved its way up the hill, stopping just metres from where she stood. Marcie glanced down and squinted her eyes to see as the glare of the warming midday sun shone bright above her. She wanted to tidy things away in her mind, put things to bed but her brain was once again racing and thinking too far ahead of the present.

The familiar broad figure of Ruaridh appeared in her line of sight and, raising a warm smile, came towards her. His embrace was all encompassing, strong, tender, comforting. She could feel him beneath his plaid shirt, strong and hard skinned from years of working in the best gym in the world. Now weatherbeaten, he still looked as handsome as she remembered. She let him go and stepped aside.

Simon was only a few steps behind, a pink shirt looking incongruous in this landscape, but his boots were well trod and worn, with solid red mud congealed around them.

His smile was broad and open and he, too, embraced her tightly. It was such a different feeling to Ruaridh. He was her home now. He looked down at her, his blue eyes flashing a sparking light, and she melted into him.

'Aye, aye,' said Ruaridh's husky Scottish brogue, breaking the silence and, hands in pockets, he surveyed the landscape as Marcie had done only moments before, his sharp eyes settling on Lochside Croft where, on cue, a tumble of blond-haired boys now fell out of the door and rushed to the water's edge.

Marcie reached behind her searching for Simon's hand, and he entwined his fingers into hers, his arm resting on her shoulder as a tap, tap, tap drew three pairs of eyes down to Swanfield. The small white car had ejected its driver at the start of the long drive and as he put his little hammer away, the *SOLD* notice was now clearly visible on the sign that had been dug into the ground near the old metal gates. She had been fooling herself if she thought she could give up a lucrative job to run a Scottish estate, but she and her fiancé's long discussions had run several scenarios over in their heads for hours and days and, in the end, Marcie and Callum's decision had involved the Balfours and Heather.

Swanfield and Strathkin meant more to Marcie than she could ever have known, but in order to move forward she knew the best, but not easiest, decision was to let the big house go.

She had walked through the house last night, feeling ghosts in every room, but missing the comforting words of Callum in her ear. She wanted his guidance from the other side of the world but realised this was one decision she had to make on her own. Living here was about community, it was about giving back, it was about being magnanimous and noble. It was about selflessness – not something she was previously known for. Lisanne was loving, but spiteful at times, and now she thought she knew why. Marcie was the new keeper of the secrets of Swanfield and she was not going to share those secrets with anyone. Marcie knew it was her uncle's guiding hand over years and years that had made her into the woman she was today, and it gave her some level of comfort knowing that what she was doing would rest easy on his shoulders.

Taking just *some* money from the sale of Swanfield meant it could be reinvested into the area. She had made plans to invest in The Strathkin Inn, to relaunching it as a sought-after destination, with camping and glamping pods positioned with the best view of the loch up on the land behind the hotel. Heather would run it with no money worries to distract her. Marcie had already employed a marketing team and sought advice from the local tourist office to put the area back on the map, for all the right reasons. Dina and Ruaridh had no issues with similar pods on the land that stretched up far behind their croft. Despite what had gone before, when Bella's sentence was over Marcie's plans were to buy the trekking centre, giving Bella a focus when she was released. She wanted the area to thrive and survive, despite all that had happened. Yes, relatives and family of those who had lost their lives would visit, but so, too, would new climbers and walkers, and riders and twitchers. And there was a whole new generation of those not wishing to take long-haul flights to destinations far afield when such beauty could be found on their own doorstep who would visit and possibly stay.

Marcie had been gifted Sweet Briar by her uncle, and, when it was time, she would perhaps return to raise her own family there. And, who knows, maybe her own daughter would one day capture an elusive Balfour boy.

# A LETTER FROM THE AUTHOR

Huge thanks for reading the first book in the Loch Strathkin Series – *Secrets of Swanfield House*. I hope you were hooked on not only Callum's journey but also the return to Strathkin of Marcie Mosse as she reconnected with her childhood friends. If you want to join other readers in hearing all about my new releases and bonus content, you can sign up for my newsletter!

www.stormpublishing.co/elayne-grimes

If you enjoyed this book and could spare a few moments to leave a review, that would be hugely appreciated. Even a short review can make all the difference in encouraging a reader to discover my book for the first time. Thank you so much!

I have been lucky enough to live and work in several countries, but it was my time spent living in the Highlands that inspired me to write about its magical scenery and fascinating places. Over dinner one night, a friend told me about a neighbour of his who had a very similar personal story to Callum, and I found myself creating a whole life journey around the few sentences he shared with me. Characters were born and places imagined, and then, when I was lucky enough to go on a writing retreat, everything and everyone suddenly came to life. Now, I find myself creating little vignettes around each of the people who live in the stunning village of Strathkin, and more than one of my friends has asked if they could visit the area where it really all began. If you find yourself in the Torridon area of the western Highlands, I'm sure you'll recognise the scenery and think you've been transported to the lovely village setting of my novels.

In the meantime, if you want a little glimpse into where I am, what I'm doing and where I'm taking my characters next, you can catch me on Insta and on X.

Thanks again for being part of this amazing journey with me and I hope you'll stay in touch – I have so many more stories and ideas to entertain you with!

Elayne x

x.com/ely_438

instagram.com/ely_author

# ACKNOWLEDGEMENTS

In 2020, I was lucky enough to be able to travel to Italy to take part in a writing retreat that quite literally changed my life. I will be forever grateful for the leadership and encouragement of the amazing Edana Minghella who ran the retreat with such fun and playfulness. My fellow writers and I needed no encouragement to stay in the stunning Palazzo del Duca in Tuscany run with such immense pride by the wonderful Mirella Di Muro. I believe we're still apologising for the wine consumption that made a huge dent in their wine cave but made us write so imaginatively. The friends I met on the retreat are even more supportive today, so thank you to Le Scrittrici of Susan Tackenberg, Moira Black and Kristin Burniston, who have also gone on to great creative and personal success. Susan and I were lucky enough to continue our own little mini writing retreats, which consisted mainly of trying to make it to cocktail hour unscathed.

I am not alone, I'm sure, in thinking that if you want to write, your first thought must be to find a group of like-minded people who will support and encourage you, as writing is a lonely profession. My thanks must therefore also go to the many authors of the Edinburgh Writers' Forum, which is one of the most fantastic and supportive group of people I have had the pleasure of meeting. If you have any inclination to write, please seek out a similar group where you will be welcomed and nourished in your writing life. These groups are amazing.

Claire McLeary, my fellow writer and Gindolier, thanks for your suggestions. You were right. To my two wonderful early readers – Helen Sturrock and Kirsty Mooney – what fun we've had along the way, so thank you both for not only your support but for the many healthy discussions about Ruaridh's beard, amongst other things. To Ivy Hartnell for proofing and for being so positive about my characters. Your favourite survived.

A big thank you must also go to all those friends who have offered their spare rooms, villas, cabins, lodges and kitchen tables for me to write on and in when I needed to escape to plot or plan. And, to those people who have allowed me to steal their names, portmanteau their names and plunder their birth certificates, I am immensely grateful to you all.

Thanks must also go to Oliver Rhodes at Storm Publishing for taking a chance on my writing and to my wonderful editor, Kate Smith, for persuading me to make the changes I initially resisted but that have turned this book around and into a much better read. I owe you a lot of gelato!

Finally, to my sister Juliet, whose encouragement and belief has been never failing. You know I am immensely grateful. See you on board soon. And, of course, Skips x

Printed in Great Britain
by Amazon

49172613R00178